Hallmark
PUBLISHING

SOUTH
BEACH
love

NEW YORK TIMES **BESTSELLING AUTHOR**
CARIDAD PIÑEIRO

South Beach Love
Copyright © 2022 Caridad Piñeiro

This is a work of fiction. Names, characters, places and incidents are either the product of the author's imagination or are used fictitiously, and any resemblance to actual persons, living or dead, business establishments, events or locales is entirely coincidental.

ISBN: 978-1-952210-69-3

www.hallmarkpublishing.com

CHAPTER 1

NEW YORK CITY

T HE CITY BUS HIT A pothole and sent a tsunami of dirty rainwater rushing toward the pedestrians at the curb. Tony Sanchez dodged and jumped to try to evade the wave but failed miserably. He stared down at the splotches of nasty brown and black on his freshly laundered jeans and hoped the rest of his day wouldn't be as horrible.

Shrugging deeper into the shearling collar of his leather jacket to battle the damp bite of the late spring day, Tony hurried down Park Avenue toward his Chelsea restaurant. He had been up at the Hunts Point Produce Terminal Market at the crack of dawn to select only the finest fruits and vegetables so he could plan the menus for the next few days.

As he walked, his sneakers squished noisily, soaked by the heavy rain that not even an umbrella could keep at bay. His wet jeans clung to his legs and chilled him to the bone. A stinging breeze rushed eastward on 23rd Street from Waterside Park and hit his face like tiny ice needles. He shivered with the wet cold and yearned for the warm summer days that still seemed so far away.

It had been a difficult winter and spring both personally and professionally. His longtime girlfriend, a fellow chef, had walked out on him, claiming that he spent more time at work than he did with her. He couldn't argue with her. Work *had* dominated his life lately because he'd suffered an assortment of setbacks at his restaurant. But even if work hadn't commanded so much of his time, it had been rough being involved with another chef. There had been too much professional rivalry between them, and both of their long hours had made the relationship difficult. It made him wonder if he could ever find a woman who would be able to deal with the life he led. A woman who would be strong enough to be at his side and help build a family.

He shook off the gloomy thoughts and rushed the last few steps to his place. The wintry wind chased him into the restaurant, but he shoved the door closed and shook the rain off his coat and umbrella. The musical clang of pots and pans and animated chatter coming from the kitchen announced that his crew was already hard at work. It pulled a broad smile from him and dispelled any lingering negativity from his earlier thoughts.

He pushed through the swinging door into the kitchen where his sous and station chefs and the rest of his staff were busy prepping all that they'd need for that day's meals including the stocks and sauces that were essentials for the various dishes they prepared. When he entered, heads shot up and several people shouted out greetings to him, but others just grimaced and buried their heads in their work. He understood. He'd been tough on them lately. Maybe tougher than he should have been.

He smiled and waved a greeting, but then grew serious

once more when he entered his office and eyed the foot-high pile of paperwork stacked in the center of his desk.

"Why does it seem that the stack grew from last night?" he murmured to himself and hurried to the small closet at one side of the room where he kept an extra set of street clothes and his chef's garb. He always kept a change of clothes handy, because you never knew what might happen in the kitchen.

Tony peeled off his wet clothes and slipped into his chef's duds, hoping that he'd be able to get into the kitchen today—something that hadn't happened a lot lately, with all the administrative obligations of running the restaurant. Changes in minimum wages, an increase in his rent, and the fact that he was no longer that week's celebrity chef had all contributed to lower profits at the restaurant and more work for him to keep things running smoothly.

He waded through the papers in the pile to triage what needed immediate attention and what could wait until tomorrow. Just below the first few bills lay a thick envelope with his name elegantly lettered in hand-scripted calligraphy. The return address was his sister's and he wondered what was inside.

A faux wax seal on the other side bore an ornate R for his sister's married surname and he opened the envelope to reveal a liner in pale peach dusted with glitter that spilled out and anointed his desk with sparkle. Not his conservative lawyer sister's usual tastes, but as he removed the invitation he realized why.

"What's with the glitter, *jefe*?" his sous chef Amanda asked as she entered his office.

"It came in an invitation to my niece Angelica's *quinceañera*." Tony held the card out so Amanda could read it.

"Whoa, very fancy. This is one of those high-end hotels in South Beach, isn't it?"

"It is. My sister does everything big. He also knew that Sylvia, a perfectionist, would put on quite an amazing event."

"You'll have a nice time then." Amanda handed him back the invite.

Tony drew in a long breath and nodded. "Thanks. How can I help you?"

Amanda smiled. "Just wanted to confirm we got the meat shipment you ordered, and everything is good. No issues, like last time."

"Awesome. Thank you," he said. When Amanda left, he set the invitation aside and got to work, although he was distracted with thoughts on how he'd take the time off.

By late afternoon and well past the lunch rush, Tony had dealt with the most urgent matters on his plate. He was about to head into the kitchen to see how lunch clean-up and dinner prep were going when his cell phone blared out conga beats to trumpet: his sister's ringtone. Since he hadn't spoken to her in close to two weeks and he was sure she was calling about the invitation, he swiped and answered. "Sylvita, *como estas?*"

A heavy sigh escaped her as she said, "I could be doing better, *hermanito*."

Hermanito. "Little bro," only he wasn't so little anymore—not that Sylvia got that. To him, she would always be the little brother she bossed around. Before he could reply, Sylvia barged right on. "You know it's Angelica's *quinceañera* in a little over two months, right? You did open the invite, didn't you? Or is it still sitting in a pile of papers on your desk?"

Guilt the likes of which only family could rouse

swamped him. "Of course, I got it and opened it, *hermanita*. Hard to believe she's growing up so fast," he said. His niece Angelica was a good kid who, as he recalled, played a mean game of dominos. He had always loved spending time with her.

"She is growing up way too fast. You'd know that if you and Javi visited. What's it been? Three years since you came down?" she said, piling on more guilt. At least this load wasn't his alone. She'd do the same to their older brother Javier who had spent even less time with the family in recent years thanks to the obligations of his tech start-up on the West Coast.

"I know I haven't been good about visiting—"

"And *mami* and *papi* miss you so much. Our parents aren't getting any younger, you know," Sylvia said. In his mind's eye he pictured them and his siblings. They'd always been so close, but for the past few years….

"I'll try, Sylvita. I'd like to see everyone."

His words were followed by a long silence before his sister blurted out, "I need your help, Tony. This event is really, really, important to Angelica and to the family."

There was a tone in his sister's voice he rarely heard. Desperation.

"Is everything okay, *hermanita*?" he asked, worry replacing guilt.

He could picture her shrug as she said, "This *quince* is a big deal, and it's not just about celebrating Angelica becoming a woman. Esteban's real estate business could use a boost and a lot of Miami's elite are coming to the party. We need to make the meal something really special and I know you can do that," Sylvia said. His heart warmed a little at the confidence in her tone, her faith in his cooking.

"You want me to help? Like plan the menu? Cook?"

5

Tony asked, wanting to be absolutely certain about what his sister was asking.

"*Sí*. I know you're the only one who can do it right. And handling the food would mean you'd have to come in early. You could take some time off and visit—maybe stay for the month. See *mami* and *papi*. Get to know your nieces and nephews better. Before you know it, they'll be all grown up and gone."

His sister was laying on the guilt in layers as thick as frosting on a cake, and he couldn't deny that it had him wanting to give in. But he had so much to do at the restaurant that he wasn't sure he could swing it. *So much to do, like the paperwork I hate?*

"*Por favor, Antonio*," his sister pleaded which surprised him. She wasn't normally the type to beg.

"I'm not sure I can take that much time off," he said, thinking about all the work he'd have to do before he left and all that would be waiting for him once he returned.

With an exasperated sigh, Sylvia said, "You and Javi. It's like herding cats to get both of you to come home."

"Is Javi going to the *quince*?" He couldn't remember the last time that Javi had visited Miami or for that matter, come East.

"It sounded like he was, but you know Javi. Absent-minded genius."

"Workaholic," he added.

"Just like the two of us, *hermanito*. We're all over-achievers," Sylvia said and they both laughed. He missed how they could laugh together. Fight together. He just plain missed her. His parents. His old friends.

"I can't make any promises, but let me think about it, okay? Regardless of whether I come in early to handle the menu, I'll be there for the party." It was the least he could do. The *very* least—which again roused guilt.

Sylvia wasn't the kind to ask for help and that she was doing so was quite telling.

"I'll take that...for now. *Hasta luego*."

Knowing Sylvia, she'd be calling again tomorrow for a more definitive answer, but by then he hoped he'd be able to figure out whether he could take the time off to help her out. And if he couldn't, how to say "No" without starting a family war.

Sara's brother handed her the last of that week's meat order along with a receipt for the purchase. "I think that's it for now."

She peered at the sealed tray holding the lollipop lamb chops and smiled. "Tell Manny he's the best. These chops are gorgeous. Perfectly butchered."

Matt grinned and chuckled. "That's why he loves you, Sara. Which reminds me—I forgot something for you. Be back in a little bit."

As Matt hurried from the room, Sara placed the lamb on a shelf in the walk-in refrigerator at the back of her restaurant's kitchen and slipped the receipt into her apron pocket. Hands on her hips, she glanced around at the fully-stocked shelves and an immense grin erupted on her face. When she and her partner had first opened their restaurant two years ago, they'd barely been able to afford enough product to put together a menu every day, but with the restaurant's quickly growing clientele that had all changed. In fact, the business was going so well that she hoped to either expand the space or find a bigger one. They had even talked about the possibility of opening a second location.

"Don't you look pleased with yourself?" Matt teased and handed her a package wrapped in butcher's paper and tied with twine.

"I most certainly am. Just look at all this," she said as she accepted the bundle from her brother. From the familiar shape beneath the wrapping, she immediately knew what it was. "A tomahawk steak? For me?" she said and at her brother's nod, added, "That's a lot of meat for just one person to eat."

Matt wrapped an arm around his sister's shoulder. "If you want, I know a few guys who'd love to share it with you."

Sara rolled her eyes. "Always matchmaking, but no thanks, bro. I'm just way too busy lately." The restaurant demanded most of her attention, so she barely had time for a personal life. She had friends and family, but still… once in a while, she was lonely.

"All work and no play, Sara," Matt warned and hugged her hard.

"I'll survive. Anything new with you?"

"Since three days ago? Same ol' same ol'." As they walked out of the refrigerator and headed to Sara's office, Matt added, "But I may have found a place for that party that Dolores is insisting on."

"The *quinceañera*? Is that what it's called?" Her sister-in-law Dolores had mentioned it when she'd gone to her brother's for Sunday dinner.

"That's it. The *quinceañera*. Sweet fifteen to me."

Sara could tell her brother wasn't quite buying into the whole idea, but she could understand why it was such a big deal for her sister-in-law.

"Dolores's family lost so much when they came here from Cuba," she reminded him. "It's important to her

8

to keep her traditions alive—and this sounds to me like a fun one."

She sat behind her desk and Matt plopped into the chair across from her. "You mean an expensive one, don't you? And Samantha is inviting a lot of kids from that fancy prep school she's going to –"

"On a scholarship since she's so smart, just like her aunt," she teased.

Her brother laughed and shook his head. "Stubborn like you, also. I'm not sure Samantha's as into this idea as Dolores, but she'd do anything for her mom."

"And you would too. You said you may have found a place?"

Matt quickly bobbed his head. "There's a fancy yacht club up on the Miami River that I deliver to. Someone cancelled their wedding—which means they forfeited the deposit. Since they've already made some money on it, the owner is being nice enough to let me have it that day for a reduced price."

"I've been to that place for an event. It's a gorgeous location," Sara said, picturing the stunning views of the Miami River and surrounding luxury homes along the banks near the yacht club.

"I may need help with the catering and stuff. Can I count on you to assist?" Matt arched one eyebrow.

Sara hesitated and disappointment bloomed on her brother's face. Before he could say another word, she jumped in with, "Things are crazy here, but I'll find a way. Besides, I'm sure you're inviting lots of big shot types—"

"There's a ton of them that are parents at that fancy school," he half-groused.

"All the better to help both of us grow our businesses, right?" she said, warming to the idea as she gave both a pep talk. "You'll feed them the best meat and fish available and my food will be irresistible. Before you know it, they'll be knocking down our doors for more," she said. In truth, if there were a lot of high-powered people at the party it would be good for both of them.

"Thanks, Sara. You're the best," he said and hopped out of the chair to come around and give her another big bear hug.

"Anything for family, Matt. You know that." She returned the embrace before shooing him away good-naturedly. "Now go. I've got a lot of work to do if I'm going to take time off to help you."

"Yes, chef," he teased, echoing the response he'd heard coming from her kitchen staff so many times.

"Get out of here," she said with a dismissive wave, keeping her smile firmly in place.

Only when he was gone did she sag back into her chair as she thought about the promise she'd just made. She'd do anything for her brothers and sister, but a big event like her niece's party was going to take a lot of time. Time that was already in short supply, thanks to the restaurant's success.

But as she'd told her brother, this would not only be a wonderful opportunity to help Dolores keep her traditions, it might be a good way to grow their businesses and impress some of the local elites.

I can do this. She braced her hands on the arms of her desk chair and hopped up to return to the kitchen. She had to get to work because she didn't have any time to waste. The restaurant would open for lunch in a few hours and stay open into the night long past when many others closed. The post-clubbing late night crowd was the perfect clientele for her restaurant's small plate eclectic menu. Even the name of the place—*Munch*—told people exactly what they would get: tasty bites to satisfy their cravings.

But unlike most late-night munchies, she was proud to serve food that would be suitable in any high-end starred restaurant. It was what had made her place a favorite spot in the South Beach area, and why she'd often thought that they should open another location. But despite the restaurant's success, she still didn't think they could swing a new storefront without additional financing—and securing that financing was a dicey proposition in the restaurant business, especially if you were young and female. There was a decided bias in favor of male chefs. No one expected a woman to be able to succeed at all, much less grow and expand.

And if she did expand the business, she could kiss her personal life goodbye.

With a heavy sigh, Sara set aside those thoughts and started prepping the menus for the next few days. She'd have to have all her ducks in a row if she was going to keep her promise to her brother and that meant being uber organized and talking to her partner to see what could be done to free her and some of her staff for Samantha's party.

It was going to turn out perfectly, with zero hiccups if she could help it. The best *quinceañera* ever…one that the guests would remember for some time to come.

CHAPTER 2

Angelica Rodriguez rushed toward the cafeteria, her heels tapping out a staccato beat on the marble of the hallway floors. Her friends would already be waiting for her at their usual lunch table. Located next to the windows that faced a stand of palm trees and the bay, it was a prime place to eat and only the coolest kids shared those prized tables.

The room was packed and as Angelica rushed in, heads turned and whispers chased her. Her confusion only increased as she caught sight of her two best friends huddled over papers they guiltily tucked away into their notebooks as she reached the table.

"*Que pasa?*" she asked, eyes narrowed as she examined the apprehensive looks on Maya and Daisy's faces.

"Nothing."

"*Nada,*" they responded, almost in unison, but Angelica knew something was definitely up.

She jammed her hands on her hips and cocked her head at a defiant angle. "You know you *chicas* can't keep a secret from me."

Maya, the more pliable of her friends, reluctantly

opened her notebook and pulled out a pale pink envelope. She placed it on the table and slowly slid it across to Angelica.

Angelica peered at Maya's name in flowery script and then gingerly picked up the envelope. A sudden hush in the cafeteria made her pause and look around. Like meerkats coming out of their burrows, her classmates had perked up and focused their attention on her.

So not good. Angelica sucked in a breath to brace herself. She withdrew the notecard in a pale pink that matched the envelope. The embossed gold lettering in the center simply said, "You're invited…"

She flipped open the card and couldn't believe what she was reading. Another *quinceañera* – from her biggest rival, Samantha Kelly, no less – and just a day before her *quinceañera*. It wasn't even close to Samantha's birthday. She was almost certain that Samantha had a summer birthday when school was out of session.

Whirling, the invite fisted in her hand, she marched toward Samantha's table where her nemesis sat with her friends. A tight smile graced her rival's lips as Angelica approached and slapped the invitation down on the table.

She crossed her arms, cocked a hip and said, "Really? The day before mine? It's not even close to your birthday!"

"Sorry, but it was the only day we could get. By the way, here's your invite," Samantha said, whipping an envelope out of her knapsack, and handing it to Angelica.

Anger clouded her vision for a millisecond before she reined it in and plastered a smile on her face. She couldn't let everyone see how upset she truly was. "*Gracias*, Samantha. *No sabía que eres Latina.*" She'd said the words in Spanish as a subtle jab, but they were true all the same. She genuinely hadn't known the other girl had a

Latino background—the name "Samantha Kelly" wasn't exactly typical.

Samantha's smile tightened even more, and she tilted her chin up in challenge. "*Mi mama es de Cubaa.*" A Cuban mother explained it. Well, explained the choice to have a *quinceañera,* anyway. Nothing could explain her terrible timing.

"Great. Wonderful. Thanks," Angelica bit out, spun, and stomped to where her friends sat, expectant looks on their faces.

When she neared the table, she snapped her hand up like a cop directing traffic. "Not one word. Not one," she warned, still flummoxed by Samantha's actions. To keep the discussion from going there, she said, "Are you guys going to soccer tryouts this afternoon?"

Maya grimaced and shrugged negligently. "Probably even though I'm sure I won't make the team."

"Way to be positive," said Daisy as she stuffed a potato chip into her mouth.

Maya chuckled and said, "I *am* being positive. I'm positive I won't make it."

Angelica likewise laughed and wagged her head. "At least you're trying. You never know what will happen."

"I know that you and Samantha will make the team," Maya said.

Daisy jumped in with, "And you'll have to kick her butt to be the team captain again."

"Again and again," Angelica murmured. It seemed as if she and Samantha were always battling for the top spot at everything. Soccer team captain. Which Angelica had won last year. Student class president which Samantha had won earlier that semester. Class valedictorian which was most definitely up for grabs.

Best quinceañera ever? she wondered. *For sure it would*

be her *quinceañera!*

Tony peered past the crowds lining the sidewalk in the airport's pick-up area, ignoring the bright plumage of the tourists in their tropical-colored shirts, the locals in their everyday T-shirts and shorts, and the fashionistas who paraded along the curb in designer clothing as if the area was a Milanese runway. He worried that he'd be hard-pressed to find his petite sister, but then a tricked-out lime green Jeep whipped up to the curb and stopped with the squeal of chrome-rimmed tires.

The driver honked and waved. He did a doubletake, wondering if he was seeing things, until his sister hopped down from the Jeep and emerged through the crowd like Moses parting the Red Sea. She launched herself into his arms, nearly knocking him over with the force of the embrace.

"*¡Hermanito!* I can't believe you're really here," she said, then stepped back and examined him as she settled onto four-inch-high heels that still only brought her up to his chin. A stylish romper in a bright floral pattern – a shocking deviation from her usual power suit - complimented her Cuban curves; bare, toned arms; and the heavy gold chain and medallion around her neck. Her thick dark hair was in messy knot on top of her head, and she had the barest hint of laugh lines around her mouth and eyes.

He raised his brows in disbelief at her statement. "*¿De verdad?* Even though you called every day until I finally said 'Yes'? And don't you roll your eyes at me," he said as he circled his index finger around her expressive face.

Sylvia laughed, grabbed hold of his hand, and hauled him toward the Jeep. *She might be tiny, but she is mighty*, he thought as they wove through the crowd to her car.

"Admit it, Tony. You wanted to come home. You missed us. You missed Miami. You missed *me* most of all," she teased and pinched his cheek in that annoying way she always had since they were kids.

At the curb, she jerked open the tailgate of the Wrangler with one powerful pull.

"You got three of the four right, *hermanita*," he kidded as he hoisted his suitcase to load it into the cargo area of the Jeep.

"When did you get this?" he asked as he walked to the passenger side, thinking that despite the bright color, a sure Sylvia trademark if there ever was one, it just wasn't what he would have guessed to be his sister's kind of ride. He couldn't imagine her pulling up to an important business lunch in this beast.

"A few weeks ago, after someone totaled my sedan," she said as she climbed into the driver's side. "I told myself no one is going to mess with me in this," she added with a definitive bop of her head that shook loose some strands of hair from her top knot.

"No one with half a brain would mess with you anyway, Sylvita."

She expertly pulled away from the curb, gold bangles dancing on her wrists as she threaded into a narrow opening in the traffic. Her very feminine hands, sporting multiple rings and bright pink nail polish, looked incongruous on the masculine leather of the steering wheel.

His sister shot him a look her eyes wide. "If that's the case, why did it take you so long to agree to come and visit?"

He shrugged. "I had things to get in order. It's not easy to just up and leave the restaurant for a month."

"And I appreciate that you did. Hopefully you'll also get to relax a little while you're here," she said, navigating through traffic like a Formula One race car driver. Even though his seat belt held him securely, Tony braced one hand on the dash and gripped the console with the other to steady himself in the seat. He sucked in a breath as they barely avoided the bumper of one car. His heartbeat jumped in his chest as Sylvia accelerated past a lumbering bus, pressing him back into the seat with almost G force strength.

"I could start relaxing right now if you'd just slow down," he said and muttered a prayer after a near miss with another of the airport buses.

With wave of her hand that had the bangles musically dancing, she said, "*¡Cálmate!* You'll be home before you know it."

"I'll be dead before I know it," he mumbled to himself. He finally relaxed as they left the congestion of the airport behind on the highway to Miami's Little Havana. Their parents had refused to leave the area even though all the kids had moved out to the suburbs along with a good number of their friends.

"*Mami* and *papi* are so excited that you're staying with them, but if they get to be too much you can always come stay with me," Sylvia said as she shot him a quick look.

It was all Tony could do to hold back his laughter. If anyone was going to be too much it was Sylvia. She had likely planned every day of his stay in the same way she would prepare for a courtroom trial.

"Angelica is excited also!" she forged on without giving him a chance to speak. "We can hardly wait to see what ideas you have for the menu. It's so important for Angelica, Tony."

"And not for you?" he asked, peering at his sister. More than him and Javi, Sylvia had always needed attention and affirmation.

With a delay that roused worry again, she said, "I'm done trying to please everyone, Tony. Now I want to please myself, without worrying about what everyone else thinks. But Angelica is in that difficult teen mode. You know, All Drama All the Time."

"And it's drama because…?" he asked, emphasizing the question with a lift of his brow.

"She lost the election for Class President to another girl who is suddenly having a *quinceañera* the day before Angelica's. Plus, they're battling to be captain of the soccer team and class valedictorian." She sighed. "You know how it is."

Tony chuckled and shook his head. "Sorry, but it's been a long time since I was a hormonal fourteen-year-old girl."

Sylvia bopped him on the arm and shot daggers at him with dark brown eyes like his own. "Be serious, Tony. She just wants things to go well. We all do. There will be lots of important people there, so it'll help Esteban with his real estate business. Mine, too."

A social event like this would be a big help in building his reputation and getting some clientele if he decided to relocate to Miami, not that he was *really* thinking about it. At least not that much. But he had to admit he preferred the warm Miami spring over the chilly one in New York City.

As they drove the last few miles to Little Havana and his parents' small cinder block home just off *Calle Ocho*, he fisted his hands to keep from reaching for his smart-phone to check on his employees yet again. Instead, he listened as his sister started listing all they'd have to get done in the short time left before the big event. Luckily his one and only expected contribution was the menu.

"The theme is Miami Spice. We're hoping you can do what you do best. Upscale nouvelle Cuban food."

"So what I usually do," he said and wondered why doing the same recipes suddenly didn't seem so appetizing.

His sister side-eyed him. "Is everything okay with you?"

He hesitated for a heartbeat, but this was his sister. The one who, despite her need for attention, always seemed to know what was right for her loved ones. Who would fight tooth and nail to *make* things right for them, no matter what?

"Things have been rough lately," he reluctantly admitted.

"Financially? Esteban and I could help you out, *sabes*," she offered without any reluctance.

He smiled at her generosity. "*Gracias*, but no. I'm okay that way for now. I broke up with Dina –"

"*Gracias a Dios.* She wasn't the right woman for you," Sylvia said and made a face. Tony thought that thanking God for the breakup was a little extreme—but his sister tended to be all or nothing when it came to her personal relationships. She loved you or she couldn't stand you. And Dina…well, Sylvia certainly hadn't loved her.

"According to Dina I wasn't the right man for *her*. Besides, we were both always working crazy hours on different shifts. It's hard being involved with another chef. As for the restaurant, lately I'm always getting pulled out of the kitchen for paperwork. That's just not my thing."

"And now I've pulled you away for a whole month," she said, clear regret filling her voice.

They had just reached their family home and as Sylvia parked and killed the engine, he reached over and hugged her. "I'm glad you did. I think I need the time away even if it's making me antsy. Now I know how new parents feel the first time they leave their baby with someone else."

"It's not easy, *hermanito*, but you'll survive," she said and returned his embrace.

Tony had no doubt he would, but would his restaurant? Although he had trained his sous and line chefs well, concern knotted his gut. But he didn't want his sister worrying about him. "I'll survive being away from the restaurant, but will I survive your *quinceañera*?" he kidded.

The squeak of a screen door and an excited "*¡Mijo!*" filled the air.

Sylvia laughed, leaned close, and whispered, "Trust me that the *quince* will seem like a piece of cake compared to dealing with *mami* and *papi*. Prepare for them to lay the worst case of Cuban guilt ever on you."

He grimaced and steeled himself because he knew his sister wasn't wrong. Barely a day after Sylvia had called to ask for his help, his parents had begun phoning and texting repeatedly with reminders about how much they missed him. About how long it had been since he'd been home and how everyone he knew, including Javi, was going to be at Angelica's *quinceañera*.

On that last point, Tony had some doubts. He'd spoken with Javi, who'd said he had something big going on and might not be able to get away. His older brother had been gone from Miami even longer than Tony had.

"Maybe I should stay with you," he said until his sister whipped out a big thick binder from the back seat and handed it to him.

"What's this?" he asked, staring at the flags and colorful papers making the pink binder bulge almost beyond its capacity.

"Our plans for the *quinceañera*. Read them. Memorize them. There will be a quiz in the morning," she teased and chucked his chin to close the surprised "O" of his mouth.

"You're an evil woman, Sylvita."

She poked him in the chest, so hard he thought he might find bruises that night. "And don't you forget that."

As if I could, Tony thought and braced himself to greet his parents.

CHAPTER 3

S ARA SCRUTINIZED THE MATERIALS THAT her sister-in-law Dolores had spread across the kitchen table of their modest suburban home in Kendall. Samantha sat next to her looking none too pleased with what were apparently her mother's plans for the *quinceañera*. Her niece slouched in the chair; arms held tight across her chest.

"Do we have to do all this?" Samantha said with a flick of her hand in the direction of the assorted papers and photos.

"It's tradition, Samantha. Each step of the *quince* means something," her mother said patiently and sat next to Sara to explain, emphasizing each stage of the ritual with what looked like family photos.

"Is this you?" Sara asked, pointing to an image of a young girl who bore a strong resemblance to her sister-in-law, minus the bifocals and stray grey strands that were beginning to emerge in Dolores's thick mop of nearly black hair. The young girl in the photo was dressed in a lovely ivory gown whose fabric cascaded in gentle waves down to intricate beadwork all along the hem. The sparkle of the tiara gracing her dark head couldn't compete with the gleaming smile on the young teen's face. She held a small bouquet of multi-colored roses with bright pink and yellow ribbons that playfully dangled across her slim, almost childish hands.

"It is. I remember this day so well. I walked into the hall with my court and my *chambelan*," Dolores said, her tones dreamy and wistful.

"Was that your boyfriend?" Sara asked, and reached for another photo of Dolores with an awkward young man in an ill-fitting black suit that looked almost funereal.

Dolores shook her head. "It was *mi primo*—my cousin—who offered to be my escort. My parents were very old school and I wasn't permitted to date."

"*Los abuelos* are so lame," Samantha said as she leaned forward to look at the photos, her attitude warming as she glanced at the picture of her mother. "I'm glad they moved into the twentieth century so I can date."

Dolores jabbed a finger in her daughter's direction. "Don't think you'll be running around all over with boys just because you turned fifteen. Right, Sara?"

Sara eyeballed mother and daughter and decided not to get involved. "This is your court? Like ushers and bridesmaids at a wedding?" she said

Dolores nodded and handed Sara the photo of the group of youngsters. "Very similar. The whole ritual is intended to show that a girl is now a young woman and available for marriage."

"OMG, mom, that is so Victorian," Samantha said with a chuckle.

Dolores nodded, joined her daughter in laughter and continued with her explanation. "Each step of the tradition is to reinforce the idea of womanhood. Samantha will change from flat shoes to heels and give away her 'last doll' to one of her cousins to show she's setting aside childish things and becoming an adult."

"Can I get like six-inch heels? Louboutins?" Samantha said and mimicked the heel height with her thumb and forefinger.

"Two," Dolores said with her fingers close together.

"Four," Samantha shot back. Instead of arguing, Dolores neutrally replied, "I'll think about that."

Samantha pumped her fist in triumph and Dolores continued.

"Samantha and her father will dance." At that Samantha popped out of her chair.

"Like this?" she said, imitating her father's awkward "Dad Dance", prompting laughter from all of them, especially since Sara could well imagine her brother clumsily moving to the music. He hated to dance, and it was only on rare occasions that he would partner with his wife or daughter.

And who will you dance with? the little voice in her head challenged, but she ignored it, her mind solely focused on the *quinceañera* traditions and the meal she'd prepare.

"Hopefully not that bad, *mija*," Dolores said with a chuckle.

Dolores described how each of the important women in Samantha's life would present her with jewelry to mark her passage into womanhood.

"That sounds so lovely," Sara said and pictured herself gifting Samantha during the ritual.

"That's kinda nice," Samantha agreed and picked up one of the photos and examined it. "What are you going to cook, Aunt Sara?"

"Samantha, *por favor*. Your *tia* only just said she'd do this. She needs time to think about it, decide what to do."

Sara flipped through the photos again, trying to

process all the steps and meanings in the tradition, grappling with what she could do to honor an event that was so important to Dolores and Samantha. "This is all so new to me." *And so foreign*, she thought. She recalled her own very simple backyard party when she turned sixteen. Burgers, hot dogs, chips, soda, and an ice cream cake had been the Kelly family celebration staple for almost every occasion.

"Is there a theme? I didn't have a theme for my Sweet Sixteen, but some girls did," she explained.

Mother and daughter shared a look again, one of seeming agreement. It was Samantha who spoke up first.

"Since *mami* is all about tradition, we thought why not Old Havana as a theme? We were going to work on centerpieces and decorations that would bring back the feel of the Fifties before the *abuelos* had to leave Cuba."

Sara liked the idea while worrying about it at the same time. "Do you want traditional Cuban foods?"

"You can do that, right? I mean we know that's not normally your thing, but I'd be delighted to share some of my family recipes with you," Dolores said and worried her lower lip with her teeth, obviously sensing some unease on Sara's part.

"I do Latin food in the restaurant, just not big traditional plates. I'd love to learn from you, and I think Samantha would as well," she said and glanced at her niece. "She can cook with us so she can someday pass down the recipes to her kids."

Samantha held up her hands in a "stop" gesture. "Don't rush the kids, *Tia*. I'm only fourteen. But I think I'd like to learn my family's recipes," she admitted and reached out to hold her mother's hand.

When Dolores slipped her free hand into Sara's and Samantha copied the gesture, forming an unbroken circle between the three, Sara knew that no matter what, everything was going to turn out well.

Days later, Tony woke in the warmth of his old bedroom where the air conditioner rattled out barely cold air. It had never really been able to keep up with the Miami heat and humidity even when it had been brand new almost twenty years ago.

Sucking in a deep breath, he stared at the network of hairline cracks in the ceiling, wondering if it had been a good idea to agree to his sister's plea. He had escaped the mounds of busy work in New York only to find himself trapped beneath the even greater piles of colorful paper and girlish lace. No matter how he tried to extricate himself from the *quinceañera* planning and focus on what he really wanted to do—cook—he found himself getting sucked into all other kinds of things of organizing and coordinating tasks, just like what he'd been hoping to avoid in New York.

He also had to deal with his parents who must have been the model for millennial helicopter fathers and mothers. No matter how many times he tried to tell them he was fine, they were in constant hover mode to the point where if he didn't feel himself drowning because of all the *quince* preparations he was being smothered by their well-meaning concern.

Shooting out of the bed, he rushed into the hallway, eager for a shower so that he could get ready for the day quickly and head out—maybe even escape both his sister and parents for just a few hours. Maybe even check out his old haunts to see where he could order the products for the menu. He had been tossing around several different recipes in his head and needed to test them out before he committed to doing them for the *quinceañera*.

As he entered the hall, his mother poked her head out from the kitchen with what had become a perpetually worried look on her face. "*Mijo*, are you okay? You look tired."

"I'm fine, *mami*," he said and managed to get to the bathroom door before she could launch another assault of questions—but he didn't quite manage to make it inside before she spoke again.

"*Por favor, Mijo*. Let me make you something to eat," she said as she walked toward him in her house coat and slippers.

"*Mami, por favor*. I don't want to be a bother. I'll run down to Versailles and get a *cafecito*," he said and closed the door before she followed him into the bathroom.

Leaning against the door, he murmured, "Patience, Tony. This too shall pass."

He managed to shower, dress, and run out of the house without a new barrage of questions and maternal worry although his father tossed him a hairy eyeball as he hurried out the front door. A look that said, "Mind your *mami*," as his father sat in his recliner, reading the newspaper and sipping what was probably his third *cafecito* of the morning. How anyone could ingest that much caffeine and sugar without a heart attack had always baffled Tony.

As Tony walked down the block and toward *Calle Ocho* it occurred to him that like his parents, the neighborhood looked older but still vital. The small cinder block homes were in nice shape, some gaily painted in teal, mango, and coral tropical colors that screamed "Miami." Postage stamp-sized lawns were thick with the varieties of coarse grasses that could handle the brutal Florida heat. Assorted annuals and colorfully leafed crotons completed the picture he remembered of the Little Havana area in which he'd grown up.

The heat and humidity were already noticeable in the early morning hour and his T-shirt clung to him with sweat. By noon the weather would drive people into their air-conditioned cars, homes, or stores.

At the corner the street became commercial, lined with all kinds of mom and pop shops, the same but different from the ones of his childhood. *La Carreta* with its kitschy sugar cane cart still tempted passing pedestrians with the aromas of garlic, onion, and roast pork, but he pressed on to the next block and Versailles with its famous take-out window—*La Ventanita*. One went there not only to get coffee and food, but also news about everything Cubano that could be happening in either Miami, Havana, or Washington.

He lined up, mouthwatering at the thought of a *café con leche* and a slab of buttered, toasted Cuban bread. As the patron at the front of the line stepped away and walked toward him, he realized it was his childhood best friend, Rick Kelly. The Kellys had lived just a block or so away from his parents' home. He and Rick had grown up together in the neighborhood and had also roomed together in college.

"Rick? *Mano*! It's been too long," Tony said, grasping the other man's hand and bro hugging him. Rick wore the familiar T-shirt for his family's wholesale meat company and work-worn jeans.

"Too long for sure, man. What are you doing here? Why didn't you let me know you were coming down?"

Rick said and took a sip of his coffee, wincing at the heat of it.

Tony shrugged. "Family stuff. I'm sorry, I should have messaged you. Do you have to run?"

Rick gave his watch a quick look. "I've got time. I'll wait for you by that counter," Rick said with a jerk of his head at the area behind the take-out window.

Tony resumed waiting in line—but not for long, since the servers worked at almost lightning speed, prepping coffee orders and toasting not only the slabs of Cuban bread, but also the trapezoidal Cuban sandwiches loaded with ham, roast pork, Swiss cheese, pickles, and mustard that some customers took with them for lunch later in the day.

In no time he had his toast and coffee and was standing next to Rick, dunking the bread; eager for that first sip of coffee sweet with sugar, milk, and the buttery remnants from the toast. He took a sip and sighed. "I forget how good the simple things are," Tony said.

Rick nodded and dunked his own piece of bread. "Fancy chef like you needs to spend more time with us common folk," Rick said, but there was no bite in his words, only humor. "How are things up in the Big Apple?"

"Crazy busy," he replied with a shake of his head.

Rick stared at him hard. "Even I can see that's not busy in a good way."

Rick had always been able to cut to the chase even when they were kids. "Too much paper-pushing and not enough cooking," Tony admitted and took another bite of coffee-soaked bread that filled a hole inside him that wasn't only about physical hunger. Sitting there listening to the rapid patter of Spanish of the patrons and the welcoming comfort of the familiar smells all screamed "home." Even if "home" came with a *quinceañera*-crazy sister and niece, and over-protective parents.

Rick shoved the last piece of bread into his mouth and around the mouthful said, "You're welcome to cook at my house anytime. Or we can go down to Sara's. She's a chef too, you know."

He didn't know. While he'd kept up with Rick and they messaged relatively often, Rick's little sister Sara had fallen off his radar. His memories of her consisted of a tomboyish girl who used to tag along with them whenever she could which often annoyed his friend. His mental image of her was dominated by freckles, braces, and long hair that Sara had always thought had too much red. Secretly, Tony had always liked the vivid color streaked through her thick locks. It reminded him of her no-nonsense temperament.

"Where's her place?" Tony asked and sipped his coffee.

"On Collins not far from Lincoln Road. You should drop by sometime. It's called Munch and it's awesome."

Munch. The name made him wonder just what kind of restaurant he'd find. Certainly not gourmet dining, but hopefully not the kind that catered only to people too drunk to notice they were being fed slop. Not that he expected that of Sara who had always been top of her class in everything she did. It made him smile as he remembered the way she'd tilt her chin up defiantly whenever Rick had said she was too little to do something. Nothing had ever phased her, and he wondered if she was still like that. There was only one way to find out.

"I'd love to see Sara again. Let me know when you're free. It would be great to spend more time with you while I'm here," Tony said as he noticed the other man sneak another quick glance at his watch.

"I'll drop you a line. I'm sorry I have to run. Matt can

be a real pain if I'm late to work." Rick clapped Tony on the back and stuffed the last of his toast into his mouth.

"Some things never change," Tony said, recalling the many times Rick's older brother Matt had gotten on Rick's case about grades, dates, and just about everything else. Which made him wonder how much Sara had changed in the over ten years since he'd last seen her: at his and Rick's college graduation.

With another bro-hug and repeat of the promise to get together, Rick hurried to a van parked at the curb and Tony settled back against the counter, enjoying the ballet of the servers filling the orders at the window; the symphony of them singing out the tickets; and the ring and slam of the money drawer and tinkle of change dropping in. Comfortingly familiar scenes much like the ebb and flow of the pedestrians beyond the window and the shops lining *Calle Ocho*.

Tony finished his own breakfast and braced himself for the return home. He'd hoped to avoid the craziness he'd been experiencing in New York with this trip back to Miami, but it was almost as busy with all the preparations for the big event. "Almost" being the key word since it still wasn't as bad as it had been in New York with the mounds of paper, equipment breaking, line chefs quitting, and everything else that had convinced him to come home to Miami for a short vacation.

Only Miami isn't home, he reminded himself. *Not anymore.* And things *did* change, he realized as he glanced around at the different stores on *Calle Ocho* and heard the mélange of Spanish accents that clearly marked some of the speakers as non-Cubans. Puerto Ricans, Mexicans, Dominicans as well as people from various South American countries were changing a neighborhood that had once been predominantly Cuban making him feel as if *Calle Ocho* was no longer the place he remembered. But change was good and just like this place had given his family a chance, he was pleased that others were also getting that opportunity.

As he drifted away from the counter and onto the sidewalk, he once again considered whether Sara had changed and speculated about the restaurant she owned. There had been obvious pride in Rick's voice when he talked about it, but brotherly love might have influenced his perspective. Of course, there was only one way for him to really know what was up: Tonight, he'd run over to *Munch* and see for himself.

Turning the corner, he spotted Sylvia's Wrangler sitting in the driveway and stopped dead. He hadn't been expecting his sister until later and dreaded diving back into that ocean of pink and lace *quinceañera* planning so soon. Pivoting on his heel, he headed back toward *Calle Ocho*.

Coward, his inner voice chided, but he quickly shot it down with, *He who fights and runs away, lives to fight another day.*

It was about time he started doing what he'd come to Miami to do—cook.

With a few quick taps to pull up the ride-hailing app on his phone he had a car on the way to take him to the local produce market. It was only a couple of miles away, but he felt that was maybe too far to walk in morning air that was already uncomfortable for someone used to the cooler New York weather.

In no time the car arrived to drive him to a local fruit store that had been in Little Havana for as long as he could remember. While not large, the stand had always used to have a good assortment of in-season fruits and some of the best milk shakes in the city.

In less than ten minutes he stepped out of the car and into the business. Much like at Versailles, customers ordered coffees, toast, shakes, and other items at a counter and then moved to a sitting area on one side of the building. He headed to the other part of the store and strolled through the stalls holding various fruits. At least three different kinds of mangoes. Mamey. Papayas. Plantains in stages ranging from a very ripe yellow to unripe green. Bananas, lemons, oranges, and melons mingled with coconuts, pineapples, and other tropical fruits. In one tall stand long stalks of fresh sugar cane waited to be crushed for the sweet grassy-flavored *guarapo* beverage so many Latinos enjoyed.

Tony smiled, recalling many a Saturday shopping excursion when his mother would buy a smaller piece of sugar cane for him to chew on while she picked up fruits and vegetables for the week.

Recognizing a familiar wizened face standing by a door to a back room, Tony walked over and greeted the man. "*¿Como estas, Luis?*"

"*Chico, que bueno verte,*" the old man said with a smile that displayed one gold tooth.

"It's good to see you too, *viejo*, I'm hoping you can help me out with some supplies."

"For Angelica's *quinceañera*?" Luis pulled the stub of a pencil from behind one ear as well as a small worn notepad from the pocket of baggy khaki pants that were barely held on his thin frame by a cracked leather belt. As usual, he wore an immaculate white T-shirt. Tony had always wondered how he kept it so pristine with all the manual labor he did.

"*Sí,* for Angelica's *quince*." Tony was reminded again that Little Havana was a lot like a small town tucked inside the big city. News traveled quickly within the community, and it was no wonder that Luis would know about his niece's party.

Tony launched into an explanation of what he would need for the menu he was contemplating as well as when and where he would need it. The old man bobbed his head up and down and scribbled notes in the pad and then said, "Let me check and see what I can do for you."

"*Gracias*, Luis. I appreciate it. Lucy still making *batidos*?" Tony asked and peered toward the counter where sure enough, an older woman with a helmet of coiffed white hair prepared milk shakes for a line of customers.

"She is and you'll break her *corazón* if you don't go see her," Luis said and jabbed the stub of the pencil in Tony's direction.

"I wouldn't miss her—or her *batidos*—for the world," he said and hurried over to the counter.

When Lucy caught sight of him, she handed the metal mixer glass to one of the clerks and waddled over in his direction. He met her halfway and engulfed her in a bear hug, lifting her off the ground. As he did, the older woman tittered and crooned, "*Amorcito*. You've been away from home for too long."

"I've been busy, *mi amor*," he teased right back and dropped a chaste kiss on her cheek.

"Is your *favorito* still mango?" she asked, slowly walking back to the counter. There was a slight hitch in her walk as if one leg pained her, reminding him that Luis and Lucy were getting older much like Little Havana and his parents.

His throat choked up and his heart ached with that realization. Stifling his sadness, he followed her and said, "Still mango, Lucy."

The older woman smiled and scooped small chunks of

fruit from a bowl into a metal mixer glass before adding condensed milk, regular milk, and sugar. She placed the glass into the blender and whirled it until the contents were frothy, then added crushed ice and blended it some more before pouring the shake into a glass for Tony. She stood there, expectant, while he drank it.

"*Delicioso*, Lucy. Even better than I remember," he said and wiped away his shake moustache with a napkin.

Lucy stroked a cold hand across his cheek. "It might not be so hard to remember if you visited more often. Your *mami* misses you."

Of course, I get the guilt trip, he thought. He should have remembered that his mother still shopped here, and that Lucy and she were also both regulars at their local church's rosary night.

"I miss her too, Lucy. I promise I'll be better," he said and hoped he'd be able to keep that promise.

Now that he was armed with the sweet, delicious, ice-cold mango shake, he decided he could brave the Miami weather for the almost two mile walk back to his parents' home. Luckily, a stiff breeze at his back propelled him there and mitigated the heat.

When he turned the corner onto his parents' block, he once again caught sight of his sister's Jeep, but he couldn't run away again. It was time to face whatever her latest demand was head-on. As he pushed through the door, the excited chatter of his mother and Sylvia talking snared his attention as did the harrumph from his father, who was still in the same position as he had been earlier that morning—the same position he spent most of his time in, just as he had for years. Newspaper in hand, bifocals halfway down his nose as he sat in his decade-old recliner. His father peered over the edge of the glasses and at a squeal from one of the women in the kitchen, he said, "*Hijo*, you better get in there before they get *mas loca* and have you feeding all of Little Havana."

Since Tony thought that the plans had already gotten well-past crazy, he sucked in a breath and girded himself for whatever new insanity awaited him.

CHAPTER 4

"CHEF, THERE'S SOMEONE OUT THERE who says he's an old friend."

Sara peered over the half wall that separated her restaurant's open kitchen from the dining area. As her hostess jerked her head in the direction of the front door, Sara craned her neck to see an older, but unquestionably memorable face, at the hostess podium. A face she had dreamed about more than once as a teen.

"OMG," she heard from beside her. "Is that Tony Sanchez? *The* Tony Sanchez?" said Jeri, her business partner, fellow chef, and long-time best friend. Inches shorter than Sara, Jeri had to rise on tiptoes to peer over the half-wall.

"None other," Sara said as she grabbed a towel to dry her hands and shot a quick look at a starstruck Jeri. Her aqua blue eyes were wide with surprise in a face of flawless *café con leche* skin. "Can you handle things for a few minutes?"

At Jeri's nod, Sara rushed out to greet Tony. She told herself not to make too much of how his smile widened when he spotted her, or how his eyes, those melty chocolate-colored eyes, warmed as he settled his gaze on her.

But it was impossible to stop how her heartbeat raced with the knowledge that he was here and seemingly happy to see her.

Hugs had always been freely given by the Sanchez family, but she held her hands out to him to avoid a hug, uncertain of how she'd react to the embrace. "It's been way too long, Tony." *Nine years and eight months, give or take*. Not that she was counting.

Liar, she told herself. Even though Tony had left Miami behind, she'd eagerly followed all his accomplishments. Even dared to wonder if he'd ever make Miami his home again.

Tony took both her hands in his and playfully wagged them. "You've grown up, *chiquitica*."

She laughed and tried to ignore the tingle building where her hands rested in his. Slowly she eased her hands free. "I couldn't stay ten forever. You look good," she said and prayed it didn't sound too much like flirting. To cover for it, she blurted out, "What brings you to Miami?"

"Family," he said and glanced around the restaurant. "I ran into Rick the other day and he mentioned you had a place, so I decided to come by and say 'Hello.'"

"Well, hello," she said, feeling more and more like a smitten teenager with every passing second. "Monica will get you a table." She waved at the hostess and when the young woman came by, she said, "Please seat Tony as soon as you can."

He raised his hand in a 'stop' motion. "*Por favor*, no special treatment."

Sara peered around the dining room. Every table was full inside and a quick look through the windows confirmed the outdoor seats were all taken. Plus, there were quite a few people milling around outside waiting to be seated.

"It may be a while," she said with an apologetic grimace.

Tony mimicked her action, scrutinizing the restaurant and outdoor area. "I can wait. I've got all night. And if I'm still here when the rush is over, maybe we can grab a coffee later?"

Coffee? With Tony? Butterflies erupted in her stomach, but she somehow got the word out. "S-s-s-ure," she stammered and without waiting for his reply, she rushed back to the kitchen before she embarrassed herself even more.

"You're blushing. I've never seen you blush before," Jeri kidded as Sara resumed the final plating of the nearly complete orders.

"It's the heat in the kitchen," she said.

"Sure, Sara. The heat and not..." Her friend paused and looked over the wall to where Tony waited outside, just beyond the entrance to the restaurant. "That hot guy you obviously have a crush on."

"Not a crush," she said and jerked tickets off the board to place them and the finished plates on the counter. Like clockwork her servers came over to pick up the meals and take them to their respective tables.

"Sure thing, Sara. Whatever you say," Jeri teased as she finished up an order of sliders by topping them with slices of perfectly grilled *foie gras*. When she was done, she passed the plates to Sara for the final touch of caramelized onion compote before a toasted brioche bun top completed the slider and the order went up on the counter.

"Please, Jeri, leave it alone," she pleaded and with a reluctant nod, her partner returned her focus to the new orders while Sara prayed that she wouldn't make a fool of herself with Tony when it came time to chat with him. She'd tried to keep her crush a secret from him and if he'd ever noticed it, he'd been gentleman enough not to mention it.

She wanted to keep it that way.

He had his restaurant and life in New York and she was here in Miami and never the twain would meet.

But in the back of her mind, she wondered, "What if?"

It had taken an hour for Tony to finally get a table. Despite the wait and the late hour, patrons still milled around outside for a spot at Sara's restaurant while others enjoyed their meals at metal bistro-style tables. At the center of each table was a galvanized metal tin with miniature orchids in full bloom along with a small votive candle. It made for a romantic setting despite the bustling crowd. At the corners of the fenced in outdoor space sat sago palms in large earthenware pots. All around the base of the palms a riot of color cascaded down from various flowering plants.

The place suited Sara, or at least what he remembered about her. She'd always been friendly and a hopeful romantic. He'd caught her reading romance novels more than once when he and Rick had dropped in unannounced for a swim at the Kellys' backyard pool. He'd even suspected that she'd kind of had a crush on him, but he hadn't acknowledged it because she was just a kid—not to mention, his best friend's younger sister.

But she's grown up, and very nicely.

He drove away that thought. No matter what, she was still Rick's sister and a chef to boot. He had no intention of repeating that mistake.

After the hostess flagged him down and led him to a table along a wall that provided a clear view of the kitchen, she quickly advised him that Sara would be sending him a plate with all of her favorite dishes and some wine for him to sample.

"Thank Sara for me, please" he said and sat back to soak in the ambiance of the interior.

The décor was simple. Sports photos and menus from various locations in Miami, some of them long gone icons, hung on the bright walls. The tables and chairs were a mix of rustic and industrial. Rough-hewn wooden tabletops blended with metal legs and bases. Metal chairs with tapered legs and curved backs matched the charcoal color of the table legs. Overhead, warehouse-style hanging lamps had shades in a mix of bright colors and cast warm light over the space.

It reminded him of one of the first places he had worked during one of his summers off from school. As a good son to immigrant parents, he had gone along with his parents' demands that he get a college degree, but with every free second, he had done everything he could to prepare for becoming a chef. Once he'd gotten his business degree, he'd struck out to follow his own dreams.

But he'd never realized Sara had the same dreams and he wondered when she'd made that decision. He peered toward the open kitchen where he could see the chefs busily preparing dishes for their customers. In the familiar cadence of professional kitchens, Sara called out the tickets and the chefs answered back to confirm the orders. She smiled at her people as they brought up the dishes for completion, but as she worked her expression became determined, almost fierce. Her grey-green eyes narrowed and focused intently on the plates. Full lips thinned until she worried her lower lip while she worked. She clearly cared deeply about the plates that would be served to the diners. *Her diners.*

She placed a completed dish up on the counter and it was efficiently whisked away by the waitstaff.

Her smile returned then and her gaze softened. *She is lovely*, he thought. The little girl with the scraped knees, braces and too-red hair had blossomed into a stunning woman. *Not to mention, a competent one*, Tony thought and smiled at how smoothly the kitchen seemed to be running.

Barely minutes later, one of the waitresses came over with a bottle of wine and a plate with an assortment of appetizers.

The name of the restaurant and the menu he had perused while waiting outside had told him that Sara specialized in small plates of comfort food, but with fine dining twists. The plate before him had what looked like mac and cheese balls, a slider, and roasted asparagus wrapped in crispy prosciutto along with what he guessed was *aioli*, probably for the asparagus.

The smells were enticing, and his mouth watered in anticipation. He picked up one asparagus spear and dipped it into the *aioli*. *Delicious*, he thought as the flavors of the garlic-scented mayonnaise blended with the delicate asparagus and slightly salty prosciutto. He quickly finished off the other spears before turning his attention to the mac and cheese balls.

Crunchy breading on the outside gave way to a burst of comforting melty cheesiness in the center. His experienced palate detected a mix of multiple cheeses. Hunger and eagerness driving him, he snared the slider and bit in. Another explosion of flavors greeted him, but the finishing touch that pushed the slider into gourmet caliber was the thin slice of perfectly grilled foie gras taking the place of a more predictable cheese.

He was so intent on the fantastic appetizers that he hadn't taken a sip of the wine, a Long Island Cabernet Franc. The wine was lighter than a Sauvignon, less acidic, with a stronger perfume and notes of cherry, cassis, and pepper. A perfect complement for his meal.

Impressive, he thought and wondered when Sara had decided to become a chef and what had inspired her to create food like what he had just eaten. Deceptively simple, comfort foods that were also inventive and gourmet which normally didn't go together.

It made him admire her and want to get to know the woman she had become even more.

"Is everything okay, chef?" the young waitress asked as she came by to switch out his empty plate.

"More than okay," he said with an enthusiastic nod. Like before, his plate was filled with a trio of samplings from the dinner menu. A square of lasagna, a petit filet wrapped in bacon, and several beer-battered fish nuggets rested beside a pile of French fries.

Although he wanted to dig into the food immediately, his appetite whetted by the appetizers, he held back to watch as Sara came out of the kitchen and made her way to various diners, stopping to chat with them and share a laugh. Her manner was easy and genuine with a full smile as her head tilted back and her body relaxed. Her grey-green eyes were alight with pleasure as she chatted with one man and a blush of color came to her cheeks at what he hoped had been a compliment about her food.

Once again, he was struck that this was no longer the tomboy he'd known. Womanly curves filled out her chef's clothing. Her red hair, always the bane of Sara's young existence, had mellowed like a copper penny into a rich cocoa brown with streaks of gold and auburn. The pigtails he'd used to pull out of annoyance were gone, replaced with a sleek cut that emphasized her heart-shaped face and the full lips that still created that marvelous smile.

He waited for her to come by his table, but she only shot him a shy smile that whispered "later" and warmed something inside of him. Something that made him feel both excited and worried. Excited because he wanted to get to know more about her. Worried not only because she was Rick's little sister, but because she was a chef.

When she returned to the kitchen, he finally gave into his desire to sample more of Sara's amazing cooking.

Each dish was perfect, from the sweet, more-than-likely home-made ricotta in the lasagna to the light and crunchy beer batter around the fish nuggets. It reminded him of a London street vendor's fish and chips he'd had during a trip to receive one of his cooking awards.

His only complaint with tonight's meal was that there wasn't enough. He understood why people were willing to wait so long for a seat. Not to mention that the nature of the menu, with its small plates, variety, and—most importantly—quality, was perfect for the kind of crowd you'd get in this part of South Beach: people coming off the nearby beach, heading out for a night of partying, or coming back from a night of partying.

"Would you like some coffee? Dessert?" the waitress asked.

Tony laid a hand over his stomach. "I'd love to, only–"

"I'd be heartbroken if you refused," Sara said as she slipped past the waitress with a collection of plates and sat opposite him.

"You did mention having coffee together, right?" Sara said with a hesitant smile.

"Far be it for me to break your heart," Tony said and grinned.

Did he realize that his grin already did all kinds of things to my heart? That just sitting here opposite him is something I'd dreamed of as a teenager with a crush on my older brother's best friend?

Sara suspected that it was totally possible that Tony could one day break it if she let her feelings for him blossom again.

As Sara eased the plate in front of Tony, she smiled at the waitress. "Some coffee please, Mandy."

"Yes, chef." The young lady returned the smile.

"Thank you," Sara said and after a nod, Mandy hurried away.

"I hope you enjoyed your meal." Sara was both nervous and eager to hear Tony's take on her food. With his reputation as a chef his opinion mattered a great deal. But it also mattered on a more personal level she had to admit. She'd hate for him to be disappointed in her.

"It was excellent, Sara. And totally unexpected."

"Because of the name of the restaurant or me?" she said with a wrinkle of her nose.

A soft smile graced Tony's lips. "Never you, Sara. You were always kind of a perfectionist as a kid."

"I'm not a kid anymore, Tony," she said and the heat of a flush rose to her cheeks. She told herself not to read too much into his praise. It might only be his being nice to an old family friend.

"No, you're not," Tony replied. The husky note in his voice and the look he shot her confirmed that he *had* noticed she was a grown woman now. *But now that he has, what am I going to do about it?*

Flustered, she organized the smaller dessert plates before them and offered Tony the first choice from the sweets she had brought over.

He picked up a mini-cannoli and took a bite and murmured his approval of the treat. "Is that fresh ricotta in the filling and the lasagna?"

Sara nodded and smiled, pleased that he had noticed. She picked up the other mini-cannoli and said, "We make it every day. The shells also, as well as the fresh mozzarella for the other dishes."

"*Brava,*" Tony said and finished off the pastry. He picked up another one, a *churro,* and dipped it into a caramel sauce, one of three sauces on the plate. After taking a bite, he once again hummed his approval and ate the rest of the *churro* in a single bite.

They both reached for the second *churro* at the same time, fingers bumping together.

A zing of awareness traveled up her arm and shot through her. She jerked her hand back. Tony did the same and she wondered if he'd felt the blast. A second later, he motioned for her to take the pastry which she did.

She dipped the *churro* into the mango sauce, her personal favorite, and offered it to Tony, expectant. *Will he like it as much as I do? And why is his approval so important anyway?*

He held her hand to steady it while he took a bite and that buzz of electricity traveled up her arm again. Caused her heart to beat erratically again. She told herself not to read too much into the almost intimate gesture of sharing the food with him.

"Love the sauce. Is that ginger in there?" Tony said.

She nodded, pleased, and double-dipped the remaining piece into the mango sauce so that she could have a taste, as well, forcing herself to ignore that his tempting lips had just been on it. "A little lime zest as well."

Tony took the final churro and swirled it around in the last sauce, a chocolate chili pepper mix. He presented the last pastry to her for the first bite.

As her gaze met his over the long cylinder of the *churro*, sharing the sweets suddenly felt like a too-intimate act. She eyed the sweet, coated with the spicy chocolate sauce she'd made and then glanced past the bite to Tony. He waited there, an expectant smile on his face. A second later he said, "They say never trust a chef who won't eat their own food."

"They say a lot of things, but they might be right with that one." With a chuckle, she took a bite and the warm heat of the ancho chili powder she'd mixed into the chocolate teased her tongue. As she had done before, Tony swirled the remaining piece of the *churro* in the chocolate sauce and popped the last bite into his mouth.

"Wow, that is wonderful. A perfect balance of sweet, spice, and heat," he said.

She dipped her head in gratitude. "Coming from you, that's quite a compliment."

"It's well-earned. Everything I tasted today—all your favorites—were fantastic," he said and looked all around the restaurant. "Judging from the crowd, they love your food too."

Sara peered at her customers and smiled. "I've been lucky."

"Talented," Tony corrected and continued. "How did you decide to be a chef?"

Sara was more than pleased by Tony's praise. She was about to tell him that he was the reason she'd embarked on that career when the waitress returned to the table. "I'm sorry to bother you, chef, but you're needed in the kitchen."

"Thank you, Mandy," she said before turning her attention to Tony. "I'm so sorry," she apologized, truly regretting that she had to leave him since they'd been having such a good time. A time she wanted to repeat, but she hesitated the barest second before blurting out, "Maybe we can do this again sometime?"

He grinned and his eyes twinkled with surprised pleasure. "How about dinner tomorrow? When do you close?"

She grimaced. They stayed open for the after-party crowd and it had become their custom to share a meal after they were done rather than before service. "Two a.m. is when we normally do our 'family meal' for staff. You're welcome to join us." That would make it far less dangerous than having dinner alone with him.

Although he seemed a bit disappointed—at the late hour? Or at the idea that it wouldn't be dinner alone?—he smiled and said, "That's usually when we do ours at my place as well. I'd love to join you."

She was both pleased and anxious about his response. "I look forward to it."

She rushed back to the kitchen while breathing a sigh of relief that she hadn't made a complete fool of herself in front of Tony.

Jeri, who had just finished plating an order when Sara entered, tossed her a wry grin. "Looks like the chef approved of more than just the food."

"Shut up, Jeri," she said playfully and snapped a kitchen towel at her fellow chef. "Let's get back to work."

"Yes, chef," Jeri said with an impudent chuckle and Sara couldn't help but laugh as well.

The night hadn't gone as she'd expected what with Tony visiting, but thankfully his visit had ended well. *Very well*, she thought, already looking forward to seeing Tony again. But even as she contemplated that, she warned herself not to get too involved with the handsome chef. He was only visiting and wouldn't stay for long. And he was Rick's friend which complicated things even more.

It was better that she keep it at a friendly level with Tony. *Just friends*, she tried to convince herself as she turned her attention back into prepping meal orders. She had to focus on her business, her niece's *quinceañera*, and nothing more. Especially not the handsome and talented Tony Sanchez.

CHAPTER 5

Roberta Lane stared at her editor as if he'd sprouted two heads. "You want me to do a story on what?"

Marco Ramirez placed the two invitations on her desktop. "I want you to cover these two *quinceañeras*—as well as any others that you can find—for a story on how these traditions are making a comeback in Miami."

She spread her hands wide in a pleading gesture. "I don't know a thing about...about—" She grabbed one of the invites, struggling to recall the name of the events.

"*Quinceañeras*," Marco repeated, enunciating each syllable.

"All right, but again, I don't know a thing about what a *quinceañera* is," she said.

"They're like a Sweet Sixteen, but at fifteen instead."

Roberta grimaced. "I don't do kids, Marco, you know that. My kind of lifestyle is charity events, weddings, art gallery openings—the kind of parties attended by the crème-de-la-crème of South Beach."

Marco glared at her from beneath his furrowed brow. "Get off your high horse, Roberta. I hired you from the free local newspaper."

"And I've worked hard to prove that I can do much more than that," she reminded him.

With a frown, he said, "Don't get so full of yourself. You'll do as I say if you don't want to end up doing the classified ads again. Besides, these two events are going to be attended by some of Miami's better-known residents, including *moi*."

These kinds of events were out of her wheelhouse. A *quinceañera*? She'd have to research just what that meant, which would take a lot of time from her other assignments. But as she looked at her boss, it was clear she wasn't getting out of this one. Continuing to argue wouldn't change her boss's mind, but it *would* tick him off. Better to stop protesting now, and just try to get through this story as quickly and painlessly as possible. She bit back a sneer and picked up the two invites. "At least they're in nice locations. I'll get the interviews set up and arrange with the photographer to get some shots of the girls preparing for the parties and then later at the events. Is there anything else you'd like me to do for the story?"

Marco cupped his jaw, thoughtful as he considered her question. "It would be good if we could find an exciting angle. Something that will draw attention to the magazine. We need a boost in readership."

Without waiting for her reply, Marco left her office.

"An exciting angle, huh?" she murmured to herself and examined the invitations again.

She quickly jumped on the Internet to try and find out more about the two girls. Thanks to some articles in a local paper about a soccer championship, she realized that they went to the same exclusive prep school. Two teen girls having big parties within a day of each other. *Drama*, she thought, recalling her own teen years.

"You want gossip, you'll get it, Marco."

CHAPTER 6

As Samantha rushed out of the high school building, she caught sight of Angelica sitting on the
ledge of a planter by the curb, apparently also waiting
to be picked up after soccer tryouts. Most everyone else
had already left.

Angelica's head was bent over a notebook, focus-
ing so intently on whatever she was drawing that she
didn't notice as Samantha walked up to her. Samantha
couldn't avoid seeing the colorful images that Angelica
had sketched in the notebook once she neared her rival.

"What's that?" she asked, intrigued by the drawings.

Angelica's head snapped up and she laid her hand
over the paper to hide what she was doing. "Just some
doodles."

Samantha shrugged and tried not to let Angelica's
attempt at secrecy bother her. "Looked interesting. Are
they for something at your *quinceañera*?"

Angelica hesitated for a too long moment before
showing her the pictures and blurting out, "They're
favors. I was thinking of putting together a small bottle
of sour orange juice, a grinder with dried garlic, and a

packet of cumin seeds. Miami spice, get it?"

Samantha nodded and chuckled. "Totally." Because Angelica had shared, she said, "I'm still trying to figure out my favors, but mom and I are doing centerpieces with cigar boxes, flowers, and vintage postcards from Havana."

Angelica narrowed her gaze, as if in thought, and said, "How about for favors, you go with chocolate and candy cigars? You could wrap them in a bundle like they do with some of those fancy cigars our dads like to smoke."

Samantha imagined exactly that, with brightly colored ribbons to hold the candies in place. "Thanks. I like that idea. What are you doing for your centerpieces?"

Angelica did an uneasy lift of her shoulders and flipped to another page in her notebook. It was filled with images of spice jars and bottles similar to what she had been drawing for the favors, but the designs were not as elegant or balanced.

"Pretty bad, right?" Angelica said after Samantha's prolonged silence.

"Not so bad," Samantha replied with a shrug. She pointed to one design in particular. "Why don't you use real fruit instead of the bottles? Make it like a still life with oranges –"

"—limes, lemons and everything else you use to spice up Cuban food," Angelica jumped in, whipping to a new page in the book and immediately starting to sketch.

"And you could mix in orange blossoms and other flowers in between the fruits," Samantha added, picturing how lovely the centerpiece would look.

The blare of a car horn shattered the picture that had formed in Samantha's mind and grabbed their attention. Angelica's mom screeched to the curb in her new lime green Wrangler. She seemed surprised to see Samantha and her daughter chatting and waved awkwardly.

Samantha returned the greeting as Angelica hopped off the ledge, shoved her notebook into her knapsack, and hurried toward her mother's car. But as she reached the door, Angelica turned, smiled and did a slight wave of her hand. "Thanks, Samantha. See you tomorrow."

Samantha returned the wave and offered a hesitant grin. "See you."

The Jeep rushed away from the curb with a squeal of tires just as Samantha's mom pulled up in the family's late model sedan. As Samantha slipped into the passenger seat her mother said, "Was that Sylvia Rodriguez? She always had a lead foot. It's a good thing she's a lawyer so she can get out of all those tickets she must get."

"Yes, that was her—she just picked up Angelica after tryouts," she said.

Her mother scrutinized her intently. "Everything okay with you and Angelica?"

Samantha tilted her head and pondered her mother's question for a moment. "Surprisingly yes. More than okay actually," she admitted. It was quite a surprise, considering that just three days ago Angelica had been all Drama Queen over the *quinceañera* invite.

Her mother opened her eyes wide. "*De verdad?*"

Samantha nodded and chuckled. "For realz."

With a tilt of her head, her mother said, "That is truly a surprise."

As her mother pulled away from the curb, Samantha murmured, "Most definitely." But as surprising as it was, she couldn't deny it had been nice to be able to talk to Angelica, almost like she was a friend. In truth, she wished they could be friends instead of rivals since they had so much in common. They were both good students and enjoyed the same sports. They had a number of other friends in common, but rarely spent time together with them.

Maybe today is the start of a change. A good change, she thought, but didn't say since it was still too new and uncertain.

"Isn't that wonderful, Tony?" Sylvia gushed and slid a business card across the table toward him.

He perused the card from the reporter for a local lifestyle magazine. *Roberta Lane. Lifestyle Columnist. South Beach Style.*

"She's interested in doing a story on *quinceañeras*?" he asked, wanting to make sure that he understood.

"*Sí.* They're apparently making a comeback in the area and she wants to cover a few of them and share why families think it's important to keep up the tradition. She heard about Angelica's *quinceañera* and wants to include us in the article. This will be amazing," Sylvia almost gushed.

From inside the family room, where his father sat in his recliner reading, he heard a grunt and a mumbled, "*¡Locura!*"

He had to agree with his father. But then again, his sister had wanted the party to be a big splash. And he couldn't deny that it could work out well for him, too—being back in the limelight might help his career even if he was staying in New York.

"It's a good thing, Sylvia," he said and pushed the card back across the surface of the table.

"I hear a 'but' there, Tony. This will give all of us a lot

of publicity. She'll probably want to interview you since you're the hometown boy who made it big."

He shrugged off his sister's compliment. "Some say success is 25% talent and 75% luck. I was lucky, *hermanita*."

"And I've heard success is 10% inspiration and 90% perspiration. You worked hard for what you accomplished, Tony. You deserve your success." Sylvia picked up the card and tucked it into her binder which had somehow grown even larger and pinker and was threatening to burst at the seams. He was worried that if it did bust open, it would litter most of Little Havana with lace, confetti, and glitter.

"*Sin duda*," his mother said, jumping into the conversation as she walked into the room to prepare some coffee.

"*Gracias*," he said and rose from the table to help his mother get the espresso maker down from the topmost shelf in the cabinet. "*Mami*, why do you put it where you can't reach it?"

His mother jerked her head of perfectly coiffed white hair in the direction of the family room and in a guilty whisper said, "Because getting it down for me is the only way I can get your *papi* to move from that *sillón*."

Tony leaned back to peer out the door of the kitchen to the family room and where his father sat in the recliner. He held a different newspaper in his hands while the noise from a Miami Marlins baseball game on the television played in the background. Cubans loved their baseball, especially his father who claimed to have once tried out with Castro for the Yankees.

With a nod to his mother, he called out, "*Papi, mami* needs your help."

The newspaper rattled and the chair groaned as his

father rose and muttered under his breath, "*Esa mujer.*
I told that woman to leave it on the counter. Why can't
you get it, Antonio?"

"I'm busy with Sylvita," Tony shouted and hurried
back to his chair. His father shuffled in, rose on tiptoes
to get the coffee pot, and handed it to his wife. As he
did so, he brushed a kiss across his wife's cheek and
hugged her. "*Amorcito, por favor*, keep it on the counter."

She tucked herself against his side and returned the
kiss. "*Amorcito*, how else can I get you to move?"

His dad mimicked a dancing pose and said, "We
could go to the senior center tonight. They're having a
mamba band and I heard they're really good."

"Are you asking me on a date, *querido*?" his mother
said, a delicate hand splayed across her chest as she
batted her eyelashes.

"*Dios mio*, please stop," his father teased and kissed
her again.

"Aren't they cute?" Sylvia said and Tony couldn't help
but laugh. It *was* cute that his parents could still be so
flirtatious with each other.

"They are. It must be nice," he said, almost wistfully,
wondering what it would be like to have such love for
so long.

"You'll find someone, Tony. Maybe here while you're
in Miami," Sylvia said and opened her binder to pull
out some of the papers.

With Sylvia's words a picture of Sara flared to life.
That smile and the tingle when they'd touched, which
he'd tried to ignore. The way a lock of her coppery hair
feathered onto her forehead, making him itch to brush it
away. The cute little wrinkle of her nose, reminding him
of the young girl who'd chased after Rick and him. But
he immediately tamped down that spark of awareness.

"My life is in New York, *hermanita*," he said, even if he was enjoying his time in Miami way too much for the time being.

"Your *unhappy* life is in New York. I know you and I can tell that you're not enjoying what you've been doing." Sylvia pushed a few of the papers in his direction, namely the draft of the menu he had worked up with her a few days earlier. She gestured to the papers and said, "*This* is what you want to be doing. Cooking. Every day."

"And what makes you think it would be any different here? Running a restaurant is always going to come with responsibilities outside of the kitchen, no matter where it is," he challenged, perusing the menu and mentally making lists of what he would have to order to be able to prepare and serve the meal to the nearly two hundred guests attending the party.

"It can be different if *you're* different, *hermanito*. You're trusting your chefs and manager back in New York. You can trust people here and you'd be closer to family so we could help. Maybe you could even get a partner," his sister said as she yanked out a seating chart from the binder and started moving around the adhesive notes with people's names.

"A partner like my ex?" he said with a huff, earning a glare from Sylvia.

"Dina was a huge mistake you should have seen coming. She was just riding on your coattails and on top of that, she resented your success." Sylvia ripped a sticky note off one table to move it to another. At his questioning look, she said, "I heard the other day that these two friends had a fight a few months ago and aren't speaking."

"Maybe I should have known what would happen with Dina," he said, hating that his sister could be so right about a relationship she'd only seen from long distance while he'd been right there, up close and personal, and had still been so wrong. His bad judgment and fear of repeating it were the main reasons why he hadn't dated since the breakup. That, and all the work at the restaurant. But for the next few weeks he'd have the time to explore new recipes and possibly a new relationship.

Like taking time tonight to go hang out with Sara. As two chefs who appreciated talent. As two long-time friends and nothing more.

But even as he told himself he shouldn't pursue her, for a moment he was tempted to mention seeing Sara to Sylvia since he'd always trusted his sister's judgment. But he held back. Nothing could really happen with Sara since he had a life and restaurant back in New York. At the thought of it, he jumped up from the table with a worried, "I have to call the restaurant and see what's up."

He hurried back to his room, whipped out his smartphone, and speed-dialed his sous chef Amanda who answered on the second chirp. "How's it going?" he asked.

"Fine, *jefe*. Ramon is doing a great job managing everything and we're holding down the fort," Amanda said.

"Are you sure you don't need me for anything?" Tony asked, worried about his absence was impacting the restaurant.

"You've done a great job of training us. No reason for you to cut your vacation short, unless you're homesick," Amanda teased, and in the background, the familiar cadence of the chefs answering confirmed all was well.

If truth be told, he might be more homesick once he left Miami. Even with the *quinceañera* insanity, he'd had time over the last couple of days to meet up with a few old friends, visit some old stomping grounds, and hit the beach for some delicious sun and relaxation.

"I'm glad everything's going well. Keep me posted if you need anything."

"I will and Tony..." She hesitated but then plunged on. "Lots of places have executive chefs who aren't in the restaurant all the time. We're doing well. Don't worry."

"Thanks, Amanda. I'll try not to," he said and went to swipe to end the call, but held off for a long second, almost wanting to ask yet again if things were okay. They were and he tried not to let his ego be stung too badly by the realization that they didn't need him around. But then again, if he hadn't taught his staff so well, they wouldn't be doing such a good job without him.

Without me, he thought once more and reminded himself that as Amanda had said, some executive chefs worked at more than one place, planning menus, developing new recipes, hiring and training staff, and all the other things he'd been doing at his own restaurant. If things were going fine back in New York maybe there was no reason why he couldn't think about a second location here in Miami.

One where he could be close to his family and old friends. Maybe one where he could even think about a relationship with someone. Maybe even Sara. The short time with her yesterday had been nice and he was looking forward to spending time with her tonight at her place's "family meal" after the restaurant closed. Maybe if it went well, he could get some time alone with her. He was still a little uneasy about the idea of getting involved with another chef, but his first impressions said that Sara was nothing like his ex.

He walked back to the kitchen to deal with his sister's almost frantic focus on seating arrangements. He dreaded being sucked into that part of the planning, but he had nothing else to do since they'd already had dinner and it would be hours before he would go see Sara.

Sylvia glanced up. "You're smiling, *hermanito*, Everything okay at work?"

"Couldn't be better," he said and, for the first time in a long time, he meant it.

Things were different here and as Sylvia had wisely pointed out, that meant he could be different as well.

And maybe that difference could include Sara during the time he'd be in Miami. But he also warned himself not to let it become more. He didn't want to hurt Sara when he went back to New York. He knew he needed to keep his distance from his friend's younger sister, but it was getting harder and harder to think of her as only that little freckled kid who'd tagged after them.

Sara was a beautiful, vibrant and talented woman. One who was hard to resist, but he'd do his best.

"We've hit pay dirt, Marco," Roberta said and tossed a handful of printouts onto her editor's desk.

He peered at her above the rim of his bifocals and picked up the papers. After he perused them, he murmured in interest. "We did a feature on Chef Sanchez, didn't we?"

"I checked our archives. An article two years ago when his restaurant got a big star. We also did a piece on Sara Kelly, her restaurant, and that fundraiser last year," Roberta said and leaned on Marco's desk to loom over him. "And guess which two top chefs are cooking at those *quinceañeras* you wanted me to cover?"

Marco jerked back and pointed to the printouts she'd

given him. "Sanchez and Kelly? Really?"

Roberta straightened and gestured for Marco to look up, as if conjuring a headline in the air. "Picture this, Marco. An award-winning celebrity chef competing against an up-and-coming chef to make the best *quinceañera* meal ever."

Marco's eyebrows drew together, creating a deep furrow across his forehead. "They're having a competition? Since when is this a contest?

Roberta tsked and shook her head. "You wanted an exciting angle, didn't you? We tell them we can only really feature one of them in the article. By the time I'm done with those two they'll be chomping at the bit to prove who's the best chef and get that feature."

Marco tilted his head and smiled, a very cold and calculating smile that said it all for her.

"I guess that smile means I have your approval to take the story in this direction?" Roberta asked, hands on her hips.

"Go for it. It's a win-win situation: the magazine gets a great story and I get two fabulous meals since I was invited to both events," Marco said.

Roberta smiled, snatched the printouts off his desk, and raced out of his office. She had calls to make, interviews to set up, and rivalries to stoke. Marco had made it clear she had to create gossip that would draw people to the magazine. If she did this right, the interest in this story would keep people talking for weeks.

CHAPTER 7

Sara looked beyond the half wall of the kitchen for what seemed like the hundredth time that night.

"He's still not here," Jeri teased as she finished plating one of the slider orders and placed it on the counter.

"I'm not looking for him. Just judging the crowd," she said which was a half-truth at best. Okay, maybe an outright lie. She'd spent most of the night waiting for Tony's arrival, anticipating that moment. Excitement racing through her at the thought of spending time with him.

"Finally thinning out," Jeri said with a relieved sigh. It had been an exceptionally busy Thursday night that had kept Jeri from going home early. Lately it seemed like Thursday was the new Friday.

"I know it's hard for you not to see Sophie before you put her to bed," Sara said and tackled an order of au gratin potatoes topped with melted cheese.

Jeri shrugged and arranged a chiffonade of basil on a caprese salad. "But I'm normally there in the morning and afternoon thanks to you, so I can deal," her friend said.

Sara withdrew the plate with the potatoes out of the salamander and smiled at the perfectly melted and crisped cheese on top of the equally crisp and golden potatoes. "Perfect," she murmured.

"Yes, I am, sis," said a disembodied voice from over the ledge of the wall.

She looked up to find Rick there, Tony beside him. Warmth filled her at the sight of him and Tony's smile.

"I wasn't expecting you, bro," she said, though she greeted him with a smile. She was always happy to see Rick—and she doubted that Jeri would mind either as she suspected her partner had a thing for her older brother.

"I was hoping to scrounge up dinner with you." Rick winked at Jeri before he turned back to Sara and plowed on with his explanation. "I ran into Tony outside. It'll be just like the old days." Rick slung an arm around Tony's shoulders.

Her smile became a bit forced as she said, "Great." Would it be just like when Tony had only seen her as Rick's annoying little sister? But as her gaze locked with Tony's, his dark brown gaze glittered with anything but brotherly interest. *Definitely not like in the old days*, she thought with pleasure.

"Take a seat. We're just finishing our final orders and you can join us for the family meal when we close up," she said and motioned to one of the empty tables by the door to the kitchen.

Out of the corner of her eye she watched the men as they sat, observing them in stolen looks during the next hour until they were saying goodbye to the last of their customers. Anticipation building for the moment she would sit beside Tony for the meal. She looked forward to getting caught up with his life and having him get to know her better.

As she wiped her hands on a kitchen towel and walked over to Tony and her brother, she noticed several empty plates on their table.

"I guess you couldn't wait," she teased. Rick had always been a big eater and between the hard physical labor of the business's deliveries and his daily six-mile run, he was in as good shape, maybe better, than he had been as a high school football player. *Tony has, likewise, stayed fit,* she thought, admiring the lean physique beneath the Cuban-style cotton *guayabera* shirt he wore. The pleated linen shirt was tight across his shoulders, but loose around his midsection.

Rick rubbed his stomach and said, "I'm a growing boy, sis. Jeri was nice enough to slip us a few snacks."

She turned to stare at her sous chef who blushed at the attention of both sister and brother. With a toss of her hands, Jeri said, "What can I say? He *is* a growing boy."

Sara rolled her eyes and shook her head. "We'll be right back."

She returned to the kitchen entrance where on either side of the swinging half-door there were two conspicuously posted signs. One read "No tweezers allowed." The other looked like a traffic sign and had a red circle with a red diagonal line superimposed over the pictogram for tweezers. Sara had no patience for starred chefs who only served tiny samplings of food prepared with tweezers to their customers. She wanted her diners to leave satisfied both physically and emotionally.

In the kitchen, preparation for the family meal was well underway. The various chefs made big plates of food for their kitchen staff and guests while the other employees brought together some of the bigger tables in the dining room to make one long one where they all could sit and eat.

Tony joined Rick and her employees in setting the table while Sara spooned out big bowls of the macaroni and cheese they used in their mac and cheese balls. Jeri had grilled two dozen patties and turned them into sliders while the other line chefs served up plates of ox tails, baked chicken, and a variety of vegetable dishes for the communal meal.

Tony walked over to take one of the heavy bowls from Sara and Rick did the same for Jeri, who gifted Rick with a shy smile. Sara wondered why the two of them just didn't finally do something about their obvious attraction.

Like you'll do with Tony? the little voice in her head asked.

Maybe, she shot back because she wasn't afraid of challenges.

"I always like the family meal with my staff," Tony said as he placed the bowl and a serving spoon on the table.

"Me too. I've got great people working with me," she said and motioned to them as they set up the food. "You've already met Jeri. These are my line chefs. Selena, Latoya, Brenda, Diane, and Natalie." She then introduced the rest of the kitchen and waiting staff as they all took places at the table.

Tony waited until Sara sat and then took a spot beside her while Jeri and Rick parked themselves opposite them. The other staff quickly sat down and soon the bowls and plates of food were going around the table family-style. People served themselves hearty portions of the different dishes.

Even though Tony had eaten earlier, the snacks had only whetted his appetite for more of Sara's delicious food. Since he'd already tried some of the dishes the other day, he selected ones which were new to him. A big serving of ox tails, always a favorite when his mother made them; fried string beans; and slices of what looked like an upside-down *tarte tartin* but were really beautifully caramelized potatoes with ooey gooey melted cheese on top.

"Everything looks amazing," he said and handed off the plate with the potatoes to one of the line chefs.

Rick murmured his approval as well and eyed both Sara and Jeri with pride. "That's my sis and her amazing partner and crew."

"You have to say that, or we'll stop feeding you for free," Sara said with a chuckle and wag of her head.

"He's like a stray cat. Never feed them—they'll always be coming back for more," Jeri added and playfully rubbed shoulders with Rick.

"I know a good thing when I see it, and this is good. Great actually," Rick said and shoved a large helping of mac and cheese into his mouth.

Tony laughed and forked a piece off the ox tail. The tender meat came off the bone easily and the fragrance of the sauce hit him even before the morsel was in his mouth. But as he bit down, the sweetness of the meat teased his tongue along with just the right touch of heat. After he swallowed, he said, "Don't tell anyone I said this, but this is better than my mom's and she's known as the Queen of *Rabos* in Little Havana."

Jeri pulled out her phone and mimicked sending a message. "I'm tweeting it as we speak. Your *mami* follows our feed, *sabes?*"

"I didn't know she was on social media," he replied with a laugh and picked up one of the crispy string beans.

"Maybe you would if you visited more," Rick said and then held his hands up in a "Don't shoot" gesture at Tony's glare. "Didn't mean to go there, but we do miss you."

Sara glanced between Tony and her brother. "Jeri does almost all of our social media. She loves to take photos of the dishes before they go out to the customers."

"That's a great idea—I'll have to try that at my place." He might be the chef with the star, but Sara and her staff were proving themselves possibly more worthy of that distinction. He looked down the table toward the other chefs and staff. "You've got a good crew from what I can see. Where have they all worked before?"

Jeri and Sara shared what seemed like an uncomfortable look before Sara said, "Mostly here. We train a lot of our own people, but Jeri and I went to the Culinary Institute of America in Hyde Park. It's where we met."

"And became besties," Jeri added and held her hand up for a fist bump.

Tony could see why the two women bonded. With her effervescent personality Jeri was bound to draw out Sara, who despite her fearlessness at almost every task as a kid, had always been a little shy around people. Or at least she'd been shy around him. Which told him that maybe he wasn't imagining the vibes he was reading from her now. Maybe she'd been shy because she was interested in him, and he hoped that hadn't changed.

Sara fist bumped Jeri back and smiled. "We came

home to Miami to work at some of the local restaurants. When I decided I was going to take a chance and open a place, Jeri took the leap with me."

"Never had any doubts," Jeri said and looked toward the rest of the staff. "We met women in the other kitchens and locations where we first started working, and when we opened this place, they came to work for us. Since then some of them have moved up and we've brought on women from a local shelter and trained them so they'd learn a marketable skill."

"That's not an easy thing to do," Tony said. It was hard enough running a place without also having to train people with little or no experience while doing it. It was impressive that Sara and Jeri had accomplished so much, but also that they took a chance so they could help others. Each thing he learned about Sara made him more and more interested in getting to know the complex woman she'd become.

"But totally worth it," Sara added with a determined bop of her head and his heart swelled with pride at her generosity and her humility. Others would not be as humble. Certainly not his Dina, his ex.

"Was this the first location for the restaurant?" he asked as he peered around the interior, even more intrigued now by Sara's journey.

"Come on, man. A place like this in this location takes big money," Rick said and rubbed together his thumb and forefinger. "They had to build up to it."

"We started with a food truck. Ran that for a couple of years and stashed away every spare penny. When we wanted a permanent spot, your brother-in-law found us this place and Sylvia sweet talked the owner into leasing it to us in exchange for our fixing it up," Sara explained.

"It was a mess after the last tenant. Took us a good

four months to get everything repaired and up to code. Luckily, we had help with all the work," Jeri said and beamed at Rick.

His friend raised his arm and flexed to show off work-hardened muscle beneath his sleeve. "Sweat equity."

"It's good that you had family and friends to help," he said, feeling a little left out. Sylvia had never mentioned helping Sara nor had Rick said anything about it when they messaged each other. But then again, he'd been the one who stayed away for years and had no one to blame but himself for not knowing everything that was happening in Miami with his friends and family. It was also something that only he could change and he wanted to change it.

"When the banks wouldn't," Jeri added with a frown and pushed away her now empty plate.

Tony turned to glance questioningly at Sara, but she immediately changed the subject. Motioning to his food, she said, "Did you try the potatoes? They're one of my favs."

He hadn't and since she'd seemed eager to change the subject, he dug into the dish and let his questions drop. He could understand that Sara might not like him knowing that things had been so rough for her, but it only made him think even more of her and what she had accomplished. It made him admire her strength and perseverance.

As he dug into the potatoes and brought them to his mouth, a thin string of melted cheese dangled from his fork. Rich butter, tangy cheese, both crusty and creamy potatoes, and a hint of smokiness invaded his senses when he ate the bite. Around a mouthful of food, he said, "I've got to get this recipe."

"I'd be delighted to share it with you," Sara said,

her eyes gleaming with pleasure at his appreciation for her food. But as her gaze dipped down to his lips as he licked away a bit of the cheese, he imagined more than her gaze on his lips.

"Maybe we can cook together when you have a moment," he said, hopeful that he could spend more time with her in the future. Even that it could be more than just two chefs admiring what both had accomplished.

Sara smiled and did a little shrug of fine-boned shoulders. "Are you sure? We don't do the whole fancy toque and chef's jacket thing here."

"I don't either. Makes my head too sweaty," he said and ran a hand through his hair, brushing back the thick waves that had always made the traditional chef's headwear a nightmare.

"Maybe," she said and finished the last bit of food on her plate.

He had hoped for something more than a "maybe" but didn't want to push too soon. Glancing down at his own plate, he realized that he'd eaten every heaping spoonful of food while they'd been talking. A quick look around the table confirmed others were also done with their meals. It made him sad that his time with Sara would soon be over for the night, especially considering the uncertainty in her "Maybe."

"Why don't you walk Sara home, Tony?" Rick suggested. "It's kinda late."

"It's always 'kinda late' when we're done. And why don't *you* ever walk me home?" Jeri groused and elbowed him.

Rick seemed taken aback. "Would you like that?"

"Girl shouldn't have to ask," Jeri said with a pout of full lips and a sparkle in her blue eyes.

"That's okay. We've still got all this to get cleaned up

and put away," Sara said and gestured to the table, her delicate hands graceful. There was a little wrinkle in her nose as she looked toward her kitchen and obviously thought about the work necessary to clean it up.

"You two go. Jeri and I have got this," Rick said and clapped him on the back.

Jeri offered her agreement. "We've totally got this. You two go ahead."

Tony peered between Rick and Jeri and sensed that his old friend was not only helping Tony, but also himself since he was clearly interested in Sara's partner and wanted some alone time with her. Tony didn't have to be told twice. He rose and held out his hand to Sara. "May I?"

Sara hesitated, but then slipped her hand into his. Her touch brought to life a life of dormant feelings. As she rose, she smiled at him and said, "I just have to change out of these clothes and grab my bag. Is that okay?"

"Totally," he said with a grin, happy that his night with her wasn't over.

With a tug, she guided him from the table. As she stepped away, she turned to her crew. "Good job, everyone. You really nailed it tonight. See you tomorrow."

Claps, hoots, and calls of "Thank you, chef," chased them from the dining area as they headed into an office space behind the kitchen. Her crew's happy vibes were so different from the ones he had gotten in his own restaurant lately. He blamed himself for how crabby he had gotten with his own staff. They used to have that kind of warmth in the beginning—but it had faded as his mood had taken a decided downturn with the demands of managing the restaurant.

In the back, he noticed that both Sara and Jeri had small offices with a third, slightly larger area that had two desks in it. At his questioning look, she explained, "Jeri and I share some administrative work, but we have a bookkeeper and a part-time manager for scheduling and other tasks. It helps keep us in the kitchen and gives us more free time for personal things."

Something I haven't learned to do, he chastised himself.

"That's great. I wish I could manage that," he said.

"You just have to give up some control," Sara replied matter-of-factly. She snagged some clothes from a hook on one wall. "Could you please wait outside while I change?"

He stepped back out into the tiny hallway and closed the door to her office. Leaning back against the wall, he thought about her statement regarding control. He knew she was right, but it was easier said than done. Still, maybe it would be worth the effort in the long run. Especially since he'd somehow become like a couple of those chefs he'd worked under, always shouting and berating their staff. And especially since Sara was calling to him in unexpected ways. That Miami and his family and friends were pulling at his heart.

The sound of muffled footsteps approaching the door had him straightening and when the door opened Sara stood there in faded jeans and a peach-colored T-shirt that hugged her slender curves. His heartbeat accelerated at the sight of her, looking so beautiful even in the casual clothes. Stunning, really.

"This is crazy, you know. I had to drive to work today and my car is just around the corner," she said and gestured toward the hall back to the main area of the restaurant.

"What about I do something crazy myself, like walk you to your car?" he teased and held out his hand again.

She hesitated, but then she slipped her hand into his,

and they walked out into the dining area. Part of the crew had cleared off the area and was now putting the individual tables and chairs back into place. while the others were tidying the kitchen. Everyone was working like a well-oiled machine without Sara there to bark out orders. *Like I do*, Tony thought.

In one corner Rick was helping Jeri with something that had her smiling and laughing. He was going to have to ask his friend what was up with the vibes between him and Sara's partner when he had a chance.

For now, he focused on the feel of Sara's hand in his, so soft and warm, and the shy smile she tossed at him as he looked back at her. The smile warmed his heart and he could picture seeing it more often. Could picture spending more time with both her and her staff—and hopefully alone with her. *Maybe tonight will be the start of a journey to that*, he thought, and smiled.

He pushed through the door of the restaurant and waited for Sara to take the lead. As she guided him past the restaurant's outdoor tables she turned onto Collins and away from Lincoln Road. They had barely walked a block when Sara stopped in front of a late model convertible.

Sara leaned against the side of the car. "Told you it was crazy," she said with a grin and a shrug.

Maybe it was, but he was grateful for even those few extra minutes in her company. With a smile, he swung their joined hands and said, "Like I said, I can do crazy."

"Which is this, whatever is happening," she said and gestured between the two of them with her hand. While changing, she'd added two gold rings and beaded bracelets that emphasized the fragile-looking slenderness of her fingers and wrist.

He took hold of that hand as well. She didn't protest

which he took as a good sign. "I don't know what's happening, but whatever it is feels nice."

"'Nice.' Ouch. That's like telling a girl she's cute," she said with a wrinkle of her nose, a gesture that was growing more and more familiar and was totally cute. He decided he really liked cute, but it was clear she needed more. That was fine—he was prepared to give it. She fascinated him on multiple levels, and he wanted to explore each one.

He released her hand to cup her cheek and ran his thumb across her smooth skin, soft and warm from the slight flush of color that painted her cheeks. "You're beautiful and I'm feeling...I don't know what I'm feeling except...."

She tilted her face upward and he cupped the back of her head and dug his fingers into the silk of her short hair. Thick strands of chocolate, caramel, and auburn twined around his fingers, much like her presence was winding something tight around his heart. Her grey-green eyes widened as he leaned toward her, but she didn't pull away. He took that as an invitation for more.

He moved closer until her breath spilled warmth against his lips but kept a respectable distance from her body since he didn't want to press too much too soon. It was too early for more, as much as he might want it.

"Goodnight, chef," someone called out from behind them, shattering the moment.

"Good night, Brenda," Sara said and waved at the young woman, her casual tone contradicted by the deep stain of color on her cheeks.

Tony took a step back and grabbed hold of her hands again. "I'm not going to say 'I'm sorry' for that." *No way am I sorry.* She was lovely, and each encounter only made him want to know her better.

Sara smiled shyly and crinkled her nose again. "Good, because I'm not sorry either, just confused. I mean, you're only visiting, right?"

If someone had asked him only days ago the answer would have been a resounding "Yes" only he was no longer quite so sure. But he also wasn't certain what he'd be doing when his month in Miami was over and he didn't want to make any promises to her that he couldn't keep. "Only visiting...for now."

"So for now it might be nice to spend some time together?"

Tony chuckled and cupped her cheek once again. He swiped his thumb across the blush there. "I always liked that you were the take charge kind, even as a kid."

"I'm not a kid anymore," she reminded.

Tony laughed again because there was no doubting that she was no longer that kid who had chased after him and Rick. He shook his head and said, "I think I noticed that. Since you're so good at delegating, unlike me, would you like to spend the day with me when you're free?"

Sara gave their hands a mischievous shake. "Like tomorrow morning, you mean? I'm free until dinner time since it's Jeri's turn to cover the lunch rush."

"I'm game. Pick you up at nine? We could do breakfast before we go somewhere?" he said, already looking forward to spending the day with her.

"I'd love that. Give me your phone number so I can text you my address," she said and after exchanging information, they stood there awkwardly for what felt like minutes, but was probably only a few seconds, before he finally took another step back and jammed his hands in his pockets to keep from reaching for her again. She was just too tempting and he couldn't rush this, whatever this was.

Sara dug into her bag, yanked out her keys, and jangled them nervously. "See you tomorrow."

"For sure. Drive safe," he said, watched her get in her car, and drive away. He missed her immediately. It had him wondering again whether his month in Miami would become something more.

As he turned to head back to his car, he spotted Jeri and Rick by the entrance to the restaurant's al fresco area. They were about a foot apart, not touching, but despite that there was no denying the connection between them. He waited for his friend to make some kind of move, only he didn't, which was so not like Rick.

Instead, his friend leaned close and whispered into Jeri's ear. Jeri laughed and with a quick brush of her hand against Rick's arm, she walked away, leaving Rick standing there. As Rick's gaze tracked Jeri's departure, a sad smile came to his lips and he jammed his hands into his pockets, rocked back and forth on his heels. It was almost as if he wanted to chase after her, but he held fast.

Tony joined him and clapped him on the back. "*Mano*, you've got it bad."

Rick shook his head and sighed. "It *is* bad, but I don't know what to do about it."

"Really? You should take some lessons from your sister. She always knows what to do," Tony said and walked with Rick back to where they had parked earlier that night.

Rick wrapped an arm around Tony's shoulder and squeezed, almost painfully. "Just remember that's my sister, man. Don't break her heart or I'll have to hurt you."

"I won't. Truth be told, I'm more worried I'll be heartbroken if I end up going back to New York."

Rick stopped and shot him a hard, questioning look.

"You mean, *when* you go back to New York, don't you? Not that we all don't want you to stay, but don't go saying stuff like that and getting everyone's hopes up unless you mean it."

Subconscious slip or more? he thought with a choked laugh. Although going back to New York was losing more and more appeal with each day spent in Miami.

Since the whole "Maybe I'll stay in Miami thing" was still a too new feeling, he said, "Yes, *when* I go back. And I won't hurt her, Rick. We're two adults and we know what we're getting into."

Rick started walking again, but in soft tones he said, "She may be an adult, but she'll always be my little sister. All I want is for her to be happy. I don't know why I never saw it before, but I think you'd make her happy."

It was a dangerous thing to possibly be the source of someone's happiness, and Tony wasn't feeling up to the challenge, especially since he hadn't found a way to be happy himself. "I want her to be happy too, Rick."

"Good, because otherwise –"

"You'd have to hurt me," Tony said with a chuckle.

"Only we both know I wouldn't hurt a fly," Rick admitted with a wry grin.

"It's why you're my best friend," Tony said and meant it. He might have left Miami, but Rick was still someone he could call when he needed advice. It made Tony sad to think that in the last few years, those calls and messages had been fewer and fewer in number.

Rick cuffed him on the back of the head, but the blow lacked sting. "Don't you forget that. And don't stay away so long next time."

"I won't," he said. Even though he wasn't sure about the whole Miami versus New York thing, he was sure that he had to come home more often. He missed his sister, pain that she was, and as vibrant as his parents still were, they were showing their age. And then there was Sara....

He definitely didn't know what to do about her, but he was willing to take the time to try and find out. And to find out more about what was going on in his friend's life.

"Tell me about you and Jeri. . ."

CHAPTER 8

THE ROSTER WENT UP EARLY that morning to list who had made the team after soccer tryouts. All the potential players raced into school before class started to head to the bulletin board by the gym.

Samantha stood there with two of her friends, Carmen and Lauren. Just a second later, Angelica, Maya, and Daisy arrived and flanked them. The six stood in front of the list as bodies piled up behind them to search for their names.

"You did it, Angelica! You're the team captain," Maya said in an ear-piercing squeal.

Angelica smiled, but the smile faded a bit as she looked toward Samantha.

Samantha bit back her disappointment and forced a smile to her lips. She faced Angelica and said, "Congratulations. You deserve to be the team captain."

Angelica shook her head, as if to clear her ears, maybe because she couldn't believe what she'd just heard. Apparently, neither could a number of the other girls around them who gasped in surprise.

In a wavery voice, Angelica somehow managed to

say, "Thank you."

Angelica's response didn't really sound sincere, maybe because Samantha's words had lacked real conviction, so Samantha doubled down on her comment, injecting more feeling into her words. "I mean it, Angelica. You're the better player. You'll be a good team captain."

Angelica jerked back as if she'd been slapped, clearly shocked. She fumbled for a second, but then regained control and said, "It's going to be a good year. You're a great midfielder."

"Thanks," Samantha said.

"We'll make a great team," Angelica said with real conviction and no hint of the usual competition between them, helping to ease any lingering tension.

"We will," Samantha said and put up her fist for a bump.

After the girls all exchanged fist bumps and jerked out their phones to text people with the news, Samantha walked away, smiling. She'd talked to her mother about Angelica and her mother had mentioned how the Kelly and Sanchez families had all grown up as friends in Little Havana. How they still had some ties that they valued.

It had made Samantha think a little more about how much nicer it might be to be friends. The idea didn't seem so farfetched anymore. It was why, no matter how much it hurt to admit it, she was glad she'd said that Angelica had been the right choice for team captain.

At least she was still the Class President and ahead by a few points for class valedictorian. *Some things just didn't change overnight*, she thought with a chuckle.

Sylvia had loaned Tony her Wrangler because as she put it, "You can't make a good first impression with *mami* and *papi*'s twenty-year old Buick Century."

Not that Tony was worried about anything like that with Sara. He'd already made multiple impressions over the years and as far as he could tell, he'd done all right otherwise they wouldn't be going out on this date.

Dios mío, he was going on a date. Something he hadn't done in the nearly four months since his girlfriend had walked out on him. Something that hadn't even been on his radar, but now that it was happening he was excited about it. Especially since his date was Sara.

He pulled up in front of the Art Deco building on Collins where a former hotel had been converted into condos. It boasted a new coat of bold yellow paint and gleaming white trim. The condo association had kept the neon sign with the original name of the hotel, though it had also been refurbished. The metal of the sign was painted turquoise and the neon would be a bright pink when lit.

There was no parking anywhere even after he did a trip around the block. As he neared the door to the condo again, Sara stood at the curb, smiling and clutching a vintage straw purse with colorful pink, yellow, and green flowers on its face. The purse perfectly matched the pale yellow capri pants and electric white camp shirt that made her whole outfit scream "Retro" just like her condo building.

She looked fabulous. His heart did a little jump in his chest. He grinned, excitement shooting through him at the thought of spending time with her.

He pulled up to the curb, reached over, and opened the door from inside.

"I couldn't find a spot and was going to text you.

I'm sorry."

She pointed upward. "I saw you from my balcony. You can't miss the lime green."

"It is an eyesore, isn't it?" he said as he pulled away to drive the few blocks to the News Café so they could have breakfast.

"I kind of like the color," she said

Great, he thought. *Already off to a bad start. Make her jump into your car and then tell her that her taste in colors sucks.* "It certainly makes a statement. I like how it drives and it keeps big sis safe, so that's all good."

Samantha rolled her eyes and chuckled. "Protective brothers. Gotta love them."

"You do." As they neared the restaurant for breakfast, he realized he wasn't going to be any luckier in finding a parking spot. They circled the block and went around and around several times when Sara said, "I have an idea. Head to Collins and 13th."

As he did so, he remembered the popular little cafeteria with the takeout window on the corner. Realizing what Sara wanted, he double parked. "Wait for me," he said and popped out of the car to get them Cuban coffees and toast.

It only took a couple of minutes to be handed the brown paper bag with their breakfast and he knew the perfect spot to drive to with their makeshift meal.

"Hold on," he said as he passed her the bag, opened the top on the Wrangler, and whipped out of the space. In no time they were on the causeway heading to Hobie Island Beach on the key for their impromptu breakfast picnic.

He parked the Jeep with the front-end facing Biscayne Bay and faced her. "I'm sorry about breakfast not going according to plan," he said as he accepted a coffee cup from her. She handed him a second coffee and he put the paper cups into the cup holders so they could grab the Cuban bread toasts from the bag.

Sara shrugged, grabbed her cup, and sipped her coffee. With a smile, she said, "You must have forgotten how hard it is to get a parking spot in South Beach. Besides, what could be better than this view and a Cuban coffee to get you going in the morning." She hesitated for a moment and shyly added, "And the company, of course."

"It's the perfect sugar and caffeine rush." He took a sip and sighed. "Thanks to your company, it's a great start to the day." He gestured to the view of Biscayne Bay. Cerulean waters were peaceful today, glittering under the bright Miami sun. A slight breeze rustled the palm trees all around them. There were a few wind surfers out on the waters, skimming the surface as their brightly colored sails caught the breeze.

"Definitely a good start," she said, before she bit into the long piece of buttered bread and murmured her appreciation. "Sometimes the simple things are the best things."

Tony couldn't agree more. The sun beamed into the car while the breeze offered comfort from the typical Miami heat and humidity. Appreciating her sitting beside him, a simple thing, but a wonderful thing. "Being back home has reminded me how much I miss some of those simple things. Nice weather. Family. Friends. Good food."

Sara cocked her head to one side and a reddish bang swept forward and made her skin look even creamier. She skipped her gaze across his face, examining him. "You make wonderful meals in New York, don't you?"

He did, only... "Lately the food is missing...soul. Passion and fun, like what I've tasted at your place."

She peered at him over the rim of her coffee cup, took

a sip, and then said, "I guess it's a good thing you came home. Maybe you can find what's missing."

As he looked at her, he thought, *Maybe I have.* He couldn't admit that aloud just yet, so instead he said, "Are you ready for the rest of our date today?"

"Totally," she said and grinned mischievously.

"We're off." He started the car and pulled onto the Rickenbacker Causeway, heading farther away from Miami and toward Key Biscayne. Barely five minutes later they were at the entrance to the Miami Seaquarium and Sara did an excited hop in her seat.

"OMG, I haven't been here since I was a kid. I love this place," she said with a broad smile, her eyes alight with pleasure.

"I remembered how much you used to like it. Except for that time that a seagull swooped down and stole your hot dog."

"I was totally annoyed," she said as she jumped out of the Wrangler.

"You were," He laughed as he came around to her side of the vehicle. He cupped her cheek and ran his thumb across her lips. "It was cute in a weird sort of way."

Touching her like that was a big mistake, he realized, because there was nothing cute about the feel of her lips beneath his thumb or the way her eyes widened in surprise before she shifted away from him. Obviously as affected by that simple touch as he was.

"Sorry, I didn't mean to invade your space," he said and pulled away from her, needing the space to keep from touching her again.

She shrugged. "No harm, no foul. I'm a big girl now."

Sí, I know. He kept that thought to himself. "I'll go get the tickets."

Sara laid her hand on her stomach and took a breath to calm her skittering insides. It had been an innocent enough touch, but there was no denying that her crush on Tony Sanchez was as alive today as it had been nearly a decade earlier. And if she wasn't misreading the signals, Tony no longer saw her as Rick's little sister or the ten-year-old who had tagged along with them whenever she could. Nope, Tony was seeing her as W-O-M-A-N and while it was something that she'd hoped for so long ago, now she had no clue how to handle it—or him. Especially since she wasn't sure that Tony intended to spend more than a month in Miami.

She couldn't open herself up to the kind of hurt that would happen if she let herself get involved with him and he returned to New York.

Luckily the Seaquarium was a blast from their childish past and not the kind of place intended for romance. At least she didn't think it was as they sat to watch a seal show and then worked their way to a touch pool filled with small bamboo sharks, fish, and stingrays. But as she skimmed her hand across the top of a passing stingray, he slipped his hand over hers, sending a jolt of awareness through her. She kept her hand there and, hands joined, they skimmed them over the docile sharks and stingrays until it was time to move to another exhibit.

Somehow it felt natural to twine their fingers together and walk hand-in-hand toward a natural mangrove area overlooking Biscayne Bay. They were greeted there by an assortment of colorful tropical birds that flitted through the trees. A flock of pale pink flamingos stood, knees awkwardly bent, in a shallow shore area. Tony and Sara lingered at the railing, looking at the birds and Sara said, "I always wondered if I had too much red in my hair because I loved to eat shrimp just like the flamingos. Silly, right?"

"I like the red in your hair," he said and combed his fingers through the short strands.

At his touch heat rose to her cheeks and she hoped they weren't as pink as the flamingo feathers. With a wrinkle of her nose, she said, "Thank you, but you're just being nice."

"Nope, not just nice," he said and grasped a lock of hair between his thumb and forefinger to rub it gently. "You're beautiful."

Suddenly flustered, she said, "We're going to miss the dolphin show." She grabbed hold of the hand that had been in her hair and dragged him across the grounds to the stadium for the show. Many of the seats were filled, leaving them to sit up front, close to the glass walls that surrounded the pool where the dolphins would swim. Much of the ground in that area was wet from the earlier show, but before they could shift to another section a group of kids, probably on a school trip, filled in the seats around them, trapping them in their place.

With a wince, she said, "Sorry."

Tony smiled and gave a reassuring squeeze of her hand. "It's okay. I don't mind getting a little wet. We've got the best view in the house. We'll be able to see the dolphins dive down to the bottom of the pool and then shoot up." He emphasized it with an upward swipe of his hand. He had strong hands, masculine but also elegant. The scars from small nicks and cuts, a silvery one from an old burn possibly, marked them as the hands of a blue-collar man. She was a sucker for hands and his called to her in ways that would be dangerous to her peace of mind.

The kids around them were antsy, forcing them to shift ever closer together to avoid the jostling and pushing that was going on as the adults with the group tried to control them. The two of them were so squashed that Tony had no choice but to let go of her hand and wrap an arm around her shoulders and draw her close to avoid the crowding.

I fit against him perfectly, she thought as he tucked her tightly against him. It felt right—maybe too right. It made her wonder again how strongly she'd feel his absence once he left Miami. *Too strongly to risk getting closer?* She asked herself.

The show began, only she wasn't really paying much attention to the dolphins or their handlers. She was too conscious of everything Tony. His scent, masculine with the hint of citrus. The feel of his lean body and his calloused palm as it caressed the side of her arm. The sound of his laugh as the kids jumped when a trio of dolphins came zooming around the edge of the pool, sending a small wave of water up and over the top of the wall.

She looked at him, exploring the strong line of his jaw and defined cheekbones. There was a small scar beneath one eye, and she remembered that he'd gotten the cut when he'd been on the football team with Rick. His lips. *Sigh*, how she'd dreamed as a teenager about those lips.

But she wasn't a teenager anymore. She was a woman and one who wanted more than just a temporary fling with a handsome man. No matter what she was feeling now, she had to protect her heart to keep it from getting broken, but she couldn't avoid looking at him and wondering what it would be like if this thing between them became serious.

His body tightened beside her and he slowly turned to look at her. His brown-eyed gaze grew darker, more intense as he realized that she was gazing at him. *How* she was gazing at him. Suddenly he was bending closer, bringing those lips nearer....

A tsunami of ice-cold water washed over them, dousing them and all the kids around them as the trio of dolphins landed with a huge splash in the pool. For a second, they sat there stunned, water streaming down their faces, but then they both started laughing. Beside them the kids jumped up and down as they shrieked their joy at the deluge.

"Let's give a shout out to all those people brave enough to sit in the splash zone for giving the rest of us quite a laugh," the MC for the show shouted into the microphone and motioned to the group, but somehow zeroed in on Tony and her. Or at least that's how it looked to Sara.

Tony shook his head, cupped her cheeks, and wiped away water and tears from her face. "Not quite what I had pictured for our first date."

She chuckled, reached up, and brushed back the wet locks of hair from his face. "I'd say it's downright perfect."

As he grinned and slipped his hand into hers, she supposed that he felt the same way.

CHAPTER 9

TONY'S FAMILY WANTED UPSCALE VARIATIONS on traditional Cuban foods served at the *quinceañera*, but Tony wanted to try something new. For that reason, he'd been trying out new recipes in his parents' kitchen. Luckily, he'd paid to have it updated three years ago after his last visit because he knew how much his mother loved to cook and because the old stove and fridge were more of an obstacle than a help.

With the *quinceañera* rapidly approaching, Tony was satisfied with his final recipes, but now his family members were about to taste test so he could get their approval.

For the roast pork Tony had decided to go with a variation on an Italian porchetta, but flavored with a twist on the standard Mediterranean spices. The day before he had deboned and butterflied a pork shoulder and carefully trimmed off all the skin to make some *chicharrones* for another dish. The crispy cracklins would be perfect in some appetizer-sized tacos. Next he'd marinated the pork shoulder with a traditional Cuban mix of juices from Seville oranges, lemons, and limes, as well as garlic, cumin, salt, and black pepper.

The pork had been sitting overnight in the marinade and now it was ready for the final preparation before cooking.

"*Mijo*, what are you doing?" his mother asked from beside him. She watched with interest as he spread out the pork shoulder on a cutting board.

He grinned as he picked up a handful of the paste he'd made just minutes earlier and slathered it on both sides of the meat. "Giving the *lechon* a twist."

His mother leaned closer and sniffed the bright green paste. "Smells like *chimichurri*."

"It's my own variation. I make it with a little Fresno chile and lemon instead of the vinegar," he explained as he tucked the pork shoulder into a tight roll and then carefully placed it on a piece of pork belly that still had its skin.

"*Mijo, sabes* that your *papi* doesn't like anything spicy," his mother warned with a tsk and shake of her head.

Tony nodded, but continued with his preparation of the porchetta. "I know, *mami*, but it's not really spicy heat, just some warmth. I'm betting you guys will love it later for dinner. And if you do, we'll make it for the *quince*."

His mother pulled back a bit to look at him. "You won't be home for dinner?"

He grinned while wrapping the pork belly around the marinated pork shoulder. "I have a date with Sara."

"Do you think that's wise, *Mijo*?" his mother asked after a long pause, one brow arching up in challenge.

Surprised, Tony said, "I thought you'd be happy. Our families have been friends forever."

A dip of her head and an uneasy shrug warned that she wasn't so much unhappy as conflicted. "We love

Sara, but it's sudden. And Sara is such a joy and so good to her parents and siblings."

"Not like me and Javi," he said, well aware that the absence of the Sanchez boys pained his family and friends.

His mother tsked again and laid a hand on his arm as he made a careful checkerboard of slices through the pork skin. After, he worked to tie the strings around the pork belly and shoulder roll he'd just created. "*No, Mijo.* You and Javi take good care of us and we understand that your jobs are important to you. But I do wish we could see you more."

After being in Miami for a week, even with all the *quinceañera* craziness, he wished he'd come home more often also.

"I won't stay away as long next time," he promised as he salted and peppered the outside of the roll and then placed it on a rack sitting in a roasting pan.

"Why did you cut slits in the pork belly skin?" his mother asked as he slipped the roll into the oven, pre-warmed to a high heat.

He smiled, loving his mother's zeal for information. When they were kids, she had always brought home games and books to challenge them to learn but had learned right along with them. "It helps the skin crisp up and the fat melt to baste the meat inside."

She nodded. "I'll have to do that with the roast pork for *Noche Buena.* Do you think we'll see you this Christmas for a change?"

The holiday season in New York was one of the busiest for his restaurant and he preferred giving free time to employees with families rather than taking time off himself. But he had a family, too, and if he was in New York—and for a moment it again surprised him that it was an "if" and not a "when"—he'd man-age to find the time to come home, even if he had to hire extra help for the holidays.

"I'll be home, *mami*," he said, and his mother wrapped her arms around him and hugged him hard.

She barely came to below his chin and he realized with surprise that she'd shrunk a little. She was slight in his arms and the sudden sense of her fragility gave him more reason to keep to the promise he'd made and be home for Christmas. Maybe he could even convince his brother to take some time off from his bigshot tech CEO position on the West Coast and join them for the holidays in Miami.

As they broke apart, his mother surreptitiously wiped away a tear, peered at the oven settings, and let out a sharp cry. "Five hundred? That's high isn't it?"

He laid a hand on her shoulder and rubbed it reassuringly. "Only for forty minutes, then we'll turn it down to three hundred until it's done. The internal temperature should get to about 145 degrees on that instant thermometer I gave you. Then you'll have to let it sit for about fifteen minutes –"

His mother's laughter stopped him. "Once your father sees this, he won't wait fifteen minutes, *Mijo*. He'll be in here picking off all that tasty skin."

Tony grabbed a wooden spoon and mimicked a whack. "Just keep him away with this."

His mother snatched the spoon away and kidded that she'd whack him. "Go get ready for your date. And be good to Sara."

"I will, *mami*. Besides, we're just friends right now," he said, hoping to allay any fears his mother might have about his relationship with Sara. He didn't mention that if he had his way, they'd be more than friends. He snatched the spoon from her to toss it in the sink before she could use it on him—the way she surely would if she saw through his lie.

His mother tsked yet again. "*Entonces eres bien tonto.*"

Glancing at the clock, he realized that while his mother might be telling him he was silly, Sara was going to have some choice words for him if he didn't get moving. "I've got to run," he said, but his mother chased him out of the kitchen with another cry of "*Tonto.*"

He'd be as much a fool to get involved with Sara as he was not to get involved. A true paradox. Of course, it all hinged on whether or not he'd uproot his life in New York to stay in Miami.

So far everything at the restaurant had been going well in his absence, or at least that's what he was being told.

Someone upstairs must have heard his thoughts since his smartphone rang and the photo on his screen trumpeted that his manager Ramon was calling.

"Is everything okay?" he said immediately, his stomach in a tight knot as he waited for the bad news.

"*Calmate, jefe.* Everything is going great. We just wanted you to know that so you won't worry. Enjoy your time off and come back nice and relaxed," Ramon said.

In other words, not come back like the cranky, crazy, control freak he'd been the last few months. "I'm not worried. I know the restaurant is in good hands."

"*Gracias.* This place is as important to us as it is to you. Enjoy your time. We'd call if there was a problem we needed you to handle," Ramon said and before Tony could say another word, his manager ended the call.

He should be grateful that he could get away. Relax. Maybe even consider a second location, if he could avoid another situation where he'd be doing most of the managing. He wanted to be cooking like he had been the last few days, trying out all kinds of new recipes for his niece's big *quinceañera* celebration. It had been fun to do, like the porchetta variation he'd created earlier. He could already imagine beautiful slices of it on a plate giving each diner succulent pork in addition to the crispy skin that was a cook's treat in so many Cuban households.

Cooking was what he was meant to do and maybe, just maybe, he'd be able to figure out during his time away how to balance his life better so he could spend more time doing that.

Just like Sara had learned. She seemed to have found the right balance in her life, as evidenced by yesterday's morning outing and tonight's dinner date.

Balance, he told himself. *Letting go of my tight control on my restaurant is a good first step*, he thought as he sat down at his old school desk to write down the basics of the recipe he'd just worked on in a note book. He had at least a dozen of them, filled with the many recipes he'd tried over the years, both good and bad. He'd often thought about going through all the recipes to put together a cookbook, but he'd never had the time. Somehow, he needed to find space in his life for the things he wanted.

Like a relationship with Sara?

He drove the question back because it was still too soon.

He picked up his smartphone and speed-dialed Ramon, who answered on the first ring. "Is something wrong?"

"Not at all. I have a favor to ask. You know those notebooks on the top shelf of the bookcase in my office?" He could picture the leather-bound journals in his mind, sitting there waiting for him to share his creations with others.

"Your recipe books," Ramon said. Tony heard the creak of his door opening in the background. "I see them."

"*Bueno*. Could you please pack them up and send them to my parents' house?" He quickly rattled off the address and instructed Ramon to use the restaurant's courier account for the shipment.

"Got it. I'll get them packed up and sent out today. Does this mean you're finally thinking about that cookbook?" Ramon asked, anticipation in his voice.

Tony chuckled at the other man's excitement. "It does. *Gracias*, Ramon."

"My pleasure. I can't wait to see the finished product."

"Me either," Tony admitted and hung up, suddenly filled with more joy than he'd had in a long time.

He was cooking again.

He was finally doing something about his cookbook idea.

And last, but in no way least, he had another date with Sara. A woman who was proving to be intriguing and exciting. A woman who could possibly become more in his life.

Pleasure sprouted in his heart and he let it sink its roots deep, hoping it would blossom and grow ever greater with his time in Miami.

"Are you sure this isn't a problem?" Sara said as she whipped off her apron and left Jeri plating one of the daily specials – a saffron-scented rice ball stuffed with gorgonzola dolce, and then breaded and deep fried.

Jeri waved her off. "Puleez, girl. How many times have

you covered for me when I needed a day off for Sophie?"

"As if I could deny my adorable little godchild anything," Sara teased. "But seriously –"

"But seriously get your butt going. You know how well the training has been going for that new girl, Valerie. And Brenda can help me with the final touches on the plating."

Jeri shooed her away with a wave of her hands and Sara relented and walked into the restaurant. When a quick peek at the door showed her Tony had yet to arrive, she took a moment to greet some of her regulars and recommend her favorites from that day's specials. One older man flirted with her mercilessly, as he always did, but she knew he had eyes for no one other than his wife beside him.

"Are you sure you won't run away with me?" he teased with a wink.

"Sorry, Lou, but I'm not available," she said just as Tony slipped in through the door.

She looked his way and Lou dramatically laid a hand over his heart. "Is he the one you're breaking my heart for?"

Maybe, she thought. "Try the lamb burgers with tzatziki tonight. I ground the meat fresh this morning and the dill is from our organic herb garden."

"Thank you, sweetie, now go meet your man," Lou's wife said and motioned toward the front door where Tony waited.

"Have fun, you two," Sara said and left the elderly couple to enjoy their dinner.

As she walked toward Tony, his smile broadened and spread up into those deliciously cocoa-colored eyes. Her heartbeat picked up its pace and a pleasant warmth filled her as he held his hand out and she slipped hers into it.

With slight pressure he urged her closer for a chaste kiss on her cheek. She'd been flustered around him before, but now, she wanted to turn ever so slightly and lay her lips over his. She held back, reminding herself that this might only be temporary if he left in three weeks. But even with the constant reminders, it was getting harder and harder to deny the feelings that had reawakened with his presence. Feelings that were way more than those of a schoolgirl crush.

She'd never thought of herself as a coward. Maybe she should let this go where it might and pick up the pieces later.

"I'm looking forward to dinner tonight," he whispered into her ear as, with a light tug, he led her outside and down the side street in the direction of Ocean Drive.

"Me, too," she said with a playful swing of their joined hands. "Where are we going?"

"I have some old friends that own a place up on Ocean Drive. Juli and Adriana."

"I know them quite well. We've done a number of events together." None of those, of course, had made her as nervous as a fifteen-year-old's birthday party. That was different, because it was for family.

"Great. I like to support my friends whenever I can," he said as they turned onto Ocean Drive and walked toward the restaurant.

They strolled past the gleaming white building for the Tides hotel and then the Cardozo with its colorful pennants and awnings over the veranda. Several patrons were seated there while in one corner a chef stirred rice and other ingredients in a paella pan. The aroma of cooking seafood drifted over to Tony and Sara.

"Smells good," he said.

Sara nodded. "I love paella. I don't get to make it

often because it takes so long to cook."

"Maybe one night I can make you some," he said, and she smiled at the suggestion.

"I'd like that." It would take time to make the paella. Time which was a precious thing for them and filled with uncertainty. But she looked forward to that time together.

They continued across the street where over-sized umbrellas in bright tropical colors looked like flowers in bloom as they protected an al fresco dining area for a small bar and fast food joint.

A block further up and they were in front of Gianni Versace's former mansion—now a luxury boutique hotel, restaurant, and event space. Tourists posed for photos in front of the ornate wrought iron gates emblazoned with the designer's signature Medusa logo in gold.

As they passed yet more of South Beach's famous Art Deco hotels and restaurants, the sidewalks grew more crowded. There were throngs of people checking out menus, waiting for a table, or just strolling around while they people watched. More than once, they had to maneuver around a group blocking the sidewalk, not that Sara minded when Tony had to pull her close to avoid the crowd. She loved the feel of his strong body beside her and the hesitant smile he shot her as their bodies bumped together.

They finally reached Juli and Adriana's restaurant, and Tony paused by the hostess podium to let the young woman know they had a reservation.

"Of course, Chef Sanchez. Juli and Adriana mentioned you'd be coming. Let me show you to your table," she said. With sharp efficiency, she grabbed two menus and led them to a table up on a higher level of a veranda, right by its edge where they'd have the best view of the street and across the way, beautiful Lummus Park and the ocean beyond.

After they sat and had their menus, the hostess said, "Someone will be with you shortly."

"This is such a perfect spot," Sara said, glancing toward the sidewalks with all the activity and past them to the quiet beauty of the park across the street. There was an intimate feel to the table thanks to the privacy of the spot, and the pleasant atmosphere was enhanced by the lovely flowers in the center of the table, and the small votive candle spilling warm light across their place settings.

"It is. I'll have to thank my friends for being so thoughtful," he said.

"Juli and Adriana are great. It's funny how many friends we have in common," Sara said.

"Not just friends. We've known *each other* a long time," Tony said, his gaze settling on her in a way that had her heartbeat accelerating and those proverbial butterflies flitting around in her stomach.

"I guess we have, but not really. Not *that way*," she said, fumbling for the right words. Hanging out in her family's backyard pool or riding bikes around Little Havana didn't really count. *Or did it?* she wondered.

Tony cocked his head, processing that. With a shrug, he said, "I know what you mean, Sara, but I'm looking forward to getting to know you better in *that way*. I hope you are also."

She was, only… "I am, Tony. I've had a nice time with you the past week, but we don't have that much time until you go."

His lips quirked in a smile that seemed a little forced, almost as if saddened by the thought he'd soon be leaving. "Then let's make the most of these weeks and find out more about each other. How does that sound?"

It sounded great. Too great, she thought, worried it

might reveal too much. She shook off the thought and plowed on. "Okay, you first. How does it feel to have earned a star? It's every chef's dream."

Tony blew out a harsh breath and shook his head. "A dream and a nightmare all at the same time."

His words surprised her. Eyes wide, Sara said, "A nightmare? Really?"

He nodded and his gaze darkened, full of...sadness she wanted to say. Pain which made her heart ache for him as he said, "It was such an honor, but the pressure since then...."

Sara locked her gaze on his, searching his features. "Difficult?"

"That's an understatement," he said, but before she could continue, two women walked up to their table.

"It's so nice to have you with us," said Adriana as she leaned down to hug Tony and then offered Sara a welcoming smile. As the one who handled the business side of the restaurant, Adriana wore a flawlessly tailored designer suit. Her auburn hair was worn up tonight and called attention to her oval face and exotic hazel eyes.

"It's good to see you again, chefs," said Juli more demurely. "We've got some new recipes we're trying out and it would be my honor to get your opinions," Juli replied with a big smile.

"If you don't mind, we'll bring you some of our specials for tonight," Adriana said and wrapped an arm around Juli's shoulders.

Tony glanced Sara's way, wanting to confirm that it was okay with her and she nodded and said, "We'd love that. Thank you."

The two women walked back toward the kitchen, chatting, Adriana's arm still on Juli's shoulder, almost in a reassuring gesture.

"They're a good team," Tony said as he watched them stroll away.

Sara couldn't agree more. "Adriana has the brass to get things done and support Juli who is an absolutely amazing chef, even if she doubts herself too much sometimes."

"Do you ever doubt yourself?" Tony asked, but a waitress came over that second with a bottle of wine before she could answer.

"Compliments of Adriana and Juli," she said as she poured each of them a glass of a very expensive cabernet sauvignon.

"Thank them for us," Sara said, grateful for the interruption as much as the wine. Unfortunately, Tony repeated his question.

"So, do you? Doubt yourself?" he said and picked up his glass in a toast.

With a shrug, she raised her glass and tapped it to his. Then she swirled the wine in the glass and once it settled, held the goblet up to watch the legs form along the sides of the glass. Peering at him past the red wine and seeing that he wouldn't up until she answered, she said, "I did when I first decided to open the restaurant with Jeri. It was such a risk."

"That seems to have paid off," he said with a lift of his glass to toast her success.

She smiled and said, "Thanks. I guess I still doubt myself at times, but I tell myself there's nothing else I'd rather be doing. How about you?"

Tony chuckled and did a little nod of his head. "I doubt myself every day. Especially lately when so much of my time involves being out of the kitchen."

"It's not easy to have your own place," she said. "I'm lucky that I have Jeri and some really good office staff to help us."

"You are. It's something I have to think about trying when I go back to New York," he said, nonchalantly—not that Sara was feeling nonchalant about that possibility. Which made her ask herself what she was doing here, falling for him all over again, when he had no intentions of staying in Miami.

She was spared from having to say anything else when the waitress and a busboy brought over a sampling of appetizers for them on a trio of plates. Each plate had two perfectly crafted bites of food on it.

Sara tried the first dish, a piece of avocado topped with whipped cream that turned out to be a delicately flavored dressing. The second was a sandwich of sorts made from a thin slice of crispy potato, a tantalizing sliver of pork belly, and a circle of an orange-cherry jelly whose sweet and sour taste cut through the heaviness of the potato and pork. The last bite was a tender nugget of poached chicken covered in a chocolate-scented mole sauce with just a hint of chili.

"Amazing," she said as she swallowed the last morsel. "I feel like I just had a complete meal in one sitting."

"Heaven in each bite," Tony said with admiration.

"Juli has really upped her game," Sara said, appreciating the creativeness and flavor of the appetizers.

"She truly has grown since the last time I ate here," he replied and sipped his wine.

A few seconds later the waitress and busboy returned with their main meals. The larger samplings of the entrees were just as heavenly as the appetizers they'd been served. There was a tasty tostada topped with poached octopus and a delicious salsa. An earthy red wine demi-glace with mushrooms graced medium rare slices of filet beside luscious Lyonnaise potatoes.

In short order, they finished the meal and sat back to chat once again.

"I can't believe I inhaled all that." Tony leaned back in his chair.

"It was delicious. I'm going to have to pry that halibut recipe from her," Sara said and spooned up another little taste of the broth in which the halibut had been served. "Do you taste lemongrass in there?"

Tony nodded. "I do. I'm guessing some coconut milk as well." He examined the remains of the slightly cloudy liquid.

"Very Thai," she said which was surprising since Juli's cooking background leaned toward assorted Latin cuisines, Italian, and continental fare.

"She's spreading her wings and if this is the outcome, it's a good thing," he said.

"I guess you liked it," Juli said as she stepped up to their table, smiling, Adriana at her side, watching over her like a mother hen.

"Loved it. Is this a new direction for the restaurant?" Tony said and glanced around at the patrons enjoying their meals.

Juli and Adriana shared a look. "We're thinking about changing some things up," Adriana admitted.

"I thought some Chino-Latino dishes on the menu would be an interesting addition," Juli said and paused, as if seeking their approval. "You two know how it is. Just because something is working doesn't mean you stop being creative," she quickly added and wrung her hands together.

Sara nodded and glanced toward Tony for his take, wondering how he felt about it. "I understand," she said. "It's why we always try to have several new dishes each season."

"Totally agree," Tony said. "I've been testing out some different recipes in *mami's* kitchen while I'm visiting. I'm hoping to add at least one of them to the menu when I get back home."

Get back home, she repeated to herself. *He is going back home in three weeks.* With that thought all the joy of the amazing meal diminished.

Juli beamed at their approval and clapped her hands excitedly. "I'm so glad you understand. You'll have to come back and sample the new menu once we've finalized it."

"I'd love to do that, especially since I plan on being in Miami more often," Tony said and shot a quick look in Sara's direction.

"We'll definitely be back," she said, feeling hopeful again since Tony planned on being in Miami more often. It made her wonder if whatever was growing between them could survive a long-distance relationship. If she was willing to risk her heart to a man who would be flitting back and forth between New York and Miami.

"Definitely," Tony confirmed and met Sara's gaze head on as if to let her know he was serious about his promise. That she could trust him with her heart. A heart that raced once again, spreading warmth through her with the promise in his smile.

Adriana offered to get them some desert, but Sara waved her off. "Seriously I could not eat another bite." Tony agreed.

"All this has been fabulous and filling," he said and dipped his head in thanks.

"*Gracias,*" Juli said and after saying their goodbyes, the two women walked away, chattering excitedly about their new menu and the stamp of approval it had been given by Tony and Sara.

The waitress came over a second later to ask yet again if they wanted dessert, or perhaps some coffee, and when they demurred and Tony asked for the check, she said, "No check. Bosses' order. It's our pleasure, chefs."

"Thank you and please let Juli and Adriana know they're invited to come by *Munch* anytime as my special guests. You as well," Sara said with appreciation.

When the young woman stepped away, Tony peeled off a number of bills and left a generous tip on the table for the waitress and other staff, once again earning brownie points in her book. After he did so, he glanced at his watch and said, "It's still early. Would you like to take a stroll through Lummus Park?"

Because she was having a wonderful time and hated for the night to end, she said, "I'd love to."

He rose and held out his hand to her. As she had done earlier, she slipped her hand into his and they walked out of the restaurant onto Ocean Drive. The crowd had grown heavier and the street was filled with an assortment of vehicles cruising along despite the "No Cruising" sign posted on a nearby streetlamp. As one vintage and heavily chromed Chevrolet Bel Air convertible drove by, the sounds of Latin music blasted from its speakers and filled the night.

Tony escorted her to the curb, waited for a break in the vehicles, and then they darted across the street. They walked away from the sidewalk on one of the paths beneath the palms and sea grape trees in Lummus Park, moving farther from the noise and traffic until they were on the winding cement path that ran adjacent to a low seawall next to the beach. Beneath the moonlight, several couples strolled along the path hand-in-hand, enjoying a cool late spring night.

An inline skater zipped by, his wheels whirring on

the cement path, interrupting the quiet by the beach wall. As a sea breeze picked up, Sara shivered, and Tony tucked his arm around her shoulders and drew her close to his warmth.

"Are you okay?" he asked and glanced at her.

I am now, she wanted to say, thinking that being held by him felt even better than she had imagined as a teenager when she had fantasized about her older brother's best friend. He held her near with his muscled arm and grinned at her, awakening those butterflies in her stomach. Dragging warmth to her cheeks which she hoped he wouldn't notice in the dim light of night.

"I'm good. This is really nice," she said and rested her head against his shoulder, savoring the feel of their bodies bumping together as they walked, tucked tight against each other. *So nice. So right*, she thought and drove away any doubts or misgivings.

CHAPTER 10

IT JUST FEELS WAY TOO right, Tony thought, but this was Rick's baby sister. This was Sara of the scraped knees and braces who had annoyed them by following them around all the time. Only he was anything but annoyed right now as she leaned into him and laid her head against his shoulder. This was a beautiful woman…a woman he wanted to get to know better. Maybe even take their relationship to a different, more permanent place, because everything he'd learned about Sara—past and present—said she wasn't a temporary kind of woman.

"It is nice," Tony said, "as long as nice is a good word and not anything like cute which you hate so much." Even though he was a little afraid to complicate things by really exploring what he was feeling, he couldn't resist her. And even though he was going back to New York, he'd do whatever he could to keep his promise to come to Miami more often. Not just because of the call of home, family, and friends. Because of Sara, he finally admitted to himself.

"Nice is not anything like cute," she said with a laugh and a wrinkle of her nose, a quirk he was becoming accustomed to.

"Glad to know. That dinner was amazing, wasn't it?" And it wasn't just the food that had been outstanding. He had loved having Sara there with him to enjoy the exquisite meal and to get her take on the dishes.

"It was. Juli and Adriana have such smarts about what they do. I'm looking forward to seeing what they accomplish with that new menu," Sara said and peered at him from the corner of her eye.

"You've got smarts too, Sara. *Munch* is unique and your recipes are innovative and fantastic. What made you go in that direction?" He wanted to know more about what made her tick.

Her shoulders shifted up and down against his arm. "I'd sit in the kitchen and watch my mom and grand-mother cook. Listen to the stories my grandmother told about the Old Country. She had loved growing up in Ireland."

He remembered Sara's grandmother and the faint hint of a brogue when she spoke. Her wonderful cranberry orange scones. "She was a wonderful woman. Did she teach you her family recipes?"

"Not at first since she didn't want to encourage me after I said I wanted to be a cook. Like your family, mine wanted me to go to college. But I finally convinced my grandmother to teach me so I could pass the recipes to my kids. People remember foods like that. When they eat it, they remember the stories and their history. That's so important." The tones of her voice were full of the same passion she cooked into her recipes. Passion which she would bring to every aspect of her life, he knew. That passion was enticing. Irresistible as he imagined being the focus of that passion.

"Comfort foods that fill your soul and not just your

belly," he said, better understanding her choice and what drove her to do what she did. It was another thing that they had in common. Another thing that intrigued him and made him want to get to know her even more.

She nodded. "Foods that rouse emotions make the meal about more than just the food."

"I get that," he said. He'd once felt the same way about the food he prepared in his restaurant and lately, he was feeling that way about the recipes he was creating for the *quinceañera*.

"What about you? With your training and everywhere you've worked, what made you go Latin rather than French or Italian?"

He thought about it for a millisecond. With a dip of his head, he explained. "I worked at a number of high-end places. The chefs were torture to work for and like you, I'm not a fan of tweezers and fancy portions you need a magnifying glass to see."

She chuckled and high fived him. "Here's a 'Big No' to temperamental chefs and their tweezers."

"For sure. Anyway, many top chefs were doing French or Italian, even if they were doing the food in all kinds of over-the-top ways. I'm not French or Italian. I'm Cuban and I'm proud of our food traditions. I wanted to show people that Cuban food could be just as high-end and luxurious."

"And you've succeeded. *Paraiso Cubano* is top-of-the-line. I know it's been difficult for you since you made it big, but you deserved that star and all those awards," she said without hesitation. Inside him warmth grew with her praise. With her understanding of what he had accomplished with no hint of the jealousy or competition he'd gotten from his ex-girlfriend.

"*Gracias.* I'm humbled by your approval," he said and

placed his hand over his heart.

"I definitely approve, and I'll be eagerly watching to see what else you do at your restaurant," she said. The warmth dimmed as it occurred to him that it would be a long-distance kind of watch. Which made him ask, "And what about you? What do you want to do with *Munch*?"

She shrugged and he could see that his last words had taken some of the light from her eyes. With a shake of her head, she said, "A second location maybe because we have a prime spot now that I'd hate to lose. We have enough patronage for that, but there's the question of financing and also time. Jeri is a single mom with a little girl, and I worry it might be too much for her to handle another place."

"Unless she has someone like Rick to help her out," he said, recalling how taken his friend seemed to be with Sara's partner.

Another shrug came from her. "Rick and Jeri have a complicated situation. I hope they'll be able to work things out, but they certainly haven't figured anything out yet."

"What about you? Wouldn't another restaurant take up too much of your time?" he blurted out and wanted to bite his tongue. It would sound too much like he was asking about any other guys and heat flooded his cheeks in embarrassment.

She stopped and turned to look at him, her gaze searching his face and then darkening to emerald with emotion. "I don't have anyone in life who would mind me being busy with *Munch* or another location. Maybe if I did..."

"You'd reconsider your dream? Don't you want someone who would understand? Who could be a partner in what you did?" *Maybe even someone like me,* he wanted to say, but held back, conflicted.

A sad smile blossomed on her lips and she cradled his jaw. Swept her thumb across his cheek tenderly. "Of course, but we both know that it's not that easy with our profession. It would take a unique person to understand and be a partner."

He'd learned that with his ex. For that reason, he couldn't offer anything of value to Sara at that moment, but he could offer comfort. Understanding.

"I know, Sara. Maybe we'll both find that person in time," he said and laid his hand over hers, both taking and giving comfort with that simple touch. He took hold of her hand and they walked together again until just a block later they reached the end of Lummus Park. They turned west to walk up 14th Street in companionable silence, each lost in their thoughts about the earlier conversation, until they reached Pennsylvania Avenue and Sara's condo building.

Sara dug her keys out of her bag and then stood jiggling them until she stepped onto the small step by her front door. It put her nearly eye-to-eye with him and her gaze locked on his, searching out his features as if trying to decide what was really happening between them.

He wished he knew as he took a step closer and laid a hand at her waist, not wanting the night to end.

"Sara," he said and shifted until his lips were so close to hers that the warmth of her breath spilled against his. He imagined closing that last little distance, but held fast, not wanting to pressure her. Not wanting to hurt her if it became more.

When Sara stepped back, it was clear that their earlier conversation had troubled her, much as it had him. Even though he wanted to learn more about her, spend more time with her, he knew that it was problematic for so many reasons and so he let her drift away toward the door to the condo.

Sara opened the door, turned, and stood there, uncertain. "I guess this is goodnight. I had a lovely time. Thank you, Tony."

"I had a wonderful time also, Sara, and I meant what I said at the restaurant. I'm not going to stay away from Miami for so long again," Tony said, determined to keep his promise.

Sara leaned against the door and crossed her arms. "I believe that you mean that, Tony. And I hope it's true. I really do. I hope we can spend more time together. Get to know each other better."

If it was possible, she sounded both hopeful and defeated at the same time. "We can do that. I have a few errands to run in the next day or so, but after that –"

"You call me when you're free," she said.

Before he could say a word or do what he'd wanted to do since yesterday—kiss her like there was no tomorrow—she raced into her building and closed the door without looking back.

He stood there for the longest time, fiercely conflicted about what he was feeling and what to do about it. As a light snapped on in a window a few stories above him, he imagined that it was Sara getting settled for the night.

With a sigh he walked away and said, "Good night, *chiquitica*. Dream of me."

Sara and Dolores sat at the kitchen table squeezing citrus for the fresh juices to marinate the roast pork that Dolores wanted to be the main dish for Samantha's *quinceañera*.

"I appreciate you sharing your family recipe," Sara said as she pushed down the handle of the juicer and orange juice sluiced down into a glass. She'd lost track of how many sour and regular oranges, lemons, and limes she'd squeezed to make enough liquid for the marinade.

Dolores smiled and squeezed the last of the limes. "My pleasure. After all, I know you don't normally make traditional Cuban foods in your restaurant."

She didn't, which made her think back to the other night and what her friend Juli had said about spreading her wings and trying something new as well as her discussion with Tony about how important highlighting that cuisine had been to him. "Can't hurt to learn, and if this comes out as good as I expect it to, I hope you don't mind if I steal the recipe for the restaurant."

Dolores grinned and reached for a big pink grapefruit. "As long as you keep this secret to yourself. The grapefruits make all the difference in the marinade. My *papi* taught me that."

Sara mimicked locking up her lips and said, "They're sealed."

Once they'd squeezed a few of the grapefruits and added that juice to the rest, Dolores held up her hand. "Time to taste."

She grabbed a spoon, dipped it into the combined citrus juices and nodded. "I think we're there."

Sara didn't really know where "there" should be, so she grabbed another spoon and tasted the juices. The citrus combination was tart with just a hint of sweetness, a good mix to offset the fattiness of the pork. "Tasty," she said.

Dolores grabbed a bowl with a mound of garlic they'd food-processed earlier. She dumped it into the bucket with the juices, added a goodly amount of cumin, several bay leaves, and finally salt and pepper. "Now we're ready," she said, grabbing the bucket and gesturing toward the large leg of pork that they'd prepped. "Can you grab that?"

Sara wasn't sure grab was the right word. It felt more like dead-lifting the nearly thirty-pound piece of meat. But whatever it was, she wrapped her arms around it, hefted it against her apron, and followed Dolores as she carried the bucket out into the garage where her brother kept a second refrigerator. Dolores set the bucket down and opened the fridge door.

The lower shelves of the fridge had been removed to allow the bucket to fit. "Time to put the pork in," Dolores said and helped Sara to slowly lower the leg of pork into the marinade.

Together they wrangled the heavy bucket into the refrigerator and closed the door. "Now it sits overnight," Dolores said and clapped her hands to signal that they were done.

"Great. So what's the next recipe I can steal...I mean, that you'll share with me," Sara teased and mischievously hip-checked her sister-in-law as they went back to the kitchen.

The front door slammed shut and the tromp of soccer cleats across hardwood floors announced that Samantha was home from practice. She stomped into the kitchen and with a harrumph dropped her knapsack onto an empty kitchen chair.

Sara and Dolores shared an understanding look that said "Drama."

"How was your day, *mija*?" Dolores said calmly.

Samantha's lips pursed with annoyance. "You know that reporter I met this morning about the *quinceañera* article?"

Reporter? Article? This was all news to Sara, who peered at Dolores for clarification.

"I'm sorry, Sara. *Mija*, I didn't get a chance to tell your *tia* the good news. Sara, we got a call yesterday from a lifestyle reporter for *South Beach Style*. They're doing a piece on the resurgence of *quinceañeras* and want to include Samantha's event," Dolores explained.

It would be good news if Sara could pull off the traditional recipes and get a nice mention in the magazine. "That's wonderful," Sara said.

"Except that they're also including Angelica. You should have seen the look she gave me this morning when she saw me with the reporter and photographer," Samantha said before she opened the refrigerator, and stood there scrutinizing the offerings.

Color rose high on Dolores's cheeks and she exploded into machine-gun rapid Spanish. "¡*Esa chiquita me vuelve loca!*"

Samantha slammed the fridge door shut, empty-handed. "English, *por favor, mami.*" Her niece shot a look at Sara and said, "You can always tell when *mami* is really mad because she yells in Spanish."

Dolores lifted her pointed chin defiantly and glared at her daughter. "I did not yell. What I said is that Angelica makes me crazy. Every time I see that girl she puts on airs and seems to forget that all the parents grew up together in the *Suaguesera.*"

At Sara's confused look, Dolores explained. "The Southwest streets in Little Havana."

"I guess she's a little conceited?" Sara asked.

"She can be at times." Samantha grabbed a banana from a nearby basket of fruit. "Sometimes she's friendly, but sometimes, we seem to butt heads."

Sara wrapped an arm around her niece's shoulders and

hugged her. "Since I know what a good kid you are, I have to say she's the problem. Ignore her."

Samantha shook her head. "I've got to go study. I'll see you later," she said and left the room.

Dolores tracked her daughter's flight, full lips twisted into a grimace. "Sometimes I wonder if we did the right thing by letting her go to that fancy prep school."

Sara knew that her brother Matt often worried about the same thing. But as far as she could see, her niece was well-adjusted and had a circle of friends she could count on. "She'll be fine, Dolores. As for this Angelica, whoever she is, we'll just make sure that Samantha's *quinceañera* is the best party ever."

"*Gracias*, Sara. With you cooking, I'm sure it will be. And hopefully there will be a mention in the magazine that helps your business," Dolores said as she pulled a cookbook off a shelf. As she opened it a number of handwritten pieces of paper spilled out. Dolores gathered them up and laid them on the table neatly, passing her hand across them in a fleeting caress.

"My *mami* wrote these out for me so I wouldn't forget our family recipes," Dolores said with a sniffle.

Sara examined the pieces of paper. Yellowing with age, they had a stain or two, which gave them character. They reminded her of the recipes her grandmother had carefully handwritten onto index cards for her. "Do you mind if I snap some photos of these? And do you have photos of your mom and dad? I'd like to turn these into a cookbook to give to Samantha as my *quinceañera* gift."

The sniffles grew louder, and Dolores wiped a tear from under her eye. "That would be a wonderful gift, Sara. *Gracias*."

"It would be my pleasure," she said and hugged the other woman. After a long minute, Dolores waved away her upset and said, "Let's get back to work."

Sara nodded. "For sure. We've got to rock these family dishes and show everyone they're at the best *quinceañera* party ever."

CHAPTER 11

T HE REPORTER SAT ACROSS FROM Tony at the News
Café while the photographer flitted around like a
bee sampling flowers, shifting here and there to shoot
photos for the article.

Tony sipped his *café con leche* as Roberta Lane flipped
through her notes, pausing here and there. He watched
carefully to catch any reaction on her part, but her face
was as immobile as the marble of a Greek statue. *She'd
make a marvelous poker player*, he suspected. Finally, she
flipped to an empty page in her notepad, reached into
her purse, and took out a digital recorder.

"Do you mind if I record this?" Roberta asked, then
clicked it on without waiting for his response.

"Sure," he said facetiously—not that she caught that.
Instead, she charged ahead with her questions.

"Was it difficult for you to leave your restaurant to
come help your family with their *quinceañera*?" she asked.

"It took some planning, but I have a great crew back
in New York. Plus, family comes first, *sabes*. When my
sister called and asked for help, I couldn't say 'no'." *Although I did think about it.* But if he hadn't come down,

he wouldn't have reconnected with Sara, and that had made it even more worthwhile.

Roberta's gaze, the only animated thing on her features, narrowed as if she was deep in thought.

"Does that mean we'll see your brother, Javier, at the party?" she asked.

Sylvia had been calling Javier, but it wouldn't be the first time that his brother hadn't shown up due to work obligations. Not that Roberta needed to know that. It also reminded him that he should call Javi and check up on him.

"We're expecting that Javier will be here for the party," he said and held his coffee cup with both hands to still any motion that might tip off the reporter.

Roberta paused, and for a moment he expected her to press for more information on his highly successful CEO brother, but with a slight shake of her head, she said, "What will be on the menu for Angelica's *quinceañera*?"

Tony dipped his head and tossed out the names of some of the recipes he'd been perfecting over the last few days. "The theme is Miami Spice so I'm doing new takes on Cuban classics as well as some other Latin cuisines since Miami now has such a diverse Latino population. I've got a Cuban-style porchetta, cracklin' and tripe tacos, and *ropa vieja arepas* just to name a few."

"You're making my mouth water, chef," she said, but as her gaze slipped over him, he felt like something she thought should be on the menu. It made him decidedly uneasy and not just because he had interest in only one woman—Sara.

"*Gracias*, Roberta. I hope you'll enjoy my food when you try it at the event," he said, then picked up his cup and sipped.

"I'm sure I will, but I'm certain others in the area

would love to try your food as well. Is there any chance you might have a new restaurant in the works here in Miami? Could that be part of your reason for the visit as well?"

He laid the cup down on the table and shifted it back and forth between his hands as he considered her question. The option to come back home and open a new place had been on his mind, and Sara had made the idea of leaving Miami that much harder to contemplate. He was enjoying his time with her just way too much.

"I've thought about it," he admitted, his gaze fixed on his coffee cup to avoid giving anything away to the reporter. "Being in Miami...being home has brought back many great memories of growing up here. Most of my family and friends are still here, so yes."

"I imagine it would be a tough choice. After all, you and your restaurant have won several awards."

With a nonchalant shrug, he said, "I'm just a man who has been lucky enough to be noticed for doing something he loves."

"And doing it well. That means people know you and expect certain things, don't they?" Roberta pressed.

Was that a sly look in her eyes? Where was she going with these questions?

Cautiously, he nodded to confirm it. "They do. That's why I always try my hardest to be the best that I can be. I don't want to disappoint my customers."

Almost as if she had just hooked a fish, Roberta reeled him in. "Do you think you'll be the best chef out of all of the *quinceañera* celebrations? Even when one of the other chefs is Miami's rising young star Sara Kelly?"

Suddenly he felt like he was flopping on the dock like that hooked fish, trying to avoid Roberta's mallet, poised to smash in his skull.

"Sara is a fabulous chef. I've had the opportunity to sample her delicious food at *Munch*," he said, dodging the question even as he wondered how it was possible that Sara had not mentioned that she was working on such an event. Not that he'd mentioned his involvement in Angelica's party either. In fact, he'd never thought to ask who Angelica's apparent rival was, but now he guessed that it must be Sara's niece.

"Is she as good as an award-winning chef with a coveted starred restaurant?"

"As I said before, Sara is an absolutely wonderful chef and what she's done at *Munch* is truly an accomplishment," Tony reiterated.

"It's not the same caliber as your restaurant and skills. That's why I imagine it's important to Sara to prove she's capable of playing in the same ballpark as you. And you likewise want to show that you're the best," Roberta said, with the first hint he'd seen of a smile, albeit a calculating one, on her face.

Her pushing and questioning was starting to wear on his patience, especially since it was hitting too close to home. A good showing in front of important locals might provide him with the connections to open a second location in Miami. "It is important. There's nothing to say we can't both be the best at what we do."

"Sara's menu at *Munch* is far from the kind of high end dining your customers expect," she said, hoisting the mallet for the killing blow. He tried to wriggle out of her reach.

"Sara's menu is luxurious and top-of-the-line. What she's doing is innovative and exciting," he said without any hesitation. He'd been floored with how Sara had transformed what were supposed to be run-of-the-mill comfort foods.

Roberta narrowed her gaze, leaned back in her chair, and tapped her pen against her lips for a second. Then she leaned forward again and said, "It sounds like you're quite a fan of Sara's. Do I detect something there besides professional interest?"

"Sara is a friend. We grew up together," he said, but he was sure that this shark in reporter's clothing would find a way to twist that statement and upset Sara, which was the last thing he wanted to do.

The reporter smiled again, but it didn't reach her eyes. "I understand you've got a professional crew from the hotel working in your kitchen. It'll be interesting to see what pros do against Sara's amateurs."

"Amateurs? There is nothing amateur about the crew working Sara and Jeri's kitchen," he challenged.

"I guess you don't know that Sara and Jeri train women from the local shelters."

Sara had mentioned it in passing. And as with everything else he learned with each layer of Sara that was peeled off, it only made him like her more and more. "I do know, and I think that's a wonderful thing to do. I admire her even more for it, especially considering what I've seen happen in her kitchen."

"Thank you so much for taking the time to chat with me, chef. I appreciate it, but I want you to understand that I have limited space for the article and can only really feature one of the events in the magazine."

And from all that she'd said so far, she intended to pit him against Sara. Controlling his anger, he said, "I understand. Whatever you decide to do is fine with me."

The reporter shot a look at her photographer, who he'd forgotten was there, grabbed her digital recorder, and stood. She held out her hand and said, "Would you have a problem with us dropping by the hotel kitchen so we can photograph you at work?"

He rose as well and shook her hand but felt like he had to wipe it clean after he did so. "It would be my pleasure," he said, though he suspected he wasn't fooling anyone with his statement. She had left a very sour taste in his mouth—which seemed to have been her goal, given the way she clearly delighted in unsettling him.

"Wonderful. Well, we must be going. We have another interview to do today," Roberta said, and Tony had no doubt that Roberta would be burning rubber to get to Sara and try to box her into a corner the way she'd tried to do with him.

As Roberta walked away, he pulled his smartphone from his back pocket and dialed Sara, but she didn't answer. He left a short message asking her to call him as soon as possible so he could explain whatever Roberta was sure to misrepresent. Especially the line about Sara and he being nothing more than friends.

They were way more than that. In the short week that he'd been in Miami Sara had come to mean a lot to him. What they already shared was so much more than just friendship and he wanted Sara to know that.

Muttering a curse beneath his breath, he swiped to end the call and decided there was only one thing he could do.

He rushed onto Ocean Drive and nearly ran to Sara's restaurant.

Sara had hated to leave Jeri holding down the fort again, but the *South Beach Style* reporter had wanted to interview her at a local Lincoln Road coffee shop rather than at the restaurant. She hurried the couple of blocks, worried that she was running late because Matt had been a little tardy with his morning delivery. As she rounded the corner onto the pedestrian mall, she caught sight of a woman sitting at one of the al fresco tables outside the coffee shop. A photographer sat on the ledge of a nearby planter, looking decidedly bored.

The reporter was dressed in a curve-hugging dress in a shocking flamingo pink. Her blonde hair was styled in an elaborate knot atop her head and swept away from an unlined, perfectly made-up face. As the woman caught sight of her, she smiled in greeting, but there was no warmth there. If anything, the hairs on Sara's neck rose in warning at the look in the other woman's gaze.

Sara swept her hand down the simple lace blouse she wore, hoping it hadn't gotten too wrinkled while she had worked in the kitchen that morning. She also hoped that she wasn't dressed too casually with her blouse and faded jeans, but she'd had too much to do to change into anything more formal.

Sara marched over and stuck out her hand. "Sara Kelly."

"Roberta Lane, *South Beach Style*. Thank you for taking the time to chat with me. Can Wilson get you anything?" she said and gestured to the bored photographer.

"No, thank you," she replied politely.

Roberta jerked her head in the direction of the coffee shop. "Wilson. Large latte, soy milk, no foam, no sugar." She tacked on as an afterthought, "Please."

As if used to the rudeness, the photographer said nothing and scurried away to fulfill her command.

Sara sat across from the woman, crossed her legs, and leaned back in her chair, trying to adopt a laidback pose when she was feeling anything but. This woman set her teeth on edge.

"Do you mind if I record our interview?" Roberta said even as she snapped on a digital recorder and placed it on the table between them. A second later she whipped a leather portfolio from a designer handbag the price of which could have fed a family of four for a month or more.

"Not at all."

"This is going to be such an interesting article. After all, we'll not only get to see how two families interpret such a lovely tradition, we'll get to see what two top chefs bring to the mix. It's just a shame that I'll only really be able to feature one of you in the article."

Sara crinkled her nose with confusion. "Feature? Two top chefs? Color me confused, but I'm not sure what you mean."

"You and Tony Sanchez, Angelica Rodriguez's uncle. Didn't you know he was going to be responsible for the meal at her *quinceañera*?"

Tony was cooking? For the Angelica who was a thorn in her niece's side? Angelica was Tony's niece? She couldn't believe she hadn't made the connection before.

"That's very nice," she eked out past the lump in her throat and the chill filling her center with worry. Maybe even anger, if she was being honest with herself.

"I guess you didn't know," Roberta said, an unctuous note in her voice.

Sara forced a smile and tried to hide her upset. "Tony is a wonderful chef and I'm sure that whatever he does will be spectacular."

A toothy grin, like that of a shark before it bit you, split Roberta's face. "Do you think your group of amateur chefs—"

"They're not amateurs." Her hands tightened on the

arms of her chair. "Who called them that?"

One manicured brow inched up in response. "I guess you think you can do as well –"

"*Better* than Chef Sanchez and his crew." She popped out of her chair, so forcefully it almost fell over. "I've got to go back to my crew of *trained* kitchen staff and chefs."

"We'll be visiting with Tony in his kitchen. Can we do the same with you? I'm sure the readers –"

Can go pound sand, she wanted to say, but bit it back. "We'd be delighted to have you with us so you can see just how well we measure up."

She didn't wait for Roberta's reply although her trill of "Wonderful" chased Sara as she almost ran down the sidewalk to get back to her restaurant.

She had taken no more than a step into the building when Jeri called out, "You've got a visitor."

Tony stood by the half-wall, a look on his face that spoke volumes.

He held his hands up in apology and said, "We have to talk, Sara."

She pointed at the door. "You. Outside. Now."

CHAPTER 12

Tony did as Sara asked. Arms akimbo, he faced her and said, "You're doing the *quinceañera* meal for your niece?"

Sara copied his pose and jammed her hands on her hips. "I am. And you're cooking for yours?"

"I came to Miami because Sylvia asked me to help out. She said Angelica's party has to be the 'best *quinceañera* ever.'" He used air quotes for emphasis.

"The reporter said she can only really feature one of the parties," Sara said and tilted her chin up. Her grey-green gaze spit emerald fire at him. "I *need* Samantha's party to be the best. For my niece. For Jeri and me and our women. I am *going* to make it the best."

He tapped his chest. "Angelica's party is important to me too, Sara. I've been thinking about relocating and maybe even opening another place here. A feature in that magazine could give me the exposure I need to do that."

Sara shook her head, looked away, and dragged her hand through her hair in obvious frustration, leaving it sticking up in spiky strands. When she met his gaze again, she said, "Do you know how much harder it is to be a female chef? How hard it is for us to get financing?"

He sympathized with her predicament. He held his hands out in pleading. "I get it—"

She slashed her hand to silence him. "Please. You can't possibly understand. It's always male chefs being featured or getting awards for their 'fine dining' restaurants," she said and barely took a breath before pushing on. "You know why so few women have high-end places?"

Tony couldn't argue with her that women often didn't get the same exposure as male chefs, and he knew that lack of exposure affected quite a number of things. Like financing. "Because you can't get the funding for anything other than a small mom and pop place."

She jabbed her finger in his direction. "Bingo. I need that article to get noticed. I need to make connections so I can either expand this place or open a second location."

As much as he understood her need, he selfishly had his own needs as well. The paradox was that those needs also included her. "I'm sorry, Sara. I know you're doing good things here—"

"I am, Tony. I'm giving women a chance to get back on their feet. That's important to me and to them. And they're not amateurs." The earlier anger in her tone had been replaced with passion. With concern for her staff.

"I never said they were. That was Roberta's word, not mine. I see how well they work. I've tasted the amazing food they've made. Your food." He took a step toward her, wanting to offer comfort, but she shifted away. It chilled his heart to have her withdrawing from him.

She raked her hand through her hair again. "They are wonderful, and I plan on leading them to make the best *quinceañera* meal this town has ever seen. It's important to me, but also to Samantha and my sister-in-law, Dolores. It's a tradition that means a lot to her."

"A tradition you know nothing about," he tossed at her, equally frustrated by her obstinance.

"Wrong again, Tony. Dolores has been sharing her traditions with me and it's been amazing to learn about it and her family's recipes. Her stories about her family, and about Cuba and how they left, are fascinating."

He could well imagine. The diaspora of Cubans to the United States was a tale of love and determination, hope and loss. "It is fascinating, but it's not *your* story. It's not your food."

"Dolores is family and because of that her traditions are becoming a part of me," she said and laid a hand over her heart to emphasize the point. "It's a part of *my family* that I want to honor with an amazing meal and an awesome event."

Her sincerity was real and intense, but there was no way she was going to out-Cuban a Cuban when it came to Cuban food or traditions. "I guess we'll see who's the better chef."

"I guess we will." With a determined dip of her head, she pivoted on her heel, and escaped back into her restaurant.

The feel of her absence was immediate. He didn't want to be at odds with Sara, but Roberta Lane had made anything else impossible with her manipulative interviews. But he wasn't about to just give up on their relationship entirely. Sara had grown to mean too much to him. There had to be a way for them to both get what they wanted despite this manufactured competition to be the one featured in the article. There had to be a way for them to continue to explore what they were feeling for each other and whether it could be more. Whether it could be real love.

He jammed his hands on his hips again and peered

through the door of the restaurant. Inside Sara was speaking to Jeri, who shot a quick look in his direction before hugging Sara. Jeri's gaze warned him to not only stay away, but to disappear or face dire consequences. He understood her anger and admired her loyalty to her friend, as misguided as it might be.

With a few quick strides he was on the sidewalk and moving back toward his car. He needed to return to his parents' house and doublecheck the menu he had planned. Not to mention call Sylvia let her know what was happening because things had suddenly gotten a lot more complicated than he had ever thought possible.

The knife bit deep into her fingertip. Sara yelped, dropped the knife, and applied pressure to the cut.

Dolores was immediately there and at the sight of the blood, she went into action like any good mom would do. She handed Sara a piece of paper towel and said, "Let me get something to clean that and get it bandaged."

"I'm sorry. I'm just a little distracted." Sara kept pressure on the wound and waited while Dolores rushed out to the bathroom and came back with a first aid kit. The two sat at the table and Dolores, clearly in mommy mode, opened the kit and disinfected the wound.

As she swiped an alcohol swab over the slice, Dolores said, "I've noticed that you're not your usual cheery self tonight. What's bothering you?"

Sara shrugged, then winced as the alcohol stung her finger, sucking in a sharp breath.

"Sorry. I didn't mean to hurt you," Dolores said, but

wiped the cut again just to be safe before instructing Sara to keep the pad and pressure on her finger.

"It's okay. It didn't hurt that much." Nowhere near as much as the hurt from the words she'd exchanged with Tony. Words that had really knocked her off her game. Especially the ones about Dolores's traditions and food not really being a part of her. That accusation had been eating at her because part of her felt that he hadn't been wrong. This *quinceañera* tradition didn't belong to her and neither did the food.

Dolores's fingers were sure, but gentle, as she wrapped an adhesive bandage securely around the cut. As she worked, she said, "Can I take a guess who has you frazzled? Would it be Tony Sanchez by any chance?"

Sara smoothed the bandage over the cut and checked to make sure it was secure so she could continue cooking. "I guess Roberta Lane, that snake, has been busy spreading her venom."

Dolores nodded and closed the first aid kit. "It's been hard enough keeping the rivalry between the girls in check and now this." She shook her head, dejection in the slump of her shoulders and the cocoa brown of her eyes. "Sometimes I'm sorry I pushed to have this party."

Sara laid a hand over Dolores's as it rested on the tabletop. "Don't say that, Dolores. This is a lovely tradition and it's been so wonderful for all of us to get to know more about it and your family's history. We tend to forget the past, but it's what shapes our future."

Dolores took hold of her hand and gently squeezed. "It does, Sara. And I also want to show how proud I am of what we have accomplished. Matt and I might not have the kind of money that Angelica's parents have, but we've come a long way from our tiny cinder block homes in Little Havana."

"You have, Dolores. You should be very proud of all that you've done." She had always loved and respected her sister-in-law and had a good relationship with her. Planning the *quinceañera* had only brought them even closer.

Dolores smiled and urged Sara out of her chair. "You should be as well. You've accomplished so much and not just for yourself. You're making a big difference in other people's lives. That's amazing!"

Maybe, Sara thought, but had to know whether Dolores felt the same way that Tony did about Sara's involvement in the *quinceañera*. "Tony said that these traditions and the foods aren't mine. He made me feel guilty that I'm going to be using your family recipes to boost my name. Kelly. Not too Cuban, right?" she said with a harsh laugh.

Dolores wrapped an arm around her shoulder. "So he thinks only Cubans can cook Cuban food? Didn't he train under French and Italian chefs?"

With a huff, Sara said, "Yes, he did. Part of the training, right?"

With a reassuring shake, Dolores said, "You respect my traditions and my food. You're taking the time to learn about both. That's what matters to me and not the fact that you're Irish." With a laugh, Dolores continued. "Besides, both Tony's family and mine were first generation in Cuba. Some there didn't consider us Cuban enough back then but that didn't stop us from being Cuban in our hearts."

Sara smiled, appreciating the support. Sara hugged her sister-in-law and walked her back toward the counter where she had been chopping garlic. "Well this heart—and stomach—thinks that the *mojo* you put on the *tostones* is absolutely amazing. Now I want to know how you did it."

Dolores urged Sara away from the cutting board and picked up the knife. She cut the garlic cloves, chatting as she chopped them into finer and finer pieces. "Well, there's the parsley and citrus *mojo* that's just like the marinade for the roast pork. This one is all garlic all the time."

When the garlic was finely diced, Dolores poured extra virgin olive oil into a cast iron pan. "*Mi abuela* had a little secret for this mojo," she said and added a healthy dollop of butter to the oil. "But you need to keep the heat low, so the garlic and butter won't burn."

"Got it," Sara said. Garlic joined the butter and oil in the pan and within seconds the fragrance of the garlic wafted through the kitchen. It took only a few minutes and the garlic was heading toward a lovely gold. Dolores immediately shut off the gas and shifted the cast iron pan off the range. The pan would retain enough heat to finish cooking off the garlic.

"Let it cool and then we can try it," Dolores said and walked over to the counter to bring over the plate of *tostones* they had made earlier that night by twice frying and flattening slices of green plantains.

As they sat at the table, Sara grabbed one of the now flat and thin plantains and added a liberal amount of salt. She ate a piece, loving the crispy edges, crunchiness of the exterior, and slightly creamy interior. Holding up what was left, she said, "This would make a totally awesome carrier for something. Maybe a slider of some kind."

"You do love your burgers, don't you," Dolores teased with a smile.

"I so do. I know most people don't think of them as fancy food, but they can be a perfect meal." She popped the last little bit of plantain into her mouth and her mind was whirling with possible ideas for the kind of slider that would perfectly match the *tostones*.

"Tony loved your sliders. Or at least that's what Rick told Matt," Dolores said with a knowing look.

Tony, Tony, Tony. He'd been on her mind since yesterday's blow-up. Maybe talking about him was a way to exorcise him from her brain so she could focus on what she had to do for the *quinceañera*. "He liked my food. I think he liked me and not just in a chef-way." And the feelings were mutual. Her childhood crush was long gone, her feelings those of a woman who wanted a happily-ever-after with a complex and interesting man. But definitely not a long-distance relationship.

"You've liked him since forever." Dolores rose from the table and went back to the stove where she ladled some of the garlic mojo into a small bowl and brought it back to the kitchen table for them to try.

"Did Matt tell you that too?" Her older brother could be amazingly dense at times about what to keep private.

Dolores chuckled and shook her head. "*Chica*, I have eyes of my own. It was obvious to everyone in the neighborhood, except Tony of course, that you liked him."

Sara planted her face in her hands and groaned. "Lord, was I that obvious?" When the smell of garlic teased her, she opened her eyes to find Dolores holding out a plantain with a tiny bit of garlic, oil, and butter glistening at its center.

She didn't hesitate to take it and sample the *mojo*. The garlic and butter were sweet against the fruitiness of the *tostones* and slight tang of the olive oil. "Delicious. I see how the butter adds another layer. I'll have to try that with some of my other recipes."

"Do I get a commission when you do?" Dolores said with a wink.

"For sure, Dolores. In fact, I'll credit you on the menu for any of the recipes I use."

"I'd be honored if you did that," Dolores said, but then plowed on. "What do you plan to do about Tony?"

She'd been thinking about it non-stop since the interview with the reporter. "There's only one thing I can do: Be the best."

Tony had always been able to count on his older siblings to help him when he had a sticky problem—and Sara was definitely one of the stickiest problems to come his way in a long time.

He'd be seeing Sylvia later, but now it was time to reach out to Javi and not just about Sara. No one had heard for certain when his brother would be arriving in Miami for the *quinceañera* which was now only two weeks away.

He dialed Javi, who only answered after several rings. "Tony, this isn't a good time," Javier said.

In the background he could hear others talking and he wanted to say that lately it was never a good time with Javier but bit it back. "I'm sorry, but I really needed to talk, *mano*."

A long pause followed and then the sound on the phone became muffled as his brother said, "You'll have to excuse me for a few minutes."

When Javier came back on, he was the only one on the line. "How can I help, Tony?"

Tony explained about Sara and the *quinceañera* competition that had come out of nowhere.

"*Hermanito*, that is a difficult situation. Do you care for her?" Javi asked and he could picture his brother's face, full of caring and patience much like when they were kids and Tony had needed advice.

"I do, Javi. I know it hasn't been all that long –"

"Just over a week," Javi challenged.

"But in that short time, we've really gotten to know each other. I like her. I'm totally into her and I don't know what to do about this."

"Can you separate the competition from what you feel for her?" Javi asked.

"I'm not sure," he admitted honestly. He was competitive by nature. It was how he'd succeeded in such a cutthroat business. But competing against Sara... "I'm not sure," he repeated, so confused by what he wanted and how it impacted what Sara wanted.

Javi started to speak, but then a second voice intruded. "Javi, we really need you back in the meeting. Come on, dude. This is important."

The sound was muffled again as Javi said, "I'll be there in a minute."

"Javi, are you okay?" Tony asked, worried that there was something serious going on in his brother's life.

"I'm okay, I just can't share any details right now. But I hope I'll be able to once I get home," Javi said, his tone rushed, but without worry which eased some of Tony's concern.

"Are you coming home for the *quince*?" Tony pressed, just to make sure he wasn't misreading his brother's comment.

"I wouldn't miss it for the world, *hermanito*. I miss you all and can't wait to see you."

Relief swamped Tony. "Take care, Javi. We'll see you soon."

"What are you going to do?" Sylvia asked as she sat across from Tony, sipping the *cortadito* that their mother had prepared for them.

Tony took a taste of his own and the thick sweetness of the condensed milk his mother had used coated his mouth. It would make a perfect base for a coffee-flavored ice cream.

"So?" Sylvia pressed and because he knew his sister would not leave it alone, he finally answered.

"I don't know. To be honest, being home has made me think about spending more time here." *And more time with Sara.*

"As in, you'd live here, *hermanito*?" Hopefulness colored her words.

With a reticent nod, he said, "*Sí*, as in living here. Maybe even opening another restaurant with a more eclectic menu. That'll take money and connections and that article in *South Beach Style* could be enough to get the ball rolling. That is if the reporter features Angelica's party and my cooking."

Sylvia gently held her small espresso cup, peering down at it until she softly said, "And rolling right over a speed bump named Sara Kelly. Not to mention her niece Samantha."

Obviously, Sylvia didn't like the thought of that any more than he did. "Were you aware that she trained at-risk women with no cooking experience in her kitchens so they could have more job opportunities?"

"And she helps place them in other restaurants and

hotels so they can move up," Sylvia added. "I knew. Esteban and I have attended her annual fundraiser to help offset the costs of equipment and supplies for the women."

"Saint Sara," he muttered and finished off his coffee with one big gulp. The heat of it burned like acid as it went down his throat along with the guilt that swamped him. Sara was doing something really important and didn't merit his sarcasm, only praise.

"She does it because of Bridget," Sylvia said, surprising him with the mention of Sara's older sister.

"What about Bridget?" Tony asked, puzzled by the statement.

Sylvia dipped her head to one side and hesitated, obviously conflicted. "She had a hard time both before and after her divorce. Bridget was lucky to have family that could help her, but if she hadn't had them, she might have ended up homeless just like the women that Sara helps."

"I still don't get the connection," he said, feeling like he was missing something.

"After her experience, Bridget went to some support groups and met many women who hadn't been as lucky as she was. That made her want to find a way to help them, so she started an organization that supports women in need and Sara helps in whatever ways she can," Sylvia said.

"So, if I'm the one whose featured in this article—"

"It's not just Sara who gets hurt, although I think that's a major part of it for you. Not an easy choice, is it?"

He shook his head. "Not at all. But I have a reputation to uphold and I made a promise to you and Angelica. As important as this is to Sara, I can't do anything less than my best for all of us." The truth of that didn't make him feel any better about what was happening or how this would all end. He didn't want to sabotage Sara's chance to expand her business. He didn't want to hurt Sara or her staff. And he still wanted to see where their relationship could go. But he had to support his family as well.

"You care for her, don't you?" Sylvia said, her brow furrowed as she waited for his response.

"I do. She's so talented. Bright. Funny. Unique. She's not afraid to follow her own drummer, *sabes*."

"Do you love her, Tony?"

If he did, he wasn't ready to say, especially not to Sylvia. The person he wanted to hear that first was Sara. "Maybe," was all that he was willing to admit to his sister.

"It's a start, *hermanito*. Especially if it keeps you in Miami. Now if we could only find a way to bring Javi home," she said with a wistful sigh.

"I spoke to Javi this morning. It sounded like he was in the middle of something really important, but he took the time to chat and to confirm that he'd be here for the *quinceañera*."

"*De verdad?* I was beginning to think that he wasn't going to make it," Sylvia admitted with a frown.

"He said he couldn't wait to get home and I believe him, Sylvita."

"Hmm," his sister said and took a last sip of her coffee, but Tony suspected his sister was already thinking about what to do to convince their older brother that he was better off in Miami rather than on the West Coast.

With that in mind, he said, "If anyone can find a way to keep Javi home, it'll be you, *hermanita*."

Which made him wonder if Sylvia hadn't also brought him home for the exact same reason. But he wasn't going to get angry with his sister for her machinations. If anything, he wanted to thank her for helping to restore his passion for cooking and opening him up to the prospect that something more was possible for him.

CHAPTER 13

ANGELICA SPRINTED TOWARD MIDFIELD, KEEPING the ball in control as she looked for an opening in the other team's defense. But as she dribbled to avoid a defender, her mind drifted for a split second as she imagined herself in a hideous seafoam green *quinceañera* gown adorned with immense neon-colored flowers. It was a mix of some of the designs she'd seen days earlier during another unsuccessful attempt to find her dress.

In that slight moment of hesitation, the defender stole the ball from her and kicked it to one of her strikers who took off down the field, racing straight for Angelica's team's goal.

With another quick pass to a teammate, the opposing team broke through the defense.

Suddenly, in a blur of blue and gold, Samantha disrupted the play with a sliding tackle. The ball skittered away and another of Angelica's midfielders kicked the ball back upfield to the forwards.

Angelica had barely made it back into the play when the referee blew the whistle, signaling the end of the game. Thanks to Samantha's save, they had been able to win the game by just one goal.

The two teams lined up to shake hands and after, her teammates ran off the field. Angelica held back, walking more slowly, thinking about how badly she'd played in the game and everything she still had to do for the *quinceañera* which was now barely two weeks away.

"What's bugging you?" Samantha asked as they stopped at their bench to pick up their water bottles for a quick drink before heading in.

Angelica plopped onto the bench, grabbed a small towel, and mopped her face with it. Samantha did the same, obviously intent on getting an answer. It was weird, but despite their disagreements, Angelica felt more comfortable sharing what was bothering her with Samantha than with her friends, maybe because it involved Samantha's aunt and *Tio* Tony. She'd overheard her mother and him chatting the other night about the party and about how much he liked Sara Kelly. But she couldn't get the words out.

"Thanks for that tackle out there. I really messed up by losing control of the ball," she said and passed the towel across her face again.

Samantha hesitated, clearly not expecting the praise, but then said, "Thanks and no need to apologize. Everyone has a bad day."

Angelica chuckled. "Not sure there was an apology there. My mind was on something else." She rose and started walking toward the locker room and Samantha followed.

"Like your *quince*? I get it. Lately I can't avoid thinking about it even though I want to not think about it," Samantha said, surprising her as they entered the locker room. They walked toward their lockers which were directly opposite each other.

"Me, too," she blurted out and quickly covered her mouth to keep from saying anything else, especially anything about Sara and Tony.

"Weird, right? There's still so much to do, but at least I've got my dress already," Samantha said. It was probably the worst thing she could have said at the moment because Angelica was still in search of the perfect dress and time was running out.

"Do you have a photo of it?" Angelica asked and opened her locker.

Samantha delayed, obviously having qualms about showing her the dress. It killed the fragile moment of camaraderie that had sprung up between them.

"That's okay. I get that you wouldn't want to show me the dress," she said and quickly reached into her locker for her shower caddy. She didn't want to show her upset.

The soft touch of Samantha's hand on her arm stopped her.

Samantha knew she had blown their moment with her reticence about the dress, but not for the reasons Angelica might think. Determined to set things back to right—or as right as they ever could be with An-gelica—she laid her hand on Angelica's arm.

"I don't mind showing you the dress. I just need to get out my phone," she said.

As Angelica straightened and turned her way, Samantha rooted through her knapsack and located her phone. She whipped it out and with a few efficient swipes, pulled up a photo of the dress.

She handed her phone to Angelica who peered at the dress intently. "It's gorgeous. You look wonderful," she said, true pleasure in her words.

"Thank you. I'm very happy with it," Samantha said. Her mother had sketched several designs before they had both agreed that this was the right one.

"Who's the designer? Where did you get it?" Angelica asked and passed the phone back to Samantha.

She should have expected those questions and prepared an answer, but she hadn't. As before, she wavered. And as before, Angelica got the wrong message.

"Got it," she said, grabbed her shower caddy and towel and hurried off.

Sara sighed and put her phone away. It wasn't that she didn't want to share, it was that she didn't know how to explain that it wasn't some fancy designer, but her very talented mother who had designed and sewn the dress.

Samantha sat there for a long second, uncertain as to what to do, but then she flew into action. Her mother would be picking her up soon and she had to be ready because Aunt Sara was coming over for yet more preparations.

In no time both Angelica and she were showered, dressed, and walking out with their teammates to wait for their parents. After their teammates were gone, the two sat silently on the edge of the planter ledge, both of them hunched over their phones, checking their social media streams and texting their friends. So different from the other day.

We're sitting barely inches apart and yet it feels like there's even more distance between us than ever, Samantha thought.

At the sound of a car approaching, both their heads jerked up and Samantha's mom pulled up in her late model sedan.

"See you tomorrow," Samantha said as she stood and grabbed her knapsack.

"See you," Angelica said, but there was no friendliness in her tone.

When Samantha slipped into the car, her mother said, "Everything okay? You look like you just lost your best friend."

Samantha peered back toward Angelica, who sat there, swinging her legs as she waited, her head buried in her smartphone again. She wasn't sure Angelica was a friend, but she wasn't really as bad as she'd told her aunt the other day.

"I'm okay, only...I showed Angelica the pictures of my dress and she really liked it. She asked who the designer was," she said and glanced at her mother intently, anxiously waiting for her reaction.

Her mother shot her a quick look, her brown eyes conflicted. "Did you tell her?"

Samantha shook her head. "No." There was a wealth of emotions in that one simple word.

"Does it bother you that I made your dress? Are you ashamed of that? Of me?"

Hurt was alive and huge in her mother's voice and it was the last thing she wanted. "No, *mami*, of course not. If anything, I'm so proud of how talented you are and how beautiful the dress is." She hated that she had hurt her mother because her mother was also her friend— possibly her best friend. But being the scholarship girl in an exclusive school was often difficult, especially when it came to things involving money.

Their family wasn't poor. They just weren't as rich as the families of most of the teens at the prep school.

"If I told Angelica, would you mind making a dress

for her?" Samantha asked.

Her mother jerked the car to an awkward stop at the streetlight as the light turned red. She eyed Samantha, examining her carefully. "Are you sure you want that to happen?"

With a quick shrug, she said, "It could be good for the family. For you. Angelica's mom has a lot of connections."

Her mother blew out a harsh breath. "Connections who would rather shop at the salon where I work or at those fancy shops in Bal Harbour."

"Unless you had your own salon," Samantha said. It had always been her mother's dream to have her own place. If designing the dresses for two *quinceañeras* got her name and her brand some attention, then maybe this was a chance for her mother to finally take a step toward that dream.

"It's not that easy," her mother said and started driving again as the light turned green.

She didn't like upsetting her mother, but it was for a good reason this time. "You always told me nothing worthwhile was easy. That I could accomplish anything if I wanted it enough and worked hard for it."

Another laugh escaped her mother, but it was lighter and more amused. With a sidelong glance at Samantha, she said, "It's hard to argue with such wisdom."

Samantha didn't wait to press on. "Is that a yes?"

Dolores nodded and reached out to run her hand across Samantha's cheek. "*Sí*, that's a yes. If Angelica wants me to, I'll make her dress."

CHAPTER 14

With just less than two weeks until the *quinceañera*, Tony still had plenty of time before he needed the fruits and vegetables to prepare the dishes he'd been preparing. He was pretty sure which recipes he'd be serving on that special night, but just in case there was a shortage of anything, he wanted to be ready.

At the fruit stand he walked through the stalls, checking out what was available and whether he would have to make any changes. So far there was a wealth of the avocados, mangos, passionfruit, and assorted vegetables he needed. Satisfied, he nevertheless searched for Luis to confirm that everything would be okay for the party.

The old man was busy laying out large Florida avocados into one of the bins. He was dressed as he always was, in his clean, but baggy khakis with the worn leather belt that kept them on his lean hips and a sparklingly white T-shirt.

"*Buenos días*, Luis," he said and clapped the old man on the back.

"*Buenos días*, Antonio. How are the *quince* plans going?" Luis said while he continued to stack the bright green fruits.

"They're going well. I just wanted to check and see what you've got just in case I need to make some changes to my menu," he said and helped the older man unpack the avocados.

Luis grabbed an avocado, held it up, and examined it before placing it in the bin. "You better get your order in soon. Sara was by this morning also. I expect to get her list this week."

Tony was sure the old man was up to something, but still decided to play his little game. "Do you think you'll run out of anything?"

The old man made a face. "*Por favor, chico*. There isn't a thing I can't get for you."

Luis grabbed the now empty avocado box and walked toward the storage area at the back of the store. Tony followed him and said, "So what did Sara say?"

"Sara said a lot. She needs avocados, nice ones like we just put out," Luis said slyly as they entered the backroom that was packed with cardboard boxes of assorted fruits and vegetables.

"We both know that's not what I mean," he said. When Luis thrust a box of pineapples at him, he grabbed it, waited for the old man to lift another box with the fruit, and followed him back out to the store to help him stock the bins.

"*Lo se, chico*. But maybe you should ask her yourself." Luis jerked his head in the direction of the restaurant portion of the store where Sara sat at the counter, chatting with Lucy and having a shake.

"Maybe," he said, but continued stocking the pineapples with the old man while he pondered what he would say to Sara if he went over.

Sara swirled the straw around the remains of the *mamey* shake that Lucy had insisted she try rather than her everyday strawberry one.

"Do you like it, *niña*?" Lucy asked as she washed the metal mixer glass and began to prepare a shake for a customer waiting at the counter.

Sara took another sip and tried to analyze the flavors that teased her taste buds. "I do. There are so many notes here. Sweet potato. Peach," she said and sucked up the last of the shake with a slurpy sound.

"*Es mi favorito*," Lucy said and sliced up a banana into the metal glass, then added strawberries, vanilla ice cream, condensed milk, and the ice to cool it all down.

While Lucy whirred the mixture together in a powerful blender, she raised her voice to talk over the noise. "How are you doing, *niña*? You look tired."

Sara shrugged. She had been feeling off but didn't want to share the why of it with the older woman. "Between work and the party, I'm pretty wiped."

Lucy poured the shake into a take-out glass for the other customer and afterward, came to take away Sara's empty glass. "You're too young to be so tired. I think there's more to your sad mood, isn't there?"

Sara would be hard-pressed to deny it and besides, Luis and Lucy knew about everything that was going on in Little Havana. She playfully pointed a finger at Lucy and said, "If you're going to try and get me to talk about him, forget it."

Lucy placed a hand over her heart, as if to say, "Who

me?" A second later, her gaze shifted to glance beyond Sara's shoulder.

As Sara turned, Lucy said, "Then maybe you should talk to *him* about it."

Sara's heart skipped a beat as Tony approached, his lips in a tight line. His long legs ate up the short distance between them. Thanks to the height of the stool, she had to look up at him when he reached her side. But then he sat, bringing them almost eye-to-eye.

His dark eyes were troubled, likely mirroring the concern in her own gaze. But that still didn't keep her heartbeat from accelerating or stop the urge to reach up and brush away a stray lock of hair that had fallen onto his forehead. She gripped her hands tightly to avoid doing that.

"Sara."

"Tony."

This was going well, she thought. *Not*. It made her wish for the easy camaraderie they'd shared only a week ago.

"How are you doing?" he asked and motioned to her empty glass. "Can I get you another?"

She chuckled and shook her head. "And risk a sugar coma? Thanks for the offer though. Would you like one?"

He nodded and from behind her she heard the whir of the blender that said Lucy was already making him a shake.

"What brings you here?" she said. *Lame*, she thought.

"Same thing as you," he said and gestured to the fruit and vegetable stalls behind him and to the shake that Lucy placed on the counter in front of him. He picked up the glass and took a big sip. The shake left behind an orangey-colored moustache on those lips she'd dreamed about more than once. As he licked off the remnants of the drink, she dragged her gaze from his mouth and back up to his eyes.

"Are you ready for Angelica's party?" she asked, wanting to keep things on a friendly note despite the unwanted competition that had arisen between them. She had to admit, even if just to herself, that she'd been missing him and the fun times they'd had before the reporter and her magazine article had entered their lives.

"I think so. How about you? How are things going?" He took another big gulp of the shake and then held it up to her. "Are you sure you don't want some?"

His offer made her remember how they'd so easily shared the churros just over a week ago and she wished they could restore that closeness. Regret slammed in her, but then her phone chirped with Jeri's custom ringtone. Her friend and partner would only call during Sara's free time if there was an emergency.

She held up her finger in a wait gesture, walked away from him, and swiped to answer.

"What's wrong, Jeri?"

"You need to check your Twitter feed, Sara. That reporter just posted a teaser for the article she's doing and it's exploding."

"Will do. Talk to you later," she said and faced Tony as she went to her feed. There it was.

Top Miami chefs battle it out. Should @TonySanchezChef or @SaraKellyMunch be featured this month? Cast ur vote! http://bit.ly/2KAKpp8 #SouthBeach #eatfamous #truecooks #foodie

The tweet had been retweeted over a hundred times already and when she followed the link to the article, there were close to five hundred votes split almost evenly between Tony and her. When she looked up, she realized Tony was likewise viewing something on his phone. His lips had thinned into that tight disapproving scowl again, probably because he had read the Twitter post and visited the magazine's poll.

Great, she thought as she walked back toward Tony and slipped onto a stool again. "I never expected this when I said I'd do Samantha's *quinceañera*." She'd also never imagined that the man she was falling in love with would end up being "the competition."

"Me, either," Tony said and raked his thick hair back in frustration. "That Roberta really knows how to make things difficult."

"That she does." When Jeri's ringtone erupted again from her phone, she held it up and said, "I'm sorry. I really should go deal with all this craziness."

"I'm sorry too, Sara. I don't want it to be like this between us."

There was such a hangdog look on his face that she couldn't resist saying, "How did you want it to be between us?" She waited for his reply, holding her breath in expectation. Praying for the kind of answer that would give her hope that it wasn't over between them.

Jeri's ringtone chirped again, and she muttered, "Give me a break."

Tony gestured to her phone even as his began its own symphony of noise. "I think you should go."

"I guess you should too," she said and didn't wait for any more interruptions.

Roberta Lane had sparked the rivalry the other day and with today's tweet she had ignited a full-fledged conflagration. Unfortunately, no matter what both she and Tony had wanted, there was no longer any way to avoid the rivalry.

And no matter what, she had to be better than Tony because too many people relied on her for her to fail.

Roberta did a little whoop of joy as she watched the number of retweets and comments jump on Twitter. She had clearly hit on something as she read the comments which went anywhere from supportive to the height of snark and meanness.

Sanchez sold out and abandoned Miami a long time ago. I hope Sara kicks his butt back to New York.

Chef Tony is so hawt! There's no way an amateur like Sara Kelly should be the one in ur article.

"That smirk on your face can only mean one thing," her boss said as he walked into her office holding his tablet. He turned it in her direction to show her the poll on their website. They'd hit over a thousand votes in just a few hours and Tony and Sara were still neck and neck.

She held up her phone for him and he let out a low whistle as he caught sight of the response her tweet had generated. "This is turning out bigger than we could have imagined," Marco said with a definitive nod and an "I told you so" look.

"Way better than a story just about the resurgence of *quinceañeras*," Roberta said.

"Definitely. We're going to get a lot of traction with this, but do you think you can keep up the momentum?" Marco asked. From the look on his face, she could tell he was already tallying how many magazines they'd be able to sell as well as hits to their website and the money from advertisers that any clicks would earn.

Roberta shrugged. "We're supposed to visit with the chefs to get some shots of them working in the kitchen.

Same with the girls in their dresses, but I think we should focus on the chef's rivalry."

"I agree. I hope you'll be able to stir that pot, Roberta. You've done well so far," he said and turned to walk out of her small office.

"Thank you, Marco," she said, but her boss stopped and faced her.

"Don't disappoint me," he said, making her worry about how far he wanted her to go to push the story.

Some might think she wasn't nice, but she wouldn't intentionally harm someone. Well, not usually. But she had to get a good story for the magazine. She'd gotten lucky with this one and she intended to run with it. If that meant some chefs ended the day with hurt feelings, then she could live with that.

CHAPTER 15

AFTER THE VISIT TO THE fruit stand, Tony had gone back home to work on his idea for a cookbook. He wanted it to feature not only traditional Cuban recipes, but the upscale and fusion recipes that he'd developed at his restaurant over the years. He sat at the kitchen table, the journals that his manager had sent down spread across the table along with an assortment of colored sticky notes he'd borrowed from Sylvia's *quinceañera* planner. He had chosen different colors to flag dishes he might want to include in the cookbook and to separate them according to whether they were appetizers, entrees, side dishes, or desserts. Afterward, he intended to mix-in stories and photos of his family and friends that related to the various recipes.

As he worked, he listened to the patter of his parents chatting in the room next door. It was a familiar sound, as comforting as the foods that Sara had chosen to make in her restaurant.

Sara, he thought with a sigh. She had looked lovely that morning, but tired. Troubled after seeing that reporter's tweet and the aftermath of it. He had hated seeing the worry on her beautiful face.

He was sorry he'd ever agreed to talk to the viper and not only because of the way she had twisted the *quinceañera* into a contest. He was angry because the story was supposed to have been about the girls and a wonderful tradition. It made him wonder if there was any way to turn the narrative back around and make it about the girls again.

"That's a very angry face when you're doing something you love, *Mijo*," his mother said and laid her hands on his shoulders. She rubbed them in a familiar gesture from his childhood, one she'd always used to soothe whatever upset was troubling him.

"Just trying to figure some things out," he said and grabbed another one of the journals to review the recipes, flag his selections, and place them in the right category.

"Would one of those things be Sara Kelly?" his mother asked.

It would do no good trying to lie to his mother. He had never been able to keep anything secret from her. "You know it is. This thing –"

"The article?" she said with an arch of a brow as she left him to put up a pot of coffee.

"When Sylvia asked me to come and help make this *quinceañera* the best for Angelica, I never expected that it would come to this," he admitted and flipped through his journal, his mind only half on the project. Maybe less than half as it drifted back to Sara.

"What's this?" Sylvia asked as she breezed into the kitchen wearing one of her "power suits." The black suit accentuated her petite figure while the white shirt was a perfect foil for her dark hair and eyes. Her bangles and many rings had been replaced by only her wedding band and engagement ring, giving her a totally professional look.

"Sara and the magazine feature," their mother answered for him.

Sylvia placed her purse on a kitchen chair, leaned her hands on the top rung of it, and stared at him. "I'm sorry, *hermanito*. Angelica and I wanted this to be the best party, but not for it to turn into this circus, or drag you into some kind of showdown."

"It is what it is," he said, not that he was happy about it. He missed Sara. Missed spending time with her. And he worried that whatever had been growing between them might have been squashed by the pressure created by the reporter.

"That doesn't sound like the Tony I know. The one who tossed his college degree to the winds to follow his dream," Sylvia said.

"*Y que pena*," his mother said and wrung her hands.

Sylvia glared at their mother. "It's not a shame, *mami*. Tony chose what made him happy and that's what you said you always wanted for us, *verdad*? To be happy."

"*Sí, como no*. I want you to be *feliz*," their mother said and returned to stand behind Tony and rub his shoulders. "And that's why Tony has to do something about Sara."

"*Por favor, mami*," he groused, but Sylvia cut him off.

"She's right, Tony. No matter what happens with this article, you have to find a way to make things right with Sara. We've always thought you two had a special connection."

"The Kellys and Sanchezes have been friends and neighbors forever so yes, there's a connection," he said, dodging the implication to avoid his sister's meddling. If his sister found out that things with Sara had already become more, she'd never leave it alone.

"*Mentiroso*," his mother said and tsked accusingly about the lie he'd told.

He gathered the journals and supplies to make an escape into his room and away from his well-meaning family, but didn't have a chance to move before his family started in on him again.

"You can run and hide from us, but you can't run away from what you feel for her, *hermanito*," his sister warned. Looks like his secret was out. "There are no quitters in the Sanchez family. Think about our great-grandparents leaving Spain for Cuba and a better way of life. About *los abuelos* and *mami* and *papi* and what it took to escape Cuba and make it here."

He couldn't deny the fortitude that his family had shown over the last generations. Or the strength it had taken for him to follow his own dream after finishing college. But fighting for love?

"Sara and me, it's complicated."

"Save that for your profile page. When this is all over with the *quinceañera*, you need to face up to what you feel for Sara and honestly, she needs to do the same," Sylvia said with a determined nod.

For the first time that day, a bit of hope rose. "You think Sara feels the same way?"

Sylvia rolled her eyes and shook her head. His mother was doing the same as Sylvia said, "How can you be so dense? Of course, she does."

Since his sister had always been a good judge of character and situations, he wasn't about to argue. "When this is over –"

"Why wait until it's over? Why not go now and tell her how you feel?" Sylvia said.

He wanted to shout out that it was too soon. That they'd only had a couple of dates in less than two weeks. *Love doesn't happen that fast*, he told himself. *Or does it?* He knew Sylvia was like a pit bull when she latched onto an idea, so he said, "I'll think about heading over later tonight to see her."

"Don't just think about it. Do it," Sylvia said.

His mother echoed the sentiment and reinforced it with a slight squeeze of her hands on his shoulders. "*Sí, Mijo*. Do it. We want you back home in Miami for good."

"*Mami*, don't get your hopes up. There's a lot for me to think about before I make that kind of decision," he said. Then, to avoid any further discussion, he jumped to his feet and hurried back to his old bedroom to work.

As he laid out the journal he'd been reviewing, his knees bumped against the wooden edges of the small student desk. He leaned back and the chair creaked from his weight. *I've filled out a bit since my teen years, but that isn't the only thing that's changed*, he thought.

He'd given up Miami and his family for fame and fortune...and loneliness...in New York.

His parents and sister wanted nothing more than for him to come back home and settle down and there was no doubt they thought Sara was what would keep him in Miami. As for what his heart was telling him...

He hadn't expected to find love in South Beach and he still wasn't sure he had. But like his sister had said, the Sanchezes weren't quitters. He'd go see Sara tonight to talk to her about this whole crazy competition they'd been dragged into and how he felt about it and her. That he wanted to go back to how it had been before that. To that place where they had been learning more about each other and growing closer. That he hoped that maybe, just maybe, they could allow that relationship to develop into something more.

Maybe after they talked, they could put things back to rights and avoid any of the upset that had come about because of a meddling reporter.

Sara shaped the dough for the strombolis that would be one of that night's specials. She'd always found making bread relaxing even if it was a time-consuming activity. It required patience as you waited for the rise to finish before you could properly knead it and begin the process all over again. As the dough beneath her fingers refused to take shape, she pounded it with her fist. She was feeling anything but patient.

"Are you imagining that's Tony Sanchez?" Jeri asked as she watched Sara prep the dough.

"Maybe." For good measure she pounded the dough again, relieved when it finally flattened and began to take the shape she wanted. *A good omen*? she hoped. As out of control as things had gotten, she missed Tony.

"We're going to use our homemade sausage and mozzarella in this, right?" Sara asked her partner. The last few days she'd found herself being less decisive than usual.

"That's what you said. But what's going to be the twist? We never do straight comfort food," Jeri reminded as she continued to stand there, watching Sara stretch out the dough.

"To tell the truth, I'm at a loss." The whole thing with the article had her distracted and rattled. Totally off her game and maybe that's what the reporter – and maybe even Tony – had wanted.

Jeri stared at the dough for a long hard minute. "How about we make it a breakfast Stromboli instead? Fried eggs, ham, and cheddar."

Sara smiled and went with the flow her partner had

started. "A little spinach and top it with a buttery hollandaise."

"Perfect for that very late-night club crowd," Jeri said and held her hand up for a high five.

Sara managed a listless high five and went to the line chefs to explain what they had to prep for the dish. Normally she'd pass the dough preparation on to the pastry chef if she was done with that day's dessert items, but this time she kept that task for herself. The kneading and pounding were cathartic and by the time the dinner crowd had begun, she was feeling more like her old self.

"Hey, sis. Are you done murdering that dough?" Rick said as he slipped into the kitchen, wrapped an arm around her waist, and wiped some flour from her cheek.

"I am. And what brings you here?" she said and craned her neck to look for Jeri to see if she could take a short break to chat with Rick. Her partner was in the back, assisting one of their newer trainees with some knife work.

Rick tracked her gaze and a warm smile lit up his features. "Just came by to make sure you're okay. I heard about the whole Tony Twitter thing."

"I'm fine and you'd be too if you just asked her out," Sara said and jerked her chin in Jeri's direction.

Rick shook his head. "She keeps on shutting me down whenever it gets close to that moment."

Thanks to her ex, Jeri was leery around men, especially since she also had her young daughter Sophie to think about as well. But Sara knew that Rick would never hurt Jeri the way her ex had.

She cupped her brother's cheek. "Just give her a little time and keep at it. But not in a stalkery way."

"Which I guess means I should get my butt out of this kitchen and over to my table." He dropped a quick kiss on her cheek and said, "Thanks, sis."

But as he walked out, a sudden silence swept over the restaurant and then built into a cacophony of excited chatter. The air seemed charged with electricity—so much so that it drew the attention of everyone in the kitchen toward the dining area.

Tony Sanchez stood at the hostess podium. He must have sensed the change in the mood triggered by his arrival since he jammed his hands in his pockets and rocked back and forth on his heels. He glanced around the room before shifting his gaze to hers.

She picked up a kitchen towel and wiped her hands clean, intending to tell him to go even as her heart sped up in a hopeful beat, but she had taken no more than a step when a chant began at one end of the room. A group of her regulars, pounding their fists on the tabletop as they said, "Sara, Sara, Sara."

Muttering a curse, she went to stop it because no one deserved that kind of humiliation, but it was too late. Like lightning the chant spread across the restaurant, growing louder and more animated as each table joined in.

Tony got the message loud and clear. He murmured something to the hostess, forced a smile and wave in her direction, and hurried from the restaurant. Sara wanted to go after him, but she had a restaurant full of people to feed. Despite that, she went to rush after Tony but a second later, her brother was charging after him, leaving his meal virtually untouched.

The crowd erupted into cheers and jeers, leaving Sara with mixed emotions. While she appreciated the support, she wasn't a fan of what basically amounted to bullying. Not to mention that a big part of her had been hoping that Tony being there meant there was still hope for the relationship that had been developing between them.

Jeri came over and laid a supportive hand on Sara's back. "Are you okay?"

She shook her head, unable to speak past the lump in her throat.

"Do you need to leave? We can handle things for you," Jeri said and rubbed her back.

"I can deal," she managed to say, but her voice was strangled with emotion and as she worked, a tear fell onto the dough she had started kneading again.

She picked it up and tossed it into the trash. Got out a new round of dough from the dozens they had made earlier that day. She started kneading and pounding and by the time she was finished and passed the dough to a line chef to be filled, she was satisfied that she'd worked the stupid competition to a back corner of her mind for the rest of the night. But as she had before, she wished that Tony being there was a sign that there was still hope for them.

CHAPTER 16

Tony rushed out of the restaurant, chants of "Sara, Sara, Sara," chasing him onto the sidewalk.

"Hey, bro, hold up," said a familiar voice and he half-turned to find Rick running after him. When his friend caught up to him, he said, "Sorry about what happened inside there."

Tony started walking again, away from the restaurant, and said, "Probably not the wisest move on my part to come by since that tweet went viral this morning."

Rick shook his head and clapped Tony on the back. "Definitely not the wisest. How about we go get dinner?"

Tony stopped once again and motioned toward *Munch* with his head. "Didn't you have a table in there already?"

Rick nodded and smiled. "And a very nice steak that I'm leaving behind, but I won't hold that against you. Are you game?"

Tony shrugged, but appreciated Rick's support. He had always been a good friend and it made him feel guilty that he hadn't been there for him lately. Distance had been part of the reason and he was reminded once again that he should spend more time in Miami. He wrapped an arm around Rick's shoulder and said, "I guess I owe you a meal. Is that fancy steakhouse still up on Washington and Lincoln Road?"

"It is," Rick said, and they did an about-face and strolled back toward the pedestrian mall that ran through several blocks in the heart of South Beach.

Tony eyed Rick as they walked side-by-side onto the broad sidewalks on Lincoln Road. "I never expected that my coming here for Angelica's *quinceañera* would turn into this sideshow," he said, wanting his friend to understand he'd never intentionally hurt anyone in the Kelly family. Most of all Sara.

"I know you didn't, but the harm's done isn't it? No matter who wins by getting the feature, someone loses. Maybe even both of you lose," Rick said with a heavy lift of his broad shoulders.

Rick wasn't wrong. "I want to be the one featured because it'll give me a chance to maybe open a place down here. But that also means that Sara and Jeri may lose an important opportunity for their business."

"Not to mention Bridget and the women that they both help," Rick reminded him, which only made him feel worse. It also brought to mind what Sylvia had told him about Sara's reasons for running her training program.

"Do you mind if I ask you something?" he said and risked a side glance at Rick who shook his head and said, "Shoot."

"Sylvia said hiring at-risk women for the restaurant was because of Bridget. She's okay, right?" he asked, truly worried about Rick and Sara's older sister.

Rick hesitated, but after a long look at Tony, he said, "She married a hotshot investment type who did a number on her here." He paused to tap his temple with his forefinger and continued. "And then he wiped them out financially. It took a long time for Bridget to rebuild her life. It's what made Bridget start the non-profit that helps women like the ones in Sara's kitchen."

Seeing her sister suffering like that would definitely spur someone like Sara not only to help her sister but others as well, Tony thought. Before he could say anything else, Rick added, "You know that old saying about what doesn't kill you making you stronger? Bridget is stronger now and doing really well so no need to worry."

"I'm glad to hear that. Maybe if Sara and I can survive this we'll be stronger as well," Tony said, trying to stay hopeful.

Rick let out a harsh laugh. "Considering some of the comments on those tweets and the poll, you may have to be stronger right now, bro."

That is an understatement of major proportions, Tony thought. "They've been rough on me, that's for sure. Why is everyone saying I abandoned Miami? I'm right here, aren't I?" he said, irked by those comments the most.

Rick stopped walking and the look he shot Tony bordered on condemning. "It's not like you've been around, bro. Javi too. It's been years since you've both been down."

Exasperated, he raked a hand through his hair and jammed his hands on his hips. "Not my choice, *mano*. I went where I had to so I could follow my dream."

Rick held his hands up to rein Tony in before he could continue. "None of your family and friends is blaming you for doing that, but it would have been nice for you to visit more often."

Just like his parents and sister had asked of him. "I plan on doing that, Rick. Trust me." Miami, his family, friends, and Sara were calling him home and he intended to find a way to make it work. It had seemed like a hard task at first but considering that his restaurant seemed to be doing fine, maybe not as hard as he'd originally thought.

Rick's stance softened and he started walking again. "I hope so because I'm not sure Sara would be happy with a long-distance relationship."

"If she's even interested in a relationship," he said, uncertainty causing his gut to tighten.

Rick shook his head. "For a smart guy you can be really dumb at times. Do you think she'd be hurting as badly as she is if she wasn't interested? But I know you're not the one responsible for the drama going on now, so I'm not mad at you. I don't think Sara is either, just confused."

"Thanks," he said as they reached the door of the steakhouse.

At the entrance, Rick paused and said, "Do you mind if I ask you something?"

Considering how truthful his friend had been, he didn't think there was much he wouldn't be willing to talk about. "Go ahead."

"Do you think you can get Javi to come spend more time in Miami?"

No one ever knew what Javi would do or not do. He'd always been not only an absentminded genius type, but a workaholic who was hard to corral. Plus, there had been that call the other day that had Tony worried about what was up with his older brother.

"I'm not sure. Why?"

Rick shrugged. "I always thought Javi and Bridget would be perfect together."

Tony laughed and cuffed Rick's head playfully. "Who died and made you Cupid?"

Rick gave a chagrined smile. "I guess since I can't get my love life in order, I'll help out all of you."

Tony thought about it for a second. "How about you help yourself and ask Jeri out?"

Rick pushed through the door of the steakhouse. As he waited at the hostess podium, he said, "Believe me I've tried. Every time I get close to asking her, she shuts me down."

The hostess took one look at Tony and rushed off. A second later, a chef came from out of the back and up to the podium.

"Chef Sanchez. So good to see you," the man said.

"Samuel, right? Didn't we work together at the Four Seasons?" Tony said.

The man's smile brightened and his head bobbed up and down excitedly. "That we did. We'll have a table for you in a second."

Tony held his hands up to stop him. "No need to bump us ahead of anyone, chef. We can wait."

"Absolutely not," Samuel said and waggled his fingers at the hostess who snapped two menus into his hand. "Please follow me."

"Thank you," Tony said and Rick joined in with his own, "Thanks, chef."

Once they were seated and had ordered a tomahawk steak to share, their earlier conversation resumed. "You've asked Jeri out and it's always a no?" Tony asked.

With a "go figure" shrug, Rick said, "Not exactly a 'No,' but that's just because we never get to the actual question. Before I can even ask, she's giving me an excuse or changing the topic. I know she had it rough with her ex and now she's a single mom. I get she's got a lot to do. I think we could be good together. But I don't want to take her time away from the things or the people she

169

loves. Her little girl Sophie is such a sweetie—I want to spend time with both of them."

Tony mulled over what his friend had said and then it came to him. "You should frame it that way. Don't just ask out Jeri. Ask out Jeri and Sophie. Make it a family kind of outing because let's face it, *mano*, Jeri and Sophie are a package deal."

Rick nodded. "A great package if you ask me. I'll give it a try. Thanks."

Tony leaned back in his chair and grinned. "I guess I'm not so dumb after all."

Except of course when it came to Sara and what to do about the situation they were in. But much like Jeri and Sophie were a package deal, so were Sara, her restaurant, and her special staff. It was something he had to keep in mind. As if God had heard his wish, his phone chirped with a text message from Sara.

I'm so so sorry about what happened. I would never embarrass you like that. Plz believe that.

Relief swept through him, erasing his earlier upset about the chant and igniting hope they'd be able to survive the competition. He texted back, *I know. I'm sorry it's gotten this crazy. I care about you. You know that, right?*

A very long pause followed, causing Rick to ask, "Everything okay, bro?"

He didn't know, but then Sara responded with, *I care about you as well. TTYS.*

Smiling, he met Rick's concerned gaze and hopefully said, "I think so. I think everything is going to be okay."

CHAPTER 17

SURPRISE. CONFUSION. CONCERN.

Those had been the gamut of emotions when Dolores had announced late that afternoon that Angelica and her mother were coming over so Dolores could design Angelica's *quinceañera* gown.

Sara skipped her gaze between Dolores, Samantha, and her older sister Bridget who had decided to join them for moral support. She was wondering if she was crazy to be worrying about this or if they were the crazy ones to be so calm about it.

"Are you sure about this, Sam? Isn't this like sleeping with the enemy?" Sara asked. The girls had been so intent on outdoing each other with their *quinceañera* and this was a decided change from that earlier rivalry.

Like maybe you and Tony should do? the little voice in her head challenged. But she shut it down by reminding that she had reached out to Tony to apologize. And for something she hadn't even done!

With a "so what" shrug, Samantha said, "I felt bad for her."

Sara peered at Dolores and at her sheepish look didn't

171

press further.

Her sister Bridget, ever the optimist, said, "This is a good thing for the girls, Sara. Our families all used to be really close, remember? Now we only see each other occasionally."

She did remember that they'd been closer, but that also brought back memories of Tony, her crush, and how it had become so much more...and more complicated... in the last two weeks. Still, it was a good thing that the girls were getting along and that the two families were re-establishing their relationships. They had used to have good times together and there was no reason they couldn't in the future. *Including Tony*, she hoped.

"You're right, Bridget. It is a good thing," she said, no matter how much she was still worried about the article and how hard it was for her to deal with how it had upset everything with Tony. Even though the tweet that Roberta Lane had sent out was no longer trending, the voting on the poll was still going strong. The reporter and her photographer were supposed to come by the next morning to shoot some photos to possibly use if they were the ones featured in the article. Sara had no doubt that once they did the same with Tony, the magazine would somehow use those photos to stir up even more attention for the fabricated rivalry between them.

The doorbell rang and Samantha went racing across the kitchen and out to the foyer to answer it. Dolores rose and smoothed her blouse down. She did a self-conscious finger comb of her short hair and followed her daughter. Bridget hung back as did Sara since this moment was about the two girls and their moms.

In the foyer Dolores and Sylvia were hugging like old friends while Angelica and Samantha stood there smiling.

"It's been too long," Sylvia said and then urged Dolores

away for an inspection. "You look fabulous."

The two women couldn't be more different and yet more alike. Both dark-haired although Sylvia didn't have a touch of visible grey while Dolores's had hints of salt in all that pepper. Sylvia had dressed casually, but stylishly, whereas Dolores wore a house coat whose pockets held the essentials for measuring and taking notes about Angelica's dress.

As Sylvia caught sight of her and Bridget, she came over and hugged them as well. Sara returned the embrace, buoyed by the effusiveness of it. Sylvia had always been supportive, from all her help to secure the location for *Munch* to the annual fundraiser for Bridget's non-profit.

Bridget and Sylvia likewise embraced but held onto each other longer. "*Amiga*, how are you," Sylvia asked Bridget.

"*Bien*, Sylvia. *Muy bien*," Bridget answered in her accented Spanish. Like many Anglos in Miami, Bridget had learned the language. She spoke far more than Sara did.

"Good to see you too, Sara. How are you holding up? Better than my brother, I suspect," Sylvia said, inspecting her with a motherly eye.

"I'm doing okay," she said cautiously. She'd forgotten how direct Sylvia could be.

"*Mentirosa*," Dolores said to Sylvia with a wink and held her hand out in the direction of the small studio off the foyer.

Confused by her sister-in-law's comment, Sara leaned close to Bridget and whispered, "What does that mean? *Menti*—"

"Liar," Bridget whispered back.

Heat flooded her cheeks, but she refused to acknowledge the comment or the inquiring look Sylvia gave her before they all followed Dolores and her daughter into the studio. The last thing she and Tony needed was families meddling in what was already a complicated situation.

The space had been a little-used dining room that her brother had converted into a work area for his wife as an anniversary gift. On the far side of the room there was a small drafting table. Beside the table was a professional grade sewing machine. On the opposite wall was a storage area that Rick and Matt had built which held an assortment of different fabric bolts, lace, threads, zippers, and other sewing supplies.

Dolores walked toward the drafting table where a number of sketches were spread out. "After we spoke, Sylvia, I took the liberty of sketching some preliminary designs. We can change up anything you want or start over if nothing is to your liking."

As Dolores stepped back, Sylvia and Angelica went to study the designs.

Concern twisted Sara's gut and judging from Dolores's rigid stance, she was likewise worried, but the reaction of mother and daughter was immediate and positive.

"These are awesome," Angelica said as she picked up one sketch for a closer look and then traded it off with her mother to examine another.

"Truly fabulous, Dolores. I didn't know you did anything like this," Sylvia said, wonder and appreciation in her voice.

"*Gracias,*" Dolores said with a slow dip of her head. "I'd hoped to one day have my own place –"

"Why don't you?" Sylvia asked, slipping into that focused attitude Sara recognized all too well. Maybe that wasn't a bad thing right now. More than once she'd talked to Dolores about opening her own shop, but her sister-in-law had always been hesitant to take the risk.

Sara understood the fear. She'd had it in droves when Jeri and she had contemplated opening *Munch*, but she was glad she'd taken the leap. Sylvia had helped her do it—and could help Dolores as well, she suspected.

"How hard do you think it would be to find a location, Sylvia?" Sara asked.

"It's not that easy," Dolores said, waving her hands back and forth to try and end the discussion.

"Not easy, but not impossible, either. I'd be delighted to ask Esteban to take a look and find a location. I could help with the lease. I'd also be happy to spread the word to all my friends about your work—though I doubt I'll have to say much after they see the dress. They're going to love it," Sylvia said and accepted one of the designs from Angelica.

Samantha joined in the discussion. "Come on, *mami*. You always tell me I can do anything I want to do."

"It's different for me," Dolores said and wrung her hands together.

"We can arrange for you to hire some of the women from the shelter to work for you. We can even see about getting a grant for training them as seamstresses," Bridget added.

"It would give women who aren't good in the kitchen, or who aren't interested in cooking, another opportunity for a trade," Sara chimed in.

"That's a wonderful idea," Sylvia said and then gestured with the sketch. "This is beautiful. I think Angelica would look lovely in this. *Preciosa*," she added and stroked a hand across her daughter's cheek.

"*Mami, por favor*," Angelica said, flustered. Samantha jostled her playfully and said, "Moms."

The sociable interaction surprised Sara. Considering the girls were supposed to be rivals, they seemed friendlier than she had expected. It was a good thing to see them getting along because that kind of incessant rivalry....

She stopped short at where she was going. That kind of rivalry could only lead to misery.

"Sara? Sara!" Sylvia said, snapping her attention back to the two moms and teens.

"What do you and Bridget think about the design?" Sylvia said and held up the sketch.

She scrutinized the drawing. The dress was radically different from the one that Dolores had created for Samantha, which was probably a good thing. Her niece was a few inches taller than Angelica, not to mention bustier. Angelica was built a lot like her mother, petite with slender curves and a smaller bosom. Dolores's design would emphasize her slenderness and make her appear taller.

"I think it's lovely. The girls will both look beautiful on their special days."

Bridget glanced at the sketches and said, "It is truly wonderful. You do beautiful work, Dolores. If I ever get remarried, I will definitely have you do my gown."

Sara was relieved that her sister could even think about marrying again after the experience she'd had. It gave her hope that her own situation was one that could be resolved happily.

"Wonderful, so what's next, Dolores?" Sylvia said and Sara had to bite back a laugh. She had forgotten just how bossy Sylvia could be.

"Fabric," Dolores said and gestured to the bolts of material on the opposite side of the room. She walked to one bolt of creamy vanilla-colored cloth. "I think this crepe satin would be perfect."

Sylvia met her there and lightly passed her hand along the fabric. "I love this, but I'm not the one who has to like it. *Mija?*"

Angelia likewise walked to the bolt and skimmed her hand across the crepe satin. "I love it too, *mami*."

"*Que bueno*. Did you want lace on it?" Dolores asked.

Sylvia and Angelica shared a look. "Do you think it needs lace?" Angelica asked Dolores, deferring to her judgment.

Her sister-in-law shook her head. "Some people might say every *quinceañera* gown should have lace—but I think it would weigh down the design and for you, it should be clean and elegant."

"Okay, so how do we get started?" Sylvia asked.

In a flurry of activity, Dolores had whipped out her tape measure, notepad and pencil from her house coat and began taking Angelica's measurements while Samantha watched.

"Let's leave them to this and make some *cafecito*," Sylvia said, and linked her arms with Sara and Bridget to guide them back into the kitchen.

"You haven't changed, Sylvia," Sara said with a chuckle and a wag of her head.

"Not at all, thankfully," Bridget said with a smile.

"I haven't, but *you* have Sara. You never used to be a quitter," Sylvia said with a determined look.

In the kitchen, Sara stepped away to take out Dolores's espresso pot and make the coffee. She didn't pretend not to understand the meaning. As she worked, she said, "I'm not being a quitter—I'm just being realistic."

Sylvia leaned on the counter beside her while Bridget sat at the table. "Realistic? Can you define that for me?" Sylvia pressed.

Sara efficiently filled the filter for the espresso pot and lightly tamped down the finely ground coffee. As she added water to the reservoir, she said, "Both Tony and I have to focus on these *quinceañeras*. Anything that distracts us from that focus—"

"Like exploring what's happening between the two of you?" Sylvia challenged.

"Nothing's happening," Sara said as she slipped the filter into the pot, and twisted it closed. She placed it on the stove and turned on the flame to heat the water.

Sylvia was silent for a long moment—not a good thing since it generally meant she was busily plotting a move. Sure enough, a second later, Sylvia said, "You see that pot?"

"Of course, I do," she said, earning an eye roll from Sylvia.

"That was rhetorical, Sara," Sylvia said with a shake of her head as Bridget chuckled. "As the water gets hotter, the pressure builds until *boom*." Before Sara could get in a word, Sylvia plowed on. "This thing between you and Tony has been building and if you don't release the pressure, it's going to explode and maybe not in a good way."

The sputtering of the pot warned that the coffee was ready. Sara shut off the flame and moved the coffee maker to a different range.

"You see this pot?" Sara teased. "It didn't explode despite the pressure and we're going to have delicious coffee to drink."

"You think Tony and you can deal with all this pressure and still make something delicious for the parties?" Bridget chimed in, her gaze narrowed as she peered at Sara.

"We're professionals. We work under pressure every day. We will get it done and it *will* be delicious," she said with a decisive nod.

Sylvia held her hands up as if to say, "If you say so."

She shared a glance with Bridget who likewise held up her hands, but it was clear neither of the women believed her.

Not that it mattered what Sylvia and Bridget thought. What mattered was what she believed was possible.

She was spared from further discussion when Dolores walked into the room with the two girls who were busily chatting about an upcoming soccer game. They seemed like old friends. It brought comfort to Sara again as well as hope.

And much like the two girls who seemed to be entering a new phase, as Dolores and Sylvia joined Bridget at the table, it seemed as if they were ready for a change as well. "It's been too long, Dolores. We should really try to see each other more often," Sylvia said.

Bridget echoed the sentiment. "We really should."

Dolores, normally the more reticent one, nodded enthusiastically. "We should. I worried about these *quinceañeras*—"

"Me, too, *amiga*," Sylvia confessed.

With a shy smile, Dolores said, "Maybe this will help us all reconnect like when we used to spend time together as kids."

"I can't picture you as kids," Angelica said with a shake of her head.

The two women exchanged a glance and laughed. "It was a lot of fun," Dolores said.

"It can be fun again," Sylvia said and took hold of Dolores's and Bridget's hands.

"OMG does that mean we'll have to spend more time together?" Samantha said and made a face at Angelica, laughter in her voice.

"Definitely OMG. What will everyone say?" Angelica replied with a roll of her eyes.

"That it's a good thing?" Sara said, hesitantly.

"Definitely," Samantha said, and Angelica echoed it. "Definitely."

Inside of Sara, the seeds of hope and comfort that she had felt earlier, took root and started to grow. Maybe they could survive these *quinceañeras* after all.

CHAPTER 18

T HE HOTEL KITCHEN WAS A dream. It had every gadget
that a professional chef would possibly need, well-or-
ganized stations for all the line chefs and other staff, and
was large enough to handle preparations to feed as many
as fifteen-hundred people.

Overkill for his niece's two hundred-person event,
but he wouldn't complain about the kitchen being over-
staffed and over-sized for the work he had to accomplish.
He was also grateful that the hotel was allowing him to
use their facilities and staff for the event. The fact that
the hotel might now be featured as part of the *South
Beach Style* article had upped the ante, so the hotel was
going over-the-top to make sure Tony had everything
he needed for the party.

"I really appreciate all that you're doing, Jenny," he
said to the Event Manager for the hotel.

The young woman, a pretty Cubana in a trim business suit, hugged her portfolio to her chest and smiled
brightly. "We're honored to have such a renowned chef
in our kitchen."

He dipped his head in thanks. "You've gone above

and beyond. I'm grateful you're loaning me your staff today as well so that we can run through the menu."

"Of course, chef. Whatever you need," Jenny said.

The sound of the ballroom door opening drew their attention. Another member of the hotel staff led Roberta Lane and the photographer into the space.

Tony's hackles rose at the sight of the reporter. She had that toothy shark grin on her face and a look in her eyes that warned she maybe had another horrible surprise up her sleeve. He braced himself for her imminent arrival, dreading it and what might follow.

As Roberta neared, she focused her attention on Tony and held her hand out to him. "So good to see you again, chef."

He took hold of her fingertips only, as if her touch was unctuous. "Roberta," was all he said.

"Where will you be working today?" Roberta said, totally ignoring the Event Manager standing beside him.

Tony gritted his teeth, placed his hand on the young woman's back, and said, "I'd like you to meet Jenny Gomez, the hotel's Event Manager. She's been responsible for making this all happen and we owe her our thanks."

Roberta surprised him then. With a broad smile and a shake of Jenny's hand, she said, "Yes, thank you, Jenny. I'm not sure we need to hold you up anymore."

"Of course. Let me get out of your way," Jenny said and handed Roberta a business card. "Here's my contact info just in case you need it."

Roberta took the card and slipped it into her jacket pocket. "Thank you. Chef, are you ready for the photo shoot?"

"Is it okay to get started, Jenny?" he asked in deference to the manager.

Jenny nodded. "I believe the staff is ready. Let me

go get them."

Jenny walked to the far side of the kitchen where a number of chefs and workers were busy preparing meals and other items. Approaching one man wearing the traditional chef's toque, she spoke to him for a moment and he nodded and looked toward Tony, the reporter, and the photographer.

The Event Manager returned and said, "Chef will have your staff over in a few minutes. They'll bring over the various items you requested in your e-mail."

"Thank you again, Jenny," he said and with that, the young woman departed, leaving Tony alone with Roberta and the photographer.

"You've had a few exciting days, chef," Roberta said, and he braced himself, expecting a trap.

"No more than usual," he said and shot a quick look at the photographer who as always, seemed totally disinterested in what was happening. He wondered what the man thought of his colleague—and if he ever spoke, for that matter.

"Really?" she said and reached into her purse to extract her smartphone. With a few swipes, she held up the phone to him. "This has gone viral apparently," she said as a shaky video ran on the small screen.

Tony didn't need to look to know what it was as the tinny sound of a Sara chant spewed from the phone. With a disinterested shrug, he said, "Stuff happens."

Obviously dissatisfied with his answer, she said, "No embarrassment then? What about your relationship with Sara?"

He shrugged once again. "I don't get bothered easily. As for my relationship with Sara, as I've said, I think she's a wonderful chef. A true professional." *Unlike you*, he wanted to say, but bit it back.

With shrewd eyes, Roberta examined him. With another few swipes of her phone, she held it up barely inches from his face, forcing him to view the video. She'd paused it a spot when the videographer had turned his attention to Sara.

The look on her face was one of pain and longing. As painful as it was to see her upset, the text she'd sent later that night gave him hope that she still cared for him on some level and that maybe, once they were done with the *quinceañeras*, they could once again explore the feelings that had been growing between them.

It took every fiber of his being not to respond to the video and give Roberta even more fodder for her gossip.

"Well, Tony?" she pressed at his prolonged silence, but he refused to be egged into a response.

"Chef. We're ready whenever you are."

Roberta jerked away the smartphone and glared at the chef and crew of kitchen staff that were lined up and waiting for Tony.

Tony stepped up to the man with the toque and shook his hand. "Chef Gonzalez. Thank you so much for sharing your kitchen and your wonderful staff. I've heard so many good things about you and them."

The chef's shoulders relaxed with the praise and he smiled. "Thank you, chef. Let me introduce the line chefs who will be working with us for the event."

"I'd like that," Tony said and followed along as the chef introduced each of the men and women who would man the stations in the kitchen.

From the corner of his eye he noticed the photographer shooting several photos as Tony met the staff. Roberta hung back, scribbling in her notepad. He forced himself to ignore their presence and focus on his main goal: instructing the staff on the dishes he planned on serving for his niece's *quinceañera*.

"We can work over here, chef," Chef Gonzalez said.

One of the chefs brought over a jacket for Tony and he slipped into it and then took a spot at the center of the table in order to explain each of the recipes they would be making the night of the party.

"The theme of the party is Miami Spice and we're going to prepare traditional foods with an upscale twist. Let's start with the avocado salad," he said and in no time, he had grilled the fruit and prepared the dressing. After, he demonstrated how to prepare the Cuban-style *porchetta* and other items for the menu.

All the time that he worked, Roberta and the photographer hovered by. She was taking notes while the photographer took shot after shot.

He hadn't expected them to stay that long and in the back of his mind he wondered if Roberta had some ulterior motive for doing so. She seemed to like to stir up trouble more than he liked to stir up a good sauce.

Once he was done explaining the side dishes, he hurried onto the dessert, but as he did so, he heard a murmur of something and chuckling from some of the line chefs. "Amateurs," "Sara," and "Munch" stood out and he turned and faced them.

"I won't stand for any negative comments being made about Sara and her staff. If I hear anyone behave that way, you're off the team. Is that clear?"

Some looked down or away, but all nodded to confirm their understanding.

"*Bueno*. Let's finish this up," Tony said and provided the chefs instruction on a *tres leches* cake with banana and coconut for dessert.

"It all sounds delicious. Sara Kelly is really going to have to up her game if she's going to beat this menu,"

Roberta said as she walked over.

Tony gritted his teeth and reminded himself to remain calm. "I'm sure Sara's menu will be original and delicious as well," he said as he wiped his hands with a kitchen towel and undid the buttons on the chef's jacket. He turned to the chefs and said, "I want to thank you for taking the time to walk through this with me. I'm sure everything is going to turn out perfectly the night of the party."

"Thank you, chef. We're all looking forward to the celebration," Chef Gonzalez said, and his staff echoed his sentiments.

Tony stripped off the jacket and handed it back to one of the assistants. As he walked toward the exit to the ballroom, Roberta and the photographer tagged along beside him and Roberta attempted to re-engage him in the interview.

"Do you have anything else you'd like our readers to know?"

That stopped Tony dead in his tracks. He was tempted to tell her what a conniver she was. Instead he said, "You can tell them that I'm looking forward to my niece's *quinceañera* and possibly spending more time in Miami in the future. I love my hometown and being back has shown me just how much I miss it, my family, and my friends."

Roberta's nasty, toothy smile warned she was going in for a bite. "And have you missed one special lady in particular? Could it be Sara Kelly?"

He forced a smile and jammed his hands in his pockets. "I'll see you both the night of the party. I have to run."

Without waiting, he hurried off to phone that one special lady and ask her to meet him somewhere neutral.

He didn't want a repeat of what had happened the other night in her restaurant.

CHAPTER 19

ALTHOUGH SHE'D BEEN HOPING THAT Tony would try to reach out to her again after his disastrous visit to the restaurant the other night, she hadn't expected that it would happen so soon. She had felt horrible but also felt powerless to stop the chant when the crowd had really gotten going. Once Tony had bolted out the door with her brother Rick chasing after him, there was little she could do except text her apologies.

And despite their hopeful message exchange, she was still more than a little hurt about everything that was happening, including that Tony thought she couldn't or maybe shouldn't prepare a traditional Cuban meal because she wasn't Cuban. Because of that, she had been working especially hard to learn Dolores's family recipes and the stories and traditions behind them. She had also checked out a book on the history of Cuba as well as some cookbooks that also contained family histories. Last, but certainly not least, she had sat with Luis, Lucy, and some of the patrons of their fruit store to hear their stories about the "*Cuba de ayer*"—Cuba before Castro—and what their lives had been like afterward.

She'd been fascinated by what she'd been learning and would do her best to honor them and their experiences with what she intended to prepare for Samantha's *quinceañera*. Just like Tony would do all that he could to make Angelica's party the best that he could.

Tony, she thought with a sigh. She had been surprised when he had called just a little bit earlier to ask if she had time to meet him for breakfast at the coffee shop around the corner from Munch. The same coffee shop where she'd walked out of the interview with the *South Beach Style* reporter.

"Breakfast? I'm not sure—"

"How about just a coffee? You can spare ten minutes for a cup of coffee, can't you?" he had pleaded.

She'd caved. "Ten minutes," she'd said. She didn't know if she could keep up a neutral face much longer than that. She cared too much about him, but also about being the one featured in the *South Beach Style* article.

"Thank you, Sara. I appreciate it," he said and named a time to meet.

She shot a glance at her watch and said, "Okay, I'll see you in fifteen minutes."

She ran back to Jeri's office let her know she'd be stepping out for a few minutes. Then she raced into her office to pass a brush through her hair and freshen up a bit before meeting Tony. As she stared in the mirror, she told herself that she didn't feel tired, but the dark circles beneath her eyes said otherwise. She dabbed a little extra foundation there, hoping it would do the trick and headed out to meet Tony.

When she rounded the corner onto the pedestrian mall, Tony was already sitting at a table, two take-out cups of coffee sitting in front of him. He rose as she approached and went to give her a hug, but she side-stepped him and sat down at the table. He stood there for a moment, shoulders downturned, hands jammed in his pockets, but finally sat.

"I hope you don't mind that I took the liberty of ordering for you. I didn't want to waste any of my ten minutes by having to wait in line," he said with a hesitant smile.

"I don't mind and thank you," she said, wanting to keep it pleasant between them. Because of that, she apologized again. "I'm sorry about what happened the other night at the restaurant."

Tony shrugged and picked up his cup of coffee. "There was nothing you could do, Sara."

She tapped her chest with her forefinger. "It's my place and I should have been able to control what was going on."

He shook his head. "You can't control everything. Besides, it's not your fault this rivalry thing has gotten so far out of hand."

"It's that reporter," she said and finally picked up her cup of coffee and took a sip. She murmured her approval of the sweet and creamy *café con leche*. "Perfect."

"I can't take credit for it," he teased, but then grew more serious. "Roberta and her photographer sat in on my session with the hotel's staff the other day."

Sara arched a brow. "Worried that they'll share your secrets?"

Tony chuckled as she had intended. Laughing with him had been one of the things she had loved most about their time together. "Worried she'll find some other way to stir up trouble between us. You have to understand that's the last thing I want, Sara." He reached out and laid his hand over hers as it rested on the table, his touch gentle and inviting.

She'd missed his touch. The warmth of his hand. The calloused feel of his palm against hers as she slipped her hand into his. It felt so right. Too right. "I've missed you, Tony. Missed what was happening with us," she admitted.

"I've missed you too, Sara. I thought that there was something special starting between us," he said and gave her hand a gentle squeeze.

It had been special. So so special and she wanted to find a way back to what they'd had.

"What do we do about this? About us? About the girls? It was supposed to be about them having their special day," she said, guilt and disappointment melding in her gut.

"We'll do the best that we can for Samantha and Angelica. As for us… Is there an 'us,' Sara? Would you like for there to be?" he asked, leaning toward her, his voice earnest. His dark gaze was alive with hope.

"I would, Tony, but it just seems like now is not the time for us," she said, and her throat tightened with emotion. "As much as I want there to be more, it's important to me and Jeri to be the ones featured. It's important for my ladies and for Bridget," she forced out, her eyes burning as incipient tears gathered. She had shattered the moment and hated that she'd done so.

"I get that, but I can't roll over and be second best, Sara. It's important to me too. But you're very important also. Maybe after…." With a squeeze of her hand, he rose, and grabbed his cup of coffee. "Look, it didn't even take ten minutes," he said, a sad smile on his face, and walked away.

Sara sniffled and bit back the tears. She refused to cry over this situation again. She'd done that too often in the last few days and it hadn't accomplished a thing.

Taking a deep breath, she picked up her coffee cup, took a sip, and willed away the hurt.

She understood where Tony was coming from. She didn't expect him to "roll over" but like him, she wasn't going to settle for being second best. It meant too much to everyone involved and she intended to finish on top even if the cost was her relationship with Tony.

Roberta couldn't believe her luck that morning.

She'd been running to get to the magazine's offices on Espanola Way, when her editor had texted her photos of Tony sitting at the nearby coffee shop on Lincoln Road. Someone had posted them on Twitter and she'd hurried over to try and sneak in another interview with him.

Imagine her surprise when barely a minute after she arrived, Sara Kelly had come by and sat across from him.

Roberta had drifted out of their line of sight. Unfortunately, she was too far away to hear what they were saying. But the picture of them together, holding hands, with misery all over their faces had told her quite a story.

She hadn't been wrong when she had sensed there was more than a professional relationship between the two chefs. Judging by how they'd looked, there had been something personal going on with them before she'd ratcheted up the rivalry around the *quinceañera* celebrations.

As she took in the absolute unhappiness on their faces, an unwanted emotion stirred in her gut. Guilt. She had wanted the story to go viral and had done her level best to accomplish it, but this… It was difficult to see their pain, even though she knew what her editor Marco would expect from her.

She reluctantly pulled out her smartphone and snuck around a planter filled with palms and flowers so she could surreptitiously snap off some photos of the two of them holding hands before Tony walked off and left Sara there crying.

She waited until both Tony and Sara were out of sight, then raced to her office, the desire for coffee forgotten thanks to the sudden sour taste in her mouth.

As she entered the magazine's offices, the receptionist jerked her head in greeting and said, "Marco wants you in his office ASAP."

She paused for a moment and pulled up the photos on her phone. It would only take a few swipes to erase them. Just a few…

"Roberta!" Marco shouted as he came out of his office.

He was at her side, glancing at the photos before she could swipe to erase them.

"That's golden," he said, taking the phone from her hand and scanning the images. "There's a romance here too?" Marco asked.

She reluctantly nodded. "It looks that way, but Marco—"

"No buts, Roberta."

"Seriously, Marco. This is going too far," she said, her conscience finally coming alive.

Marco jabbed his finger in her face. "This story has been bringing in a lot of website traffic for the magazine, but the hits on the poll and tweets have been dropping. This is just what we need to get things moving again," he said and thrust the phone back into her hand.

"I want some tweets and a short story on my desk within an hour. Do it or pack up your desk and go home."

Roberta juggled the phone in her hands as she watched her editor's retreating back. She told herself she could do this. It was important for the magazine and her career, and those were the things she had to prioritize, no matter what. It didn't matter that what had started as a story about the girls had morphed into something else thanks to her. Something causing pain to two innocent people. *Thanks to me.*

It doesn't matter, she kept on telling herself as she headed to her desk to fulfill her editor's command. *It doesn't matter*, she repeated even though she knew that to Sara and Tony it mattered a great deal.

Sara's cell started buzzing like a hive of angry bees. She dreaded peeking at the notifications because the experience of the last few days had taught her it couldn't be anything good. But ignoring it would risk her getting blindsided by something later.

She set down the knife at the station where she had been fileting fish for one of that night's daily specials and wiped her hands with the towel tucked into her apron waistband. Pulling her phone from her back pocket, she swiped it open and cringed at the notices that she had a slew of messages from her friends and dozens of social media mentions.

"Put the phone down," Jeri said before she walked over, and grabbed it out of her hand.

Sara wiggled her fingers in Jeri's face. "Give it back."

"You don't want to see what it is, Sara. Trust me," Jeri

said and tucked the phone behind her back.

"I do want to see it. Better that than being surprised later," she said and held her hand out for the phone.

Jeri hesitated, but relented and handed Sara the phone. She stood there, waiting, as Sara skimmed the subject lines on the messages and then headed to a Twitter feed that was going insane. It was obvious why.

Kiss and tell? Are these top chefs more than just rivals? You be the judge! http://bit.ly/2KAKpp8 #SouthBeach #eatfamous #truecooks #foodie

The preview photo beneath the tweet was a picture of them at the coffee shop. She hovered her finger over the link, hesitant to see what other photos Roberta Lane might have gotten her hands on, but finally resolved that it was better to know so she could deal with it.

She clicked on the link and it took her to the magazine's website. There was a short write-up about their meeting that would probably take longer to read aloud than the time Tony and she had spent having coffee. She barely glanced at the words because the pictures were way more compelling. Tony and her, peering at each other intently. Gazes filled with so much pain and longing. Her heart tightened in her chest and she laid her hand there as her eyes shimmered with tears. The pain was so unbearable it was almost hard to breathe, but somehow she managed a shaky breath.

"How bad is it?" Jeri asked, concern evident in her voice.

Sara's throat was so tight with emotion that she couldn't even get out a squeak. She held up the phone so that her friend could see the pictures.

"Wow. So sorry, Sara. None of that is anyone's business. I didn't realize *South Beach Style* had become such a gossip rag."

Sara jerked the phone back for another quick look and then shut off all notifications and swiped the phone closed. "Tony and me…it's complicated. I'm sorry this has all become such a mess. I know it's important to you—to us—that we're the ones highlighted in the article."

"It *is* important to me. To us. It could mean more money, more opportunities," Jeri said, apology coloring her words.

"Which means we could hire enough staff for you to spend more time with Sophie. Maybe even Rick?" Sara asked.

With a reluctant shrug, Jeri said, "Maybe. But what about you and Tony? Will you have a chance after this is all over? The last thing I want is for this to hurt you."

"He's going back to New York either way, and if I lose, I'll have to live with the humiliation here in Miami." She jammed the phone into her back pocket and hurried to her station to finish prepping the fish for that night, Jeri chasing after her.

"Or maybe he'll stay. Anything is possible, Sara," she urged.

Sara had never thought of herself as a pessimist, but when it came to Tony and what was happening, she was finding it hard to stay positive. Jeri was right that anything was possible, but….

"Maybe he'll stay even after I win this stupid contest that Roberta has whipped up. But I guess there's only one way to find out."

Jeri smiled and wrapped her arm around Sara's waist as she began to filet the fish again, her knife movements sure and efficient. "You're going to kick his butt, aren't you?"

"I am," Sara said with certitude. She was going to be the one who got the most face time in the article and let all the other chips fall where they may.

Tony was flipping through his journals, trying to search for recipes to include in his cookbook, but the words were just a blur. All he could think of was Sara and the disturbing images and article that the reporter had posted earlier that day.

His phone chirped, snagging his attention. Again. His phone had become a non-stop noise machine with a combination of text messages and calls that he had been ignoring. But as he glanced at the screen, he realized it was Javi. He hoped everything was okay with his older brother. Javi had seemed way too busy and preoccupied the last time they'd spoken. He'd been worried about his brother ever since their discussion.

"*Javi, hermano. ¿Como estas?*" Tony said.

"*Bien, hermanito.* I wish I could say the same about you. Are you okay?" Javi asked.

Am I okay? he asked himself but didn't have an answer. "I guess you saw the tweets and stuff."

"I did. Or I should say my programs did. I've got them set to alert me when anything mentions you and well...things were blowing up," Javi said with a heavy sigh. "I'm sorry, *hermanito.* I guess the Sanchez boys are doomed to have a thing for the Kelly girls."

Javi's comment reminded him about what Rick had asked just a day or so earlier about Javi and Bridget. Grateful for a way to change the subject away from him and Sara, he asked, "You and Bridget were a thing?"

Another sigh, heavier and filled with more emotion,

flooded the line before Javi said, "Water under the bridge, *mano*. She has her hotshot finance guy –"

"They're divorced and from what I understand, he did a number on her."

"She's okay, right? Because if not...." Javi didn't finish, but then again, he didn't need to say anything else to make it clear that he would tear the other guy apart if he had to. Unless he'd let his big athlete's body go to flab after becoming a desk jockey.

"Bridget is more than okay, Javi. Maybe you'd know that if you came home more often," he said and almost bit his tongue as his sister's and *mami*'s words spilled from his mouth.

Javi chuckled and he could picture his brother's smile and the way he'd drag his hand through the thick waves of his dark hair, so much like his own. "I guess I will find out once I'm home. *Hermanito*, I have news for you all. News you couldn't ever possibly imagine," Javi said, humor and happiness in his voice.

"Sounds like good news, Javi," he said and wished that he'd have good news to share soon and not about the article.

"It is. I know you're having a tough time now, but it'll get better, Tony. Sara is totally worth it," his brother said.

He couldn't argue with him. "She is. I'll try to stay positive." Even if it was almost impossible to imagine things working out well, he would hope for it with all his heart because as Javi had said, Sara was worth it.

But as he hung up with Javi, he realized hope alone couldn't make things right. *He* had to make things right. With that in mind, he phoned Sara...and the phone just rang and rang.

He told himself it was likely because she was busy and not because she was ignoring him. He was about to hang up when she answered, slightly breathless. "Tony?" she asked, surprise in her voice.

"*Sí*. How are you?" he asked, but in the background the noises of activity in the kitchen filtered over the line.

"Busy. It's been a little crazier here what with the tweets and other stuff," Sara said, but there was no obvious pleasure in that.

"I guess that's good, right?" he said, glad that something good was coming out of their misery.

"It is, but at what sacrifice?" she said, dejection in her voice.

"I understand, Sara. That's why I'm calling. I'd like for us to do something together," he said.

Silence, for barely a breath, tightened his gut with anticipation, but then she said, "I'd like that."

He expelled a relieved breath. "Is tomorrow good?"

A rough laugh greeted him. "I think Jeri and I can work things out."

Wow, he had hoped for a "yes" but now that she'd agreed, he'd have to scramble to make plans for the day. "I'll text you with the time and place. Is that okay?"

"It's more than okay, Tony. Thank you. I'm looking forward to it," she said, and hope flared into possibilities. Way more than he'd thought likely after their meeting that morning.

Armed with that, he thought about who could help him pull this off and one person immediately came to mind.

He picked up the phone and dialed. When his friend answered, he said, "I need your help, Rick."

"I hope this will work for you," Rick said as he gestured to the backyard at his suburban home.

"It's great," Tony said, looking around at the pool and beyond, to the small deck on a canal where a Seadoo sat on a lift. "Did you buy this house with someone special in mind?"

Rick shrugged which was an answer in and of itself. As Tony glanced back toward the home, with its inviting open space concept visible through the French doors, it was obvious his friend intended to have a family in this home.

"It's really nice, Rick," he said.

"But not what you expected," Rick said with a chuckle and a shake of his head.

"No way, it's definitely you. I can picture you here with a family," Tony teased and clapped his friend on the back.

"Me, too, bro. Maybe someday," his friend said wistfully.

"I appreciate you loaning me your home and helping me get everything ready. I know it was last minute," Tony said in apology.

Rick laughed and held his hand up for a high five. "If the Kelly brothers can't get it for you –"

"No one can," he said with a chuckle, repeating the jingle his friend's family used as their business slogan. He slapped Rick's hand for the high five.

Rick pointed his finger at him. "You got it and I should get going, but...take care with her, bro."

Tony nodded. "I will, Rick. You know I care for her."

"I do, but this *quinceañera* thing. It's way out of control," Rick said and then quickly added, "I won't be back until late."

"I appreciate you clearing out, but what are you

doing?" Tony asked.

Rick smiled, a broad grin filled with happiness. "I took your advice. I'm babysitting Sophie at the restaurant so Jeri can cover for Sara. She was supposed to have the morning and afternoon off."

Tony was pleased that his friend was finally making inroads with Sara's partner because it was way too easy to picture Rick here with them, in the home he'd made for a family.

"Good luck, *mano*," he said and walked with Rick to the front door.

"You too," Rick said and left to go to the restaurant.

Tony had to get going to prep everything he needed for Sara's arrival in less than half an hour. He quickly whipped up some bacon and French toast slices he filled with a spread he'd made with mascarpone and strawberries. Into the oven to warm while he made a pot of coffee and heated some milk for it.

He had just finished setting the table, complete with a vase of yellow roses, when the doorbell rang.

His heartbeat picked up its pace and his hands seemed suddenly sweaty as he went to the door. He opened it and Sara was there, a hesitant smile on her face. She held a smallish plastic container that she thrust at him. "I made some churros and cannolis since you liked them so much the other day."

And since it had been such a nice first time together, he thought and hoped that it had been her intention to restore that feeling.

"*Gracias*. Welcome, although it's weird since it's Rick's house," he said and held his hand wide to invite her in.

"A little weird, but he's so happy that he gets to babysit Sophie," she said and walked in.

"I'm glad for him," Tony said, and Sara echoed it.

"I'm glad too. Jeri and Sophie…it would be awesome for them to be together here," she said and gestured to the comfortable home her brother had created.

"It would be, and I hope…" he hesitated, not wanting to create too much pressure right off the bat.

"It'll be a nice day for us too," she said and laid a hand on his arm, offering reassurance.

"Me, too. I made breakfast. I thought that after we ate we could hang out by the pool," Tony said as Sara followed him into the kitchen.

"Or steal a ride on Rick's Seadoo," she said with a smile and wrinkle of her nose.

"I remember that time we left you behind to go on your dad's Seadoo," Tony said and shook his head. "You were so angry."

Sara chuckled. "I was annoyed. I was totally big enough to go with you, but my dad didn't think so. I think it was hard to stop thinking of me as his little girl."

The look that Tony shot her confirmed that he no longer thought of her as a little kid and her heartbeat sped up with the passion in his gaze.

"You're definitely big enough now, but I have to confess that I don't know how to use that thing," he said and gestured to the watercraft.

"But I do. It'll be fun. We're supposed to be having fun today right?" Sara said with an arch of her brow.

He grinned and nodded, but his smile faded as he said, "For sure. I don't want to be all work and no play Tony again."

She laid a hand on his arm, her touch soothing. "I think you're past that, aren't you? At least from what I've seen."

"I hope I am," he said and gestured toward the table he'd set. "But first, breakfast."

"Breakfast is my favorite meal of the day. How can I help?" she asked, but he waved her off and in no time they were sitting and eating the meal he had prepared. Sharing a coffee companionably.

Sara loved the easy time together, so much like what had been happening between them before the reporter had stirred up trouble. "This was great. Thank you. It's nice to be able to just be together without all those other pressures."

"It is." He clearly wanted to avoid additional mention of those pressures since he said, "How about a swim?"

Sara chuckled and shook her head. "How about a spin on that Seadoo instead?"

"Impatient, aren't you?" he teased, but offered her his hand as they walked out the French doors and onto the patio.

"I am so not patient," Sara admitted with a chuckle and a playful swing of their hands.

"I imagine that's how you and Jeri got so much accomplished in so little time," he said, praise for them obvious in his voice.

"Thank you. That means a lot to me," she said, appreciating his support despite all that was happening. "Let's go do that ride."

Together they walked over to the dock with the Seadoo and Sara efficiently used the lift to get the machine into the water. But as she went to go down the ladder to it, Tony said, "I think you should do the driving."

Sara arched a brow. "Really?" Most guys would insist

on being the ones at the wheel.

Tony nodded. "Really. I wasn't kidding when I said I don't know much about this thing. You don't see many of them on Manhattan streets," he said with a laugh.

Sara chuckled. She rubbed her hands together, feeling like the proverbial kid in a candy shop as she gazed at the machine. "Rick is so gonna freak out, but I'm going to love this!"

She quickly stripped off the cover-up over her bathing suit, grabbed a life vest from a storage bench, and rushed down the ladder and took a seat.

Tony pulled off his T-shirt, grabbed a life vest, and came down the stairs. He slipped in behind her, his powerful body pressed to hers. The warmth of his legs against hers, the feel of him, was distracting, but somehow she got the key in the ignition and started the engine.

Glancing over her shoulder at him, she said, "Ready?"

Tony wrapped his arms around her waist. "Ready," he said, but she detected a note of hesitation in his voice. Possibly even panic.

"Trust me," she said and drove slowly until they were out of the canal and into the more open waters of Biscayne Bay. Once they were there, her impatience took over.

She gunned the engine and the Seadoo shot off across the water, forcing Tony to hold her tightly as they both leaned forward into the speed, enjoying the spray of the salt water, rush of the bay breeze, and the feel of them, riding together. Bodies pressed close. Their breaths catching and then exploding in delight as they soared into the air, launched from the wake of a passing boat, and landed. Dipping into the trough of another wave before she expertly maneuvered into another leap into the air. Over and over, water rushing over them. Their laughter loud over the roar of the engine.

But the ride, as fun as it was, was physically trying as she piloted the Seadoo and as her muscles began to quiver from the effort and the chill of the water, she slowed the watercraft and steered it back toward her brother's home. Tony's warmth and the support of his body against hers tempering her exhaustion and the cold.

She eased the Seadoo back onto the rails for the lift and they quickly scrambled back up on the dock. After lifting the watercraft, she expertly washed it down and flushed the engine of the salt water.

"You do that like a pro," Tony teased as she rolled up the hose and stowed it after she had finished.

"Rick has taught me well," she said and faced him.

He was staring at her intently, his dark eyes filled with a mix of emotions. Droplets of water clung to his hair, wetter in some spots from the spray as they'd ridden the waves. Tousled, she stepped toward him and smoothed back the errant locks of hair.

He smiled, laid a hand at her waist and after a slight pause, he said. "I appreciate you coming today. I want to try and make things right between us."

"I want that more than anything also, Tony," she admitted.

He arched a brow and his gaze was inquiring as he said, "Even more than a feature in the magazine?"

She hesitated, wanting to be truthful. "How about we agree that it's important to both of us and leave it at that?"

He hesitated, then took a step toward her and cupped her cheek. "Agreed. You mean a lot to me, Sara. You have to believe that."

She wanted to believe—Lord, how she wanted to believe—and because she wanted this day to be one that moved them together again rather than apart, she said,

"I do. And you have to believe that I never wanted for this to become what it has."

"I do," he said, and it was way too easy to picture him saying those words in another situation. She cradled his jaw and ran her finger across the stubble on his cheek. Took a step closer and the smell of him, Tony, saltwater, and spring air, wrapped around her. Drew her ever closer until her lips were barely an inch from his and it was all she could do to resist taking the next step. But resist she did, taking a step back to meet his gaze.

There was disappointment there, but she offered him a smile and said, "Let's take this a step at a time, Tony."

He nodded and laughed. "I guess you're more patient than I am." But then he said, "A tiny step at a time... to each other."

"To each other," she repeated and hoped she could muster the patience to get them through the *quinceñera* and to that togetherness they both seemed to want.

CHAPTER 20

S AMANTHA STUCK THE LAST OF the silk flowers into the florist's foam that they'd glued into the bottom of the cigar box. She shifted the flower a little to balance out the centerpiece and smiled. In addition to the flowers and some moss over the foam, they had added vintage postcard reproductions from Cuba, tiny colorful maracas, and a few seashells. The centerpieces would look lovely at her *quinceañera*.

Across from her at the kitchen table her mother was completing her centerpiece as well. When she finished she looked up, elated. "These are going to look great."

Aunt Sara, who had been working at the stove, frying *tostones* for a dish she wanted to try out with them, looked over her shoulder and grinned. "They do look fabulous. You're definitely going to nail the Old Havana theme with those."

"Awesome," Samantha said and pumped her arm in celebration.

The sound of the front door opening and closing was followed by heavy footsteps as her father walked across the tiled foyer and into the kitchen.

Something was very wrong. The defeated droop of her father's shoulders and the dark glower on his face had her instantly worried.

Her aunt shut off the gas and set aside the frying pan as her mom rose, walked over to her dad, and laid a comforting hand on his arm.

"What is it, Matt?" her mother asked.

He sucked in a rough breath. "I think you should all sit down for this."

Mami returned to her seat and Aunt Sara sat next to her. As they had just a few weeks earlier, the three of them joined hands and braced themselves for what her father had to say.

He didn't join them at the table, but instead leaned heavily on the top rung of a chair across from them. With a lift of his shoulders that almost seemed to pain him, he sucked in a breath, slowly released it, and finally said, "I got a call from the yacht club this afternoon."

This is so so going to be not good, Samantha thought and tightened her hold on Sara's hand.

"They had a fire overnight in their kitchens. It caused major damage. The manager told me there's no way the repairs will be done in time for Samantha's *quince* in a week."

"But we can reschedule, right? They can give us another day?" Samantha said, her voice rising, trembling, with each word.

That sad look on her father's face got even sadder. "I'm sorry, Sam. They were doing me a favor giving me that date—and it was only possible because someone had forfeited a deposit. The owner says if we take another day, which they don't have until much later in the year, we'd have to pay full price for the space."

This isn't happening, she thought. "But we can do that,

right? Can't we?" she said, desperate for reassurance. Her family could probably never afford a location like the yacht club at full price, but something had made her ask anyway.

"I can help, Matt. Just let me know what you need," Aunt Sara said and met Samantha's gaze. Her aunt's image blurred in her vision as tears threatened to spill, but she would not cry. Her parents were upset enough, and she wouldn't add to that distress by crying.

"I appreciate that, but you have your own worries and I know how tight your budget is for the restaurant," her father said.

"We appreciate it, Sara, we do, but Matt is right. We'll find some other way to have the party. Maybe we can do something right here. The garden is lovely this time of year," her mother said and looked over at Samantha.

No, no, no, she wanted to say, but eked out, "Sure, the backyard. We could do that. Sure."

She was trying to stay strong for her parents but to do that, she had to get out of the room. "I have to study for a test," she said and bolted from the kitchen.

After Samantha had run from the room and up the stairs, her footfalls sounding as loud as gunshots, Sara peered between Dolores and Matt. "There has to be something we can do. I can cover some of the costs. The staff. Some of the food."

Matt shook his head. "No way, sis. It's way too much."

"But it's important to Samantha," she said. "She shouldn't have to give this up."

"I get that, but there's nothing I can do," Matt said wearily.

"What are you going to tell people? The party is supposed to be in a little over a week," Sara said.

With a reassuring squeeze of her hand, Dolores said, "We'll think of something. We just need a day or so to deal with this. Will you be okay?"

It was hard to believe that with such devastating news her brother and sister-in-law were thinking about her well-being, but then again, that's the way they were. With the Kellys, family always came first.

"I'll be okay, and I'll do whatever you need me to do. Any way I can help, just let me know. I can cook up some fabulous dishes for you on Matt's monster grill," she said, hoping to lighten the mood.

With a shrug, her brother said, "I do meat. I need a big grill to do meat."

"*Amorcito*, you can feed a football stadium with that grill," his wife teased.

"Yes, I can—and we just might for Samantha's *quince*. We'll let you know, Sara," her brother said and walked around to urge his wife to rise so he could hug her hard.

Satisfied things were going to be all right with Dolores and Matt, Sara rose to make her exit. "You let me know what you need, and I'll be there."

Matt nodded. "We know you will be the same way we'll be here for you, sis."

"Thanks," she said and headed for the door, hoping that whatever decision they made would make Samantha as happy—but now, she wasn't sure that was possible. The poor girl must be miserable.

She wished there was something she could do to take away her niece's hurt, but her brother was right that she couldn't offer much financially. All she could do was give her niece the best party food ever when it was time. That was how it should have been all along before things had gotten out of control. Samantha and her *quinceañera* first and foremost.

Everything else...*everything* else had to come second.

CHAPTER 21

T HE BALL SAILED IN SAMANTHA's direction, a soft lob that would be easy for her to control and kick back toward the forwards. As it landed, Samantha misjudged it, her kick off balance, and the ball bounded off the field.

The coach's whistle rent the air. "Kelly, what is wrong with you today?" she shouted out as action stopped on the pitch.

"Sorry, coach," Samantha said, her arms crossed protectively over her chest, her face red with exertion and embarrassment.

"Take five laps around the field, Samantha. Maybe that will get your head out of the clouds. The rest of you head on home," the coach said. The coach looked at Angelica and jerked her head in Samantha's direction as the other girl started to run the punishment laps.

Angelica understood that as captain, it was up to her to find out what was going on. But even if the coach hadn't instructed it, she would have tagged after Samantha because she was obviously not herself. She'd been distracted through all the classes they shared all day and from what she had seen at lunch, she'd been quiet and withdrawn then, too.

She sped her pace to catch up to Samantha and then fell into step beside her.

Samantha shot her a confused look before facing forward again, her arms pumping as she ran. "Coach said for everyone to go home."

Angelica shrugged and said, "You played so badly today I thought you might need help finding your way back to the locker room."

A choked laugh escaped Samantha and was quickly followed by a loud sniffle.

Angelica peeked at her from the corner of her eye. Tears streamed down Samantha's cheeks and her breathing grew more and more ragged until it was impossible for her to keep running.

Angelica wrapped an arm around Samantha's shoulders and guided her to one of the benches along the edge of the field. She joined her, rubbing Samantha's back until she finally quieted and wiped away her tears.

"I'm sorry," Samantha said.

"No harm, no foul," Angelica replied, unsure of what to do next. She asked herself what her mother would do, and the answer came quickly.

"I'm here if you want to talk."

Beneath her hand Samantha's body jumped a bit. Her friend–surprising to think of her that way, but they *had* become friends–shifted on the bench to face her. Samantha hesitated and sucked in a breath.

"I'm not going to be able to have my *quinceañera* at the yacht club. Maybe nowhere actually," she said, and her eyes glistened, tears threatening once again.

"OMG, why not?" Angelica asked, full of empathy.

"There was a fire at the place and...we can't reschedule." Another long pause followed, but with a shake of her head, Samantha finally said, "My family can't afford to pay full price for another date. The only reason we were having it there was because my dad got a deal from his friend."

Angelica had wondered how the Kelly family could afford something like the fancy yacht club. Now she knew.

"I'm sorry, Samantha. That's so not fair," she said and once again passed her hand across Samantha's shoulders as the tears fell down her friend's face.

"What can we do?" Angelica asked.

Samantha laughed roughly once more. "It's 'we' now?"

Angelica thought about it for a long moment. "Maybe. I mean this whole *quinceañera* thing has gotten out of control thanks to that stupid reporter. My *tio* Tony and your aunt Sara are both miserable because of it."

"Totally miserable," Samantha said, picked up the edge of her jersey, and dried her face.

"We can't just give up," Angelica said and stood up.

Samantha stared at her, puzzled. "What are you doing?"

"I think better when I run, and you owe Coach five laps. Are you game?"

Samantha stood and walked back with Angelica to the track surrounding the field. As Angelica started to jog, Samantha said, "What am I game for?"

Angelica smiled at her. "Finding a way out of this mess."

When his sister had called and said she was holding an

emergency family meeting, he hadn't known what to expect. He certainly hadn't been prepared to see Sara there, sitting at the kitchen table along with Matt, Dolores, Bridget, and Samantha Kelly. On the opposite side of the table sat his sister's husband, Esteban, and Angelica.

"What's up?" he asked, and Sylvia motioned him to a chair next to her husband. Then she surprised him by sitting next to him and saying, "Angelica and Samantha have something they wish to say to us."

"I don't get it," Sara said at the same time that Matt asked, "What's this about?"

"*Amorcito*, just wait, *por favor*," Dolores said and laid a calming hand on Matt's arm.

"Yes, be patient, Matt," Bridget echoed and shot her older brother a glare.

At least he wasn't the only one not in the loop, evidently.

Angelica and Samantha rose almost in unison and walked to the head of the table where they stood side-by-side. After a nervous glance between them, Samantha said, "There was a fire at the yacht club where we were supposed to have my *quinceañera* and we won't be able to have it there."

Matt jumped in, a muscle angrily jumping across his strong jaw. "Honey, that's not something to bother the Sanchezes with. Your mom and I told you we would work something out."

Samantha nodded. "I know that, *papi*, and I really appreciate all that you've done so I could have the *quinceañera*."

"What's the issue then? You don't trust us to do it?" Matt blustered, obviously upset and possibly shamed by having the family's dirty laundry aired.

Once again Dolores chimed in. "Matt, *por favor*. Let the girls finish."

"Fine. Go ahead," he said and locked his arms across his chest, in defensive mode.

Samantha dared a quick look in Angelica's direction who took up the baton and spoke.

"Samantha and I talked yesterday after practice. We had a lot of the same people invited to both parties, they were only supposed to be a day apart anyway, and there's space in the hotel ballroom for additional people."

Tony was hearing it, but he wasn't quite believing it. Were these two girls, who according to his sister had been rivals for everything, proposing a joint party? He was about to question them, but Sara beat him to the punch.

"You're saying you want to have one party for both of you?" Sara asked, clearly as confused as he was.

The two girls shared a look, nodded, and simultaneously said, "Yes."

A drawn-out silence followed until Bridget broke it. "Are you sure?"

Samantha nodded. "It makes sense. Both families will save money. You can put the money you save aside for our college funds. Maybe you can even give part of it as a donation to Aunt Bridget's non-profit."

"That's very generous of you girls to suggest, but not necessary," Bridget said.

"But what about your themes? The menus?" Sara asked, her brain apparently working much along the same lines as Tony's, since he'd been wondering the same things.

"It's a perfect mix," Angelica said and clapped her hands together. "The old meets the new!"

Samantha jumped in excitedly. "And we know how important the article is to both you and Angelica's Uncle

Tony, so we thought you could do a four-course menu and have each of you do two dishes."

"How will we decide who does what course?" Tony asked, his mind already calculating the changes he'd have to make both in terms of the courses and the number of people who would have to be fed.

Both girls hesitated again, but then Samantha blurted out, "We can flip a coin to decide."

"I guess there's not much else to discuss, is there?" Tony said. As he glanced around the table, it seemed clear that everyone was onboard with what the two teens had proposed. Everyone except possibly Sara who looked as concerned as he was. Make that three people because Matt Kelly didn't look too pleased either.

But for his part, Tony would go along with whatever his sister and niece wanted because as Sara had said the other day, their primary concern all along should have been the girls and their *quinceañeras*. Not to mention, he hoped that the next several days in the kitchen with Sara would keep moving things in the right direction.

"You're kidding me, right?" Jeri said as she and Sara walked around the kitchen the next day. It was a tradition in *Munch* for them to take this walk to make sure all the line chefs were at work on their respective parts of that day's menu. Satisfied that all was in order, she finally gave her attention to her partner.

"I'm not kidding. It's a good solution for the girls. Very adult of them," she said despite the turmoil she was feeling. She looked forward to working with Tony, but it would still be difficult to be in competition with him at the same time.

"Maybe for them, but how about for you?" Jeri said as they returned to the station they shared for the final plating of all the dishes.

"I'll survive," she said and sighed. *Or at least I hope so.*

"A coin toss, huh? When do you plan on doing that?" Jeri said as she did a last check of their station for what they would need to finish the orders.

Sara shot a quick look at her watch. "He should be here soon. We'll do the flip and tomorrow we'll talk about the dishes we plan to make and do any necessary adjustments."

A tap came on the glass door of the restaurant.

Tony had arrived.

"This shouldn't take long," Sara said and walked over to let Tony in. She unlocked the door and after he had entered, locked it up again. Lunch service wasn't set to begin for another hour so that gave them plenty of time, not that they'd need it for something as simple as a coin toss.

They stood there, hesitant. Seeing him reminded her of how nice it had been the other day, enjoying the ride over the waves and after. That almost moment. There was something about having him around that just made her feel… She didn't want to say "whole" because she didn't think any woman needed a man to complete her. But she did feel comforted. Excited. Steady. Unsteady.

"Sara?" Tony said at her prolonged silence.

"How do you feel about this?" she said.

Tony hesitated, walked over to the first free table, and gestured to it as if to ask if it was okay for him to sit.

With a nod and a wave of her hand, she confirmed it and joined him there. He held out his hands, palm up, and as she had just days earlier, she slipped her hands into his. Warm. Smooth and rough at the same time, much like their relationship so far.

He squeezed her hands and offered up a crooked smile. "You know I want there to be an us. We just have to get through this competition."

Her heart sped up a beat, because she was beginning to believe. "We were moving in the right direction. And if the girls can set aside their differences —"

"—we can too. We just have to focus on the girls and their *quinceañeras* for now. Make a truce so that reporter doesn't have more gossip for her story."

"Agreed. As for the competition to be featured, we'll find a way to keep things from getting out of hand," she said.

"Agreed," he said. Then he released her hands to reach into his pocket, take out a quarter, and place it on the tabletop. "You probably want to check it to see if it's legit."

She put her hand up and smiled. "No need. I trust you."

"Ladies first," he said and motioned to the quarter.

She picked up the coin, jiggled it in her hand, and as she tossed it in the air, she said, "Heads."

The quarter landed in her palm and she flipped it over onto the top of her hand to reveal the flip. "Tails," she said, dejected since she had no doubt which course Tony would choose as his first pick.

With a nod, Tony said, "I'll do the entrée." He held his hand out for the coin, took it, and did the second flip. He kept his hand over the coin until Sara hesitantly said, "I'm sticking to heads."

He pulled his hand away to show George Washington's face gleaming on the quarter.

"I'll take the appetizer," Sara said.

They repeated the coin toss with Sara winning the next flip and choosing the dessert course, leaving Tony to do the salad.

"I guess it's settled," Tony said and went to rise, but she stopped him.

"Not quite. I want Jeri and my people in the kitchen for my courses," she said.

With a lift of his broad shoulders, he said, "I'm sure that can be arranged. Not to mention that it would be good for *South Beach Style* to see them in action."

It was thoughtful of him to realize that. "Thank you."

"I know how important this still is. Somehow we'll figure it out, Sara," he said, and then he cupped her cheek. Ran his finger across it in a gentle caress. "You know that, right?"

"We will figure it out," she said.

He nodded and smiled. "Good. Once you've had a chance to think about your part of the menu and any changes to what you'd planned, we can meet again and see whether the courses are a good fit. Finalize a list of supplies we'll need," he said, his tone and manner welcoming and friendly, but also professional.

Encouraged about the continuing change in their relationship and what it might mean for them personally, she said, "That sounds like a plan. I should be set to go in a day or so. Call me when you're ready."

She rose and walked to the door to unlock it.

He followed her and walked out, but then stopped and faced her. "I'm looking forward to working with you, Sara."

And then he was gone, heading off in the direction of Lincoln Road.

"I'm looking forward to it also," she murmured and

couldn't keep from doing a little happy dance. Things were looking so much better than they had just a few days earlier. Sara wasn't going to pass up this opportunity not only to cook the best possible food for their nieces, but to keep her relationship with Tony moving in a positive direction because...

She cared for him, maybe more than she should. That take-charge streak in her said to grab this opportunity—and Tony—with both hands.

CHAPTER 22

WORRY BUILT INSIDE ROBERTA LANE as she read the e-mail from Sylvia Rodriguez advising her about the change in plans for the *quinceañera* parties. Her editor would not be happy, but the one thing that might keep him from totally flipping out was the fact that the two chefs would still be competing by preparing the different courses for the meal.

She'd remind him of that…via email. Not in person. She wasn't normally a coward, but she wasn't ready to deal with Marco just yet. She forwarded him the email and grabbed her purse, hoping to make an escape when he barged into her office.

"This isn't good," her editor said as he walked in, coffee cup and Cuban toast in hand. He sat before her desk; his brow furrowed. A glower covered his face.

"Isn't it?" she said, hoping to head off his anger over the change. "The girls have apparently gotten over their drama and are even donating a portion of the monies originally set aside for the party to Bridget Kelly's non-profit. This is a whole new angle for the story. People love feel-good stories."

"People love gossip and rivalries more," her editor said with a pout, took a sip of his coffee, and pointed to her with the coffee cup. "Run with what you have and make it a good story."

He rushed out of her office and she picked up her phone and dialed Tony Sanchez, but her call went straight to voice mail. "Hello, Tony. This is Roberta Lane. I just got the news about the *quinceañera* party and it's so wonderful. I'd love to chat with you about how that changes your plans. Please call me back as soon as you can."

She ended the call and immediately dialed Sara Kelly. When her phone likewise went straight to voice mail, she left her a similar message.

They were both avoiding her, and she could understand why, but they couldn't do it forever. Especially since she'd be attending the event to do follow-up interviews with everyone and to get more photos for the magazine.

Maybe then she could apologize to them for what she'd done. She hoped that would be enough to allay the guilt that she had been feeling over how the story had gone. Luckily, this new twist had things moving in a positive direction and she intended to showcase that.

Facing her computer, she sat down to write up some nicer, more positive tweets and a short article about the new *quinceañera* celebration that would be happening.

Thankfully, Dolores's kitchen didn't have the feel of a demilitarized zone considering the interactions that he and Sara had had over the last few days. Sara and he had met there to prepare the various dishes for the event so that both the Kelly and Rodriguez families could try them before they finalized the menu. It was also convenient because Dolores had been furiously working on Angelica's gown and it was ready for a first fitting.

Tony could hear the women in the other room, chatting about the dress and the party as he took his *porchetta* roast from the oven.

Beside him Sara was cooking her own pot of white rice as well as *picadillo*, a Cuban staple made with ground beef, onions, peppers, green olives, raisins, and a light tomato sauce.

"That smells great," he said, and his stomach rumbled. *Picadillo* was one of his favorite dishes and he could picture the two of them sitting to eat it together, cooking together in the future the way they were now.

Sara seemed pleased by the praise and said, "Your pork smells heavenly also."

"Thanks. I need to go outside and crank up the grill for the salad."

That drew a little chuckle from her. "Grill and salad are not two things most people put together."

He winked at her. "I'm not most people."

He hurried outside, turned on the gas grill, and in no time, he was back in the kitchen preparing the avocados for cooking.

Sara had her head in the refrigerator, checking on the desserts she had prepared earlier and brought over. "Almost set," she said and returned to stirring the *picadillo*, but then shut the gas beneath the pan.

"Interested in watching me grill?" he said and juggled handfuls of avocados.

"Sure. Let me help," she said and took some of the avocado halves from him.

Once they were outside, Tony popped up the top of the grill and held his hand above the ranges. "Temperature is just right. We're good to go."

He placed his halves on the grill and Sara did the same. They stood there, watching the fruit grill until Sara said, "Roberta Lane called me. I ignored the call. I've also been avoiding her social media."

Tony looked at her from the corner of his eye. "She called me too and I ignored her as well. I'm off social media for now."

Sara met his gaze. "You know she won't give up, right?"

He shrugged and picked up one avocado to check. Still not enough grill marks. "We'll just have to keep things calm and not give her anything to write about."

Sara looked back toward the house. "I haven't told them about our truce, have you?"

Tony shook his head. "No. I want to keep what's happening between us to us, don't you?"

Sara nodded. "I do. We've had enough interference in our relationship."

Tony smiled. "Our relationship. I like the sound of that," he said, reached out and wrapped an arm around her waist to draw her close.

Sara's nose crinkled and she leaned into him. "I like the sound of it too."

"Is it my imagination or do they look happy?" Angelica said as she caught sight of Tony and Sara in the backyard from the window in Dolores's workroom.

Samantha walked to the window and peeked out.

"Are they hugging?"

"They are. We were hoping that having to cook together might make things right between them. Looks like it's working," Angelica said and slipped out of the gown, careful to avoid the pins Dolores had used for fitting the dress.

Samantha made a face. "But are they really cooking *together*? Maybe we shouldn't have made that stupid suggestion that they split the courses as part of the contest."

"Maybe," Angelica said and grabbed hold of the top and jeans Samantha handed her. After she dressed, she said, "We don't have anything for the cocktail hour. What if we ask them to do those together?"

"And what if the dishes they cook for us aren't all that good—or we say they aren't? We can ask them to fix them. Together," Samantha said. "You know, like it's too fatty and not well-balanced. I've watched a ton of those cooking shows. I bet I can fake it."

"Me, too. I love watching cooking shows. Especially the ones where they give you all kinds of weird ingredients."

Samantha made another face. "Like crickets. Who eats crickets!"

Angelica laughed. "Major yuk."

"*Niñas*, your *papis* are here. Come on out when you're ready," Samantha's mom called out from the kitchen.

Angelica and Samantha shared a look. "I'm ready to do this. Are you?"

Samantha laughed and made a slicing motion with her hand. "I think two chefs are going to get chopped tonight!"

"*Chica*, this *picadillo* is delicious," Dolores said and covered her mouth with her hand as she talked around the bite she had taken.

"Wonderful. Better than Sylvia's," Esteban said, earning a playful elbow from his wife.

"I don't know. There's something missing," Samantha said, shocking everyone into silence, especially Sara. She thought she had executed Dolores's family recipe faithfully even if she had added her own little twist with some extra paprika.

"Aren't you making rice, too, *Tio* Tony?" Angelica said and eyed her uncle.

"I am," he said with a nod.

"Isn't that too much of the same thing?" Angelica said while she shoveled another forkful of the *picadillo* into her mouth.

"Sara and I can discuss changing that up," Tony said and glanced at her. But her attention was on the two girls who shared a conspiratorial look.

"We can definitely discuss it," Sara said, wondering what was up with the two teens.

"And think about what's missing! Something...salty," Samantha said, earning a rebuke from Bridget who had joined them for the taste testing.

"*Mija*, Sara made this just like I do, and you've never complained before," her mother chimed in.

"No problem, Dolores. There's always room for improvement," Sara said, unfazed by her niece's comments. If anything, it made her take another taste to see if

Samantha was being accurate in her assessment. *A little more salt was a definite maybe*, she thought.

After they had finished the tasting of the *picadillo*, they moved on to the avocado salad that Tony had prepared. Sara loved the play of the olive oil powder against the avocado, watercress, and balsamic vinegar. But as they had with the appetizer, the girls had "suggestions" about the salad.

"Balsamic isn't very Cuban is it?" Angelica said, but before Samantha could say anything, Tony jumped in with, "No it isn't. Sara and I will work on it."

The *porchetta* faced a similar fate, prompting both sets of parents and Bridget to chastise the girls for being rude.

Sara held her hands up to keep the parents from exacting punishment. "It's okay. Tony and I are open to suggestions. We want everything to be the best it can be for the *quinceañera*. Right, Tony?" And of course, fixing up the recipes meant time with Tony which was a win-win as far as she was concerned. She'd have to thank the girls for their thoughtfulness because she was sure that was what they had intended with their comments. Judging from the way they'd cleaned their plates she didn't think they were *actually* unhappy with the food.

"Of course, Sara. We can work on it this week and hopefully have everything ready for the party next weekend," Tony confirmed and eyed Sara, a friendly glitter in his gaze.

"And you need to think about some hors d'oeuvres for the cocktail hour too," Angelica said.

"Anything else?" Tony asked, arching a brow at his niece who shook her head.

"I think that's everything, *Tio* Tony. I know you and Sara will be able to work everything out together," she said deadpan. *Too deadpan*, Sara thought, confirming to her that the two girls were up to something.

Tony shot her a knowing look, apparently having reached the same conclusion.

"Sara and I will work together to address all your... suggestions," he said calmly.

Sara did a quick assessment of everyone at the table and said, "I assume you trust us to get everything fixed and make the right choices without another tasting session, because time is tight."

"Of course, we do, Sara," Dolores answered and at Matt's glare, Samantha remained quiet. Bridget sat there silently, but the pleased smile on her face said she had seen through the girls' ruse, unlike their seemingly oblivious parents.

Sylvia and Esteban likewise stared Angelica into silence. "We're grateful for anything that you and Tony will prepare for us," Sylvia said.

With a warning smile at the two girls, Sara said, "Then I guess Tony and I have our work cut out for us."

CHAPTER 23

Tony commandeered his parents' kitchen so that he and Sara could address the girls' plethora of suggestions.

Much like Sara, he was of a mind that the two were scheming, probably throwing Sara and him together in the hopes their relationship might be rekindled. He wasn't opposed to making time to work on recipes with her, despite being used to top dog status in his own kitchen, especially since it meant more time with Sara and a chance to move their relationship along.

"*Mijo*, Sarita is here," his mother called out in a too pleasant singsong. His mother would like nothing better than for him to be involved with a woman who might bring him home to Miami permanently. She'd apparently be even more pleased if that woman was Sara.

"Sara, *mami*," he corrected, knowing the childish endearment no longer applied. There was nothing little about Sara anymore.

Sara stepped into the room and his spirit lightened. Her outfit wasn't fancy, just serviceable jeans and a pale pink T-shirt, likely in deference to the heat that was bound to build in the kitchen. To him, she looked perfect..

"Thank you for coming," he said and glared at his mother as she stood there, waiting expectantly. "*Mami*," he warned and with a face wreathed with indignity and a flip of her hand, she left the kitchen.

Sara barely contained a laugh and humor glittered in her gaze. "She's just being...a mom."

"I don't remember your mom being such a busybody," he said, grabbing two clean aprons from a drawer and handing one to Sara.

"My mother put the mother in smother," she said with a grin and unfurled the apron.

He did the same and they stood there staring at them for a second before breaking out into laughter. The aprons bore the images of television icons Lucy and Desi with two of their more memorable quotes.

Sara hugged the Lucy one to her body and said, "Eeeewwwww."

"Lucy, you got some 'splainin' to do!" Tony said in an exaggerated Cuban accent and slipped on his own apron.

Sara smiled and as she put on her apron, she said, "And we've got some cooking to do according to the girls."

Tony huffed indignantly and wagged his head. "Seriously? You do know it was all a ploy to get us working together, right?"

Sara laughed and nodded. "Definitely, but they were right about the rice."

Tony couldn't argue with that logic. It was one of the things he liked about Sara: her honesty and straightforwardness. "I could change it up for the entrée."

Sara held up her hand. "Actually, I had an idea based on something new I tried out at *Munch* – a *toston* choriburger."

"Let me guess," Tony began while taking assorted pots and pans from his mother's cabinets so they could get to work. "It's a slider made with *chorizo*?"

Sara shook her head and took one of the larger pans from him to help. "Not just *chorizo*, but a mix of ground beef and dried *chorizo* served on two *tostones* instead of bread. I was thinking I could serve the *picadillo* over Cuban bread toast and we could do choriburger sliders as one of the hors d'oeuvres during the cocktail hour."

Tony paused in his digging through the cabinets and pondered her suggestion. "I like that idea. I was also thinking about Samantha's comment about the *picadillo* needing more salt. I know what I'm going to suggest isn't traditional –"

"Nothing about these *quinceañeras* is traditional," Sara said with a wrinkle of her nose.

Tony chuckled and ran a finger across the crinkle to smooth the creamy skin there. After, he cradled her cheek, needing the contact with her. He'd missed it so much. "True. How about adding some capers? It'll juice up the briny flavor and give it some pop."

Sara nodded, shrugged, and cupped his hand as it rested on her face. "I'm game. I was thinking maybe a citrusy vinaigrette at the base of your avocado salad instead of the balsamic. Maybe even grilling the lemons for the dressing to give it that smokiness to match the char on the avocados."

Tony smiled and nodded. "I like that idea a lot. Let's give it a try." He was enjoying brainstorming with her. It was a welcome surprise given how he was used to being the one calling the shots. Sara had a quick and inventive mind and so far, her instincts had been on the money. He suspected that together they were going to make a meal that would be much better than the one they had originally planned.

In just a few minutes they were both busy chopping and working on their two dishes, implementing the changes they'd discussed. Once they were done, they made plates to take out to Tony's parents in the living room. When they sat down to try the new dishes, they found that the tweaks they'd done had totally lifted the dishes to a new level.

"This *picadillo* is da bomb," Tony said as he ate a big forkful. "I hope you don't mind if I add it to my menu."

With a cheeky grin, Sara held her hand out to say sure. "As long as I can steal this avocado salad. I love the mix of flavors. Fruity, smoky, sharp. Perfect."

"We've got two winners, three if you include the choriburger sliders." More if they include the way things seemed to be improving between them.

"Four because you have to do your famous Cuban sandwich. Mind sharing what the secret is?" she said as she swirled her last cube of grilled avocado around in the vinaigrette.

"Sure, but you have to swear to keep it secret," he teased.

His mother came into the kitchen not a minute later with their empty plates. As Tony held up one of the nearly licked clean plates for Sara to see, he said, "I guess we do have some winners."

"Everything was *delicioso, Mijo*. Sarita," she said with a wink at Sara before leaving the room.

"Busybody," Tony said under his breath and returned to the table to chat about the entrée.

"Did you like the *porchetta*?" he asked, truly interested in what Sara's experienced palate thought of the dish. It was nice to have a chef with whom he could chat so comfortably. Not like his ex who had always been trying to outdo him. Even despite the competition they'd been forced into, he had sensed that cooking with Sara would be totally different and he hadn't been wrong. It had been fun and inspiring today.

"I really liked it, but when I was working with Dolores, she shared an old family secret from her dad that you'll have to keep secret as well. He put grapefruit juice in with the other citrus. You wouldn't think it, but it really made a difference in the sweet-sour of the marinade," she explained and mimicked juicing the fruits with her long, elegant fingers.

He couldn't resist reaching out to take hold of her hands and was grateful when she didn't pull away. He playfully swung her hands and said, "I'm game, but we'll have to let the pork marinate overnight."

With obvious reluctance and a gentle squeeze of his hands, Sara glanced at the clock on the wall. "I can stay and help with the marinade, but then I've got to get back to the restaurant for the dinner service. I'm sorry."

"No problem. Can you come back tomorrow so we can work on the menu some more?" he asked, eager to spend more time with her.

Sara grinned and then dipped her head. "I'll talk to Jeri. She's been great about this, but I have to make sure she doesn't have to do anything with Sophie."

"If she does, maybe Rick can help out again," he suggested. Maybe this would be what it took for Rick and Jeri to finally take the next step.

Sara laughed. "I guess you noticed Jeri has a thing for Rick."

Tony barely contained his laughter. "Actually, I noticed Rick has a thing for Jeri. And he cares about her little girl as well. Anyway, whatever you need, Sara. I truly mean that. I really liked working with you today."

Sara hesitated, making him worry that he'd pushed too fast, but then she nodded and said, "I liked it too. A lot. I'm glad we got to do this, and I'd love to do it again. Schedule permitting."

Inside of him something broke free that he hadn't even known was imprisoned. "I hope you can make it work."

"I hope so too," she said and surprised him by brushing a quick kiss across his cheek before dashing out of the kitchen.

He stood there, smiling, as she walked out the door. Reaching up, he ran a hand across the spot where she had kissed him, imagining that the warmth of her lips lingered there. Recalling how nice it had been and thinking about how he'd like for it to happen again. *A lot*, he thought with a chuckle.

His mother walked in then, a smile on her face that brightened as it landed on him. "*Mijo*, it looks like you had a nice time."

Since it would be impossible to deny it, he swept his mother into a big bear hug. "I had a fabulous time, *mami*." He knew the words would give his mother hope that his relationship with Sara would become more, but since he was feeling the same way, he let her and himself believe.

Angelica squirmed on the platform as Dolores finished pinning an adjustment on the hem.

"*Niña, por favor. ¡Quietate!*" Dolores said around the pins in her mouth.

"Maybe she can't hold still because she's got a guilty

conscience," Angelica's mom said and walked around, examining the dress.

Dolores peered up at Angelica and past her to Samantha, who was perched on a stool by her worktable. Pulling the pins from her mouth, she said, "I'm surprised Samantha can be so calm after the *mentiras* she told."

Both girls immediately protested, their cries vehement.

"I'm not feeling guilty."

"I didn't lie about anything."

Her mother pointed a finger in Angelica's face. "First of all, you're Cuban, which means you can never have too much rice."

"Amen," Dolores said and resumed tacking the hem and checking its length.

"And you," her mother said, rounding on a still-seated Samantha. "Tony is an award-winning chef and you challenged him on his dish."

"But balsamic is *so* not Cuban," Samantha almost whined.

With a shrug, her mother said, "Okay, I have to give you that."

"We weren't doing it to be mean. And anyway, carbs are evil," Angelica said in defense of their actions.

"Carbs are totally evil," Samantha offered in agreement. She shared a look with Angelica and said, "We did it so Aunt Sara and Tony would have to work together."

"We thought that it might help them get together again the way they were before this while crazy competition got started," Angelica said and looked down, shamefaced.

Dolores rose slowly, slipped the pins from between her lips, and stuck them into a pincushion strapped to her wrist. Her mother walked around to stand beside Dolores and crossed her arms as both women stared at them.

Samantha slipped from the stool to stand beside Angelica, clearly intending to have her back for whatever additional scolding was coming their way.

"Your *abuelita* says that Tony and Sara made some excellent food for them yesterday. Your comments seem to have inspired them," her mother said.

"And?" Angelica said, sensing there was more to the story.

Dolores and her mother shared a look. "Your *abuelita* also said that by the time they finished they were laughing and joking and your *Tío* Tony was very happy," her mother said.

Dolores clapped her hands and with utter glee said, "Do you know what that means?"

Angelica frowned, not sure what to say except the obvious. "That *mi abuelita* is a terrible *chismosa*?"

Her mother, Dolores, and Samantha all burst out guffawing. Wiping away tears of laughter, her mother said, "She truly is a gossip."

"And you girls were truly... I want to say devious, but I can't because there was some truth to what you said," Dolores added.

Samantha piped up with, "How about inspired? We really wanted to make things right with Aunt Sara and Tony."

"Totally inspired," Angelica agreed.

The two moms exchanged a quick look and then shook their heads.

Her mother said, "I guess if it works –"

"*When* it works," Angelica insisted and hopped off the platform.

Her mom walked over and linked her arm around Angelica's. "When it works, we'll hopefully see more of *Tío* Tony."

"*Tío* Tony and Aunt Sara, together—like, in a couple together," Samantha said and walked to stand beside her mom.

"And who knows, maybe new little—" Dolores began, but Sylvia shot up her hand to keep her from continuing.

"Don't press your luck, *amiga*. For now, let's just hope this little plan our daughters cooked up works."

CHAPTER 24

Tony popped the piece of crispy pork belly skin into Sara's mouth and she chuckled as she ate the *chicharrón*. The creamy heaviness of the fat was a wonderful foil to the crunchiness of the skin. "People will love this."

"Thank you," Tony said as he sat across from her, sampling the *porchetta* as well. It was so easy to sit with him. Work with him. The time together had been filled with laughter and smiles.

She stabbed a piece of the interior pork. The fresh flavor of citrus was chased by the earthiness of herbs and a hint of warmth. "They'll love this even more."

Tony nodded, picked up a piece, and ate it. After he swallowed, he said, "I can taste that hint of grapefruit. It makes a subtle and really positive difference in the marinade."

"Thank Dolores for that family secret." Sara quickly speared another piece, enjoying the entrée, but as she ate something else came to mind. With a surprised huff, she pointed to the pork with her fork and said, "This herb rub is your Cuban sandwich secret isn't it?"

Tony grinned and that smile warmed her. "That's the

secret *you* have to keep," he teased, dragging another chuckle from her. "Yes, I rub the pork when I roast it and then put a little bit of the rub directly on the pork when it goes into the sandwich."

"That explains the brightness of the flavor. We're going to do Cuban sandwiches for the hors d'oeuvres, right?" she asked.

"If you're okay with it," he said and she was glad that he was so agreeable. That things between them were progressing nicely. Maybe they were even back to where they had been before Roberta and all her nastiness.

"Totally okay with it. We can make them into smaller bites, like finger sandwiches. And Dolores makes these tasty deviled ham sandwiches, too."

"Maybe the two of us can come up with our own version?" he asked, his tone inviting.

She would have loved to keep on cooking all day with him, but unfortunately, she couldn't. "I'd love to, but I'm also out of time for today," she said regretfully.

Tony did a quick look at his watch. "Me too. I promised my manager I'd call him at two to discuss how things were going at the restaurant."

She sensed worry in his voice. "Is everything okay?"

With a shrug and a huff, Tony said, "Apparently everything is going just fine."

A big blow to his ego, finding out he's not indispensable, she imagined, and she tried to soothe it. "It wouldn't be that way if you hadn't trained them so well. You should be proud of the job you did and enjoy the freedom that gives you."

She regretted adding the last little bit, imagining what he would infer from it.

"Thank you. I appreciate that. As for the freedom... I guess that's one way to look at it. I've enjoyed being in

Miami with family and friends. You. I'd love to spend more time with you," he said, gazing at her in that way she'd wanted from him since she was a teenager. It felt amazing to be seen like that by him.

"I've enjoyed sharing time with you as well, Tony. It would be nice to spend more time with you," she admitted, but then quickly changed the topic. "What if we do *yuca* fries with some kind of dip?"

With a disappointed shake of his head, probably at her redirection of the discussion, he said, "I like that idea. Maybe we can try those and the deviled ham sandwiches tomorrow?" he asked, his tone hopeful.

"Sounds like a plan." Why was her throat tight? She'd always known he wouldn't stay in Miami.

He stood and held out his hand for her to take. "That's wonderful, Sara."

She slipped her hand into his. He squeezed it gently and took a step toward her. Brushed away one of her bangs that had slipped forward into her eyes. "I'm sorry again for all that's happened."

His gaze was so intense, so warm and inviting, like the welcome of the Miami sun, that she had to look away.

"There's no need to apologize, Tony. We just got caught up in things," she said and forced herself to look back up at him.

When she did, she realized he was closer. Almost too close.

He stepped back, jammed his hands into his jeans pockets, and rocked back on his heels. "I'll walk you to the door."

She laughed and shook her head. "I think I can manage to find my way there. Besides, you should probably clean up the mess we made before your mom gets mad."

Tony glanced back at the relatively clean counter and sink. As professional chefs, keeping things neat and organized was part of who they were. Still he teased, "You're an evil woman to leave me the pots and pans."

"Remember that," she said with quick tap of her index finger on his lips, and before he could say or do anything else, she hurried from the room.

After she said goodbye to his parents and walked out the door, she hugged her arms around herself to keep from doing a happy dance. She had to stay positive but also not read too much into what had just happened. She needed to take it one day at a time because only time would tell whether there was a future for her and Tony here in Miami.

Roberta Lane surfed from one social media account to another, checking the data to see how her postings were going. Although they were doing relatively well, none were performing as strongly as her original write-ups about the competition between the two chefs.

She checked her notes, found the number she wanted, and picked up the phone. She dialed and waited patiently until Dolores Kelly answered.

"Good afternoon, Dolores. It's Roberta Lane."

An awkward pause followed. "Good afternoon. How can I help you today?"

"We had wanted to get some photos of the girls in their dresses for the article. I understand you're making both. It must be very exciting for you," Roberta said.

"It is. I hate to rush you, but I'm at the salon and

really need to get back to work," she said and in the background, Roberta heard the sounds of activity.

"So sorry. What time is good for me to come over and get photos?" she pressed, needing to write the kind of feel-good story she hoped would make up for her earlier actions.

There was another hesitation before Dolores finally said, "Tonight. I'm doing the final fittings for the girls."

"Wonderful. How is seven? Should we meet at your salon?" she asked.

"At my home workshop. I'll text you the address," Dolores said.

A few seconds later her phone chirped to confirm she'd gotten a text. She checked the message and smiled. Dolores's address was in a middle-class suburb of Miami. Not anything like the area where she was sure the wealthy Rodriguez family lived. Not to mention that Samantha had let it slip that she was at the fancy prep school on a scholarship.

Despite what Marco wants, their differences and similarities are things I can highlight in my article in a positive way, she thought and called her photographer to schedule him for the shoot.

"You all understand the plan, right?" Sylvia said, briefing Angelica, Samantha and her mother the way Samantha imagined the sharp lawyer would counsel one of her clients before important negotiations.

"No matter what she says, smile and stay positive," Angelica repeated as her mother peered at her.

Sylvia turned her attention to Dolores, who said, "And be sure to mention the shop for some free publicity."

"But not too much. Remember we're looking to help you get your own place," Angelica's mom said.

She finally focused on Samantha, making her feel even more nervous than she had been before. "Don't let her get under our skin," Samantha repeated.

"She *did* say she was sorry. Maybe she really means it," her mother added, clearly wanting to believe the best in everyone.

"We'll see. If there's trouble brewing, trust me to jump in and steer it back to neutral ground," Sylvia said just as a knock came at the front door.

"Places everyone," her mother said like a movie director preparing for filming.

Angelica hopped up onto the platform for the fitting, Dolores grabbed her pincushion and kneeled in front of her, and Samantha leaned against the edge of her mother's desk, not wanting to wrinkle the fabric of her *quinceañera* dress. From her perch she had a perfect view of everything going on in the foyer right off her mother's studio.

With a satisfied nod, Sylvia stepped into the foyer, but her father had already opened the door for the reporter and her photographer. "Welcome," her father said, but there was little warmth in his voice.

"Thank you," Roberta said. "You have a lovely home, Mr. Kelly."

"Thank you," he said and walked away when Sylvia approached.

"Right this way, Roberta. The girls are so excited about you seeing their dresses," Sylvia said.

Roberta paused at the entrance to Dolores's workshop. "Is this where you normally work?" the reporter said.

Her mother's head jerked up at the statement, as if waiting for nastiness from Roberta, but Sylvia quickly deflected any attack. "Dolores has a wonderful workshop here. It's the perfect place for the final fittings."

"Instead of the salon where she works as a seamstress?" Roberta asked.

Without looking up, her attention focused on the hem of Angelica's gown, her mother said, "Angelica is my private client. But I also do some amazing work at my salon."

Way to go, mom, Samantha thought.

"The dress is lovely," Roberta said and looked from Angelica to her. "They're both so very different. One is elegant and the other...well, more playful."

Samantha didn't know what to make of that statement, so she straightened and smoothed down the fabric of her dress. She remembered what Angelica's mother had said. *Stay positive* and that's exactly what she was going to do.

"Playful is good and I think Angelica looks so elegant in her dress," she said.

Her friend peered over her shoulder as Samantha's mom continued checking the hem on the dress. "And you look like a princess. I wish I could wear something with more frills, but I'd get swallowed up in them."

They had been right to keep things simpler on Angelica's petite frame, but thanks to her height and curves, Samantha was able to carry more lace and layers to her dress.

"Samantha is definitely curvier, but you both look wonderful. Really wonderful," Roberta said, surprising them with her compliments.

"Wilson, can you please slip inside and start shooting some photos. We'll probably want one of the girls standing together as well. Maybe out in the backyard?"

The reporter moved aside to let the photographer pass into the room, and he snapped off several photos while Dolores finished with Angelica's fitting. Her mother stood and stretched her back out after being hunched over for so long.

"Your turn, *chiquitica*," her mother said.

Angelica hopped off and exchanged places with Samantha, but there was little to do on her dress as her mother had already given it a last look just days earlier. Despite that, her mother flitted around her, checking seams and fit. The snap, snap, snap of the camera shutter chased her around the room.

"You look lovely, Samantha. The two of you will light up the room on Saturday," Sylvia said.

"Two girls and one *quinceañera*. That is a rather unusual situation, don't you think?" Roberta said, obviously wondering how the two girls had decided to join the events.

Sylvia didn't hesitate to answer. "We owe it all to our amazing young ladies. When they first heard about the fire and that Samantha's party might be delayed for several months, they decided that it would be wonderful to combine the two events. Especially since by doing so they were able to donate a portion of the earmarked funds to Bridget Kelly's wonderful non-profit."

Apparently sensing an opportunity for additional information, Roberta said, "That's the same organization that provides Sara with her staff, right? The staff that's going to be working beside Chef Tony's team?"

Dolores set the reporter straight. "That's *Chef* Sara, Roberta. And from what I understand, both chefs are very excited about combining their talents and staffs for this event."

Roberta smiled. "They didn't look happy the last

time I saw them so I'm glad that things are working out for them."

Her statement brought about a stunned silence. None of them seemed really able to believe the sudden change of heart. Sensing that, Roberta said, "I truly mean it. I'm sorry about everything, but my editor was pushing me in a particular direction and I had no choice."

Her apology wasn't enough for her mother who said, "It's getting late, Roberta. I'm sure you understand that the girls have to get up early for school tomorrow so if you wouldn't mind, maybe you can get those other photos in the backyard so we can wrap this up," With a sweep of her arm, Dolores guided them out of her workshop, back into the foyer and a hall that ran into the open concept kitchen and living room. At the far side of the room were French doors that led to a paved patio and beyond that, lush gardens and an immense brick barbeque. Both were her father's pride and joy, besides her of course. When he wasn't at work, he was in the backyard tending to his plants or grilling some steaks he'd brought home.

"Very nice. Your landscaper does a wonderful job," Roberta said.

Forgetful of the rules not to volunteer any information that hadn't been asked for, and proud of her father's accomplishment, Samantha said, "My father does all the work in the garden."

"It's lovely. He should be proud," she said and motioned to her photographer.

"Let's take the photos so these young ladies don't look too tired for their *quinceañera* in a few days, Wilson."

The photographer jumped into action, circling the two girls to snap off a flurry of pictures. As he walked away, Samantha could have sworn she heard him say,

"You did great, ladies."

Her father had come to the French doors to watch and he led the way for Roberta and the photographer while the four of them hung back. As the front door opened and closed, Angelica threw one hand up in the air and said, "That deserves a high five!"

It deserved way more than that, Samantha thought, but joined in as they celebrated surviving the reporter and a change of heart she wasn't sure they could trust.

CHAPTER 25

WORKING WITH TONY IN HIS parents' kitchen, the two of them alone, had been way too intimate and at the end, way too tempting. When Tony called to set up their next—and last— meeting before the *quinceañera* parties, she hesitated, so conflicted about where it all might end.

"I'm really busy today," she said, almost tempted to totally bail on him. "Almost" being the operative word as she blurted out, "Maybe you can come over to *Munch* this morning."

"Sure. I can be there in half an hour," he said, but she detected a note of disappointment in his voice.

"Great. See you then," she replied, relieved.

At *Munch* she'd have Jeri and the rest of her staff around them as they worked which would hopefully avoid a repeat of that almost-kiss yesterday.

"Chicken," Jeri whispered into her ear as she passed by on her way to one of the line chefs.

Sara ignored her and returned to finely mincing the toasted coconut for the flan trio she wanted to make for the girls' party. When she was done with two of the three different flavored flans, she strolled through the kitchen to see how the line chefs and other staff were doing with the preparations for the lunch service. There was something about seeing her women at work that was a balm to her soul. It made her feel that she was accomplishing something much more important than crafting a tasty dish or running a successful business. She was changing lives.

Bolstered by that, she returned to her station to wait for Tony. *Tony*, she thought, smiling as she thought about the last few days together and how wonderful they'd been. How nice it might be if they could do that on a regular basis.

She was about to get started on another dish when she heard a knock. *Tony*.

Before she could get to the door, Jeri was there, opening it for him. As he entered, she said something to him that made him pause and look her way. With a nod, he forced a smile at Jeri and walked toward the kitchen. Once he was inside, he went straight to her and stood before her, almost uncertain, much like she was.

She decided to take the bull by the horns and grabbed hold of his hands, swinging them playfully. "Ready to get to work?"

He smiled, a broad bright grin, and breathed a sigh of relief. "Ready, willing, and able. We're doing dessert today and the rest of the hors d'oeuvres, right?"

Sara nodded and gestured to the banana flan custard she already had on the side, ready to be added to ramekins. If only she could get the caramel right.

"I planned on a trio of flans, but the third one is giving me problems." She quickly explained her issue and he listened intently, hands on his hips. He tilted his head her way, but downward, as if to better absorb what she was saying. There was nothing condemning in his stance, only concern for her and what she was trying to accomplish. She liked that and admired the way he respected her process. He was a chef with a one-star restaurant after all.

When she finished, he dipped his head and said, "I get it. The strawberries have too much water for the caramel and freeze-dried ones can be too tart."

He looked up, thinking about her problem. "What if you did a strawberry jelly?"

She considered his suggestion and it made sense. Plus, it would add visual diversity to the dish. "I like that idea. Let's try it out," she said and together they made the jelly, got it into the blast chiller, and cut out ramekin-sized rounds to place over the custard once it was out of the oven and cooled.

Once they were done, she realized that she'd been less than an ideal hostess when he'd first walked in. "I'm sorry. I put you to work right away and didn't ask if you wanted a coffee or anything."

He smiled and skimmed his hand down her arm. "That's okay, I was happy to dive right in. But now that you mention it, a *café con leche* would be great. Maybe while we chat about the rest of the dishes for the cocktail hour?"

She nodded and stepped away from him, that intimacy growing once more even though they were in a kitchen filled with people. She realized the connection she had with him had nothing to do with proximity or privacy. It was just that Tony made her feel that way. Made her want more than just time in the kitchen with him. He made her want a life filled with laughter. A life where his smile did funny things to her heart and his touch warmed her. She wanted more.

"Let me get you that coffee, plus a paper and pen," she said and hurried away to give herself some breathing room.

She rushed to her office to grab a pad of paper and a pen and then dashed back to the coffee station in the kitchen. They always had a fresh pot brewing for the workers and customers. One of the Cuban workers had also put up a pot of milk and heated it. She mixed the hot milk and coffee, adding a few spoons of sugar, and took it to her station where he patiently waited.

After he took a sip, he sighed and said, "Love it."

"Great. So, let's make a list of what we have," she said and quickly jotted down the four courses and hors d'oeuvres they'd already planned on. Which reminded her that they'd yet to work on the deviled ham for the sandwiches.

Once the list was complete, she said, "Both sets of grandparents are from northern Spain, so how about some *gambas a la plancha*."

"I like that idea. Maybe manchego with a thin slice of dried chorizo and topped with a thin slice of *membrillo*?" Tony said, caught up in her enthusiasm, but then he paused. "Is that too much chorizo? I have it in my beans and you have it in the burger."

"Can you ever have too much chorizo or rice?" Sara said since both were favorites of hers.

Tony shook his head and joined in her laughter. "Never. You know we haven't included *ropa vieja* and that's a Cuban staple also."

It was and the shredded beef in tomato sauce was one of her favorites. "We haven't done a *tamale* either and I love those."

"I do, too. So what if we—"

"Stuff the tamale with the *ropa vieja*," they said at

the same time.

Like water streaming across rapids, the ideas came fast and furious until they had to actually pare back the number of choices for the cocktail hour. But as Tony went to cross off the deviled ham sandwiches, Sara laid a hand on his to stop him.

A jolt like electricity made them both jump. Sara lost her concentration for that brief second, but quickly recovered. "We can't lose the deviled ham sandwiches. It's comfort food, isn't it?"

Tony nodded and immediately agreed. "You're right. They were at every occasion in my house. Let's get to work on it. I mean, if you want to, that is."

She gave him points for asking instead of commanding. "I'd like that. I actually baked a ham yesterday for us to use," she said and walked away to get the ham from the fridge.

When she returned to the station Tony had set up the attachment on her stand mixer so they could grind the ham. As she set the ham on a chopping board at her station, she said, "I did a guava glaze on it because the deviled ham spread always had a sweet-spicy flavor to me."

"Probably the catsup a lot of Cubans mix in," he said. "Want me to chop?"

"Please. I'm going to get some of the other ingredients," she said and went back to the fridge for the mayonnaise and cream cheese. Cornichons for a relish, fresh lemons, and parsley.

Tony had chopped and ground the ham until it resembled a slightly rough meal. He was checking the grind, passing it through his fingers to check the consistency. As she came over, he said, "What do you think?"

She examined the ground ham. "I like that coarser

texture. There's no way anyone would think it came out of a can."

"Especially when we get done with it. Good choice on the cornichons. Their tart and sweet will really work with this spread."

She nodded and started rolling lemons to break up the juice segments "Thanks. I thought so."

Tony grabbed the parsley and chopped. "I don't see any heat here. Did you have any thoughts on that?"

Sara shook her head. "I'm torn between hot sauce and chilis. Or maybe hot mustard?"

Tony made a face at the latter. "Not a mustard fan. Pickles either."

It surprised her since they were keys ingredient in Cuban sandwiches, until it hit her. "That's why you don't use them in your sandwiches. Only the marinade."

He smiled and laughed. "You're quick, Sara. Yes, that's why I only use the marinade."

She threw her head back and joined him in the laughter, enjoying how easy it was to work and laugh with him. But then she got back to work, squeezing the lemons into a measuring cup so they could do the final touch to the spread with the lemon juice when appropriate. As she worked, she said, "What about grilling some chiles? It would add that smoky flavor to the spread."

"I like that idea," he said and tossed the minced parsley into the mixing bowl. "Do you have cream?"

"I do. Why?" she asked and grabbed the cornichons to start chopping them.

"I use a little cream to soften the cheese and less mayo. Not a fan of a heavy mayo taste," he said.

She peered at him from the corner of her eye. "You've got a lot of things you dislike, don't you?"

His gaze locked with hers. "What I like is way more

important. I like the way we can work together. I like you, Sara," he said, then reached out and stopped her chopping before she could lose a finger.

"I like this too, Tony. A lot. Maybe more than a lot, but I'm here and you're going back to New York, right?"

With a shrug, Tony looked away and shook his head. "I have to go back, Sara. If only to make sure things are okay so I can decide what to do next."

"Do you mean that, Tony? Do you really think that you might decide to come back to Miami if things are okay in New York?"

He faced her and shrugged his broad shoulders. "I never pictured myself as an executive chef, running things from afar, but you make me want to think about that. About us," he said, sincerity in his voice. His brown-eyed gaze was intense as it settled more intimately on her.

"I've been thinking about us as well, Tony. I love working with you. Being with you. I think I'm falling for you, but I'm not sure I could handle a long-distance relationship," she said in a rush of words, afraid that if she stopped, she'd bottle up all that she was feeling. It was long past time that he know. That she admitted what had been growing in her heart over the last few weeks.

Tony stepped close and wrapped her in a tight embrace. He lowered his head to hers and whispered, "I think I'm falling for you too, Sara. I never expected this when I came to Miami. Never thought it would be with you, someone I've known all my life and yet, someone new and exciting and so so special."

She savored his nearness, aware of how special it was considering he would soon be leaving. Fighting tears, she said, "We'll just have to find a way to work things out, just like we did with all the recipes."

"We will. We're good together that way," he said and

with a final reassuring squeeze, stepped away since they had things to finish for the *quinceañera* in a few days.

"Where is the cream?" he asked.

"In the fridge," she said, hiding the tear that slipped down her cheek. She hated the thought of him leaving. But now she knew that it might not be forever because he loved her and she loved him.

"You're going to get burned," Jeri said while she walked by with a tray of slider buns.

"Shut up, Jeri," she warned and as Tony approached with the cream, she left her station to get some hot peppers.

By the time she returned Tony was blending the ham and his mix. He waited until she had grilled, chopped, and added the skinned and seeded chiles. Spilled in some of the lemon juice while Tony mixed again. Grabbing a spoon, he offered her a taste.

"Delicious. You try it," she said. When he did, he nodded and said, "We've got a winner here."

"We do." The 'we' being an operative part of the sentence, she realized. The rivalry stoked by the South Beach Style reporter had vanished over the last few days, replaced by a common desire to do the best they both could do.

Together. Just like they'd said the other day. Tiny steps to together.

For themselves and for the girls.

She turned to him, feeling that connection again, but suddenly Jeri was there, standing between them. Her face inquisitive and protective at the same time as she focused on Tony. Without glancing away from him, almost accusingly, Jeri waggled the wireless phone in Sara's face.

"Matt wants to confirm the final numbers with you,"

she said.

Sara held up her finger to Tony. "Give me a minute. I'll tell him to add brisket for the *ropa vieja,* more chorizo, and the ham."

She hurried to her office to get the numbers, rattled them off to Matt and augmented the order with what they'd need for the additional hors d'oeuvres. But when she returned to her station Tony was gone and Jeri was there, cleaning up the area.

Sara stopped short, shocked. "He left?"

Jeri shrugged, but avoided meeting Sara's gaze. "Jeri, what did you do?"

Her friend stayed in avoidance mode, giving undue attention to wiping down the stainless-steel counter.

"Jeri," Sara insisted.

Jeri tossed down the towel, jammed her arms across her chest, and lifted her chin in defiance. "I suggested that it was best that he leaves before you got back."

Sara shook her head. "Why, Jeri? Why would you do something like that?"

Jeri's stance didn't waver. "He's got you all twisted up, Sara. I don't want you to get hurt again."

Sara took a step back, turned away, and then marched back up to her partner. "Like you're any expert on romance? You've had your Prince Charming right under your nose for years –"

"Who? Rick?" Jeri challenged.

"Yes, of course, Rick. Don't be so dense."

Jeri blew out a harsh laugh, but then the surprising sheen of tears filled her gaze. "I know he's your brother and you love him, but Rick is never serious about anything."

She could see her friend's genuine upset, which tempered Sara's anger over what Jeri had done. After all, she understood why Jeri would see any man coming near her *or* Sara as a potential threat—to their happiness if not their safety.

Jeri's ex had been abusive and untrustworthy. Jeri hadn't deserved the way she'd been misused and abandoned. That experience had scarred her, but her reaction to it had been to withdraw from the chance of ever getting hurt again. Sara wished for more for her friend. That Jeri could learn to trust and love again. Sara reached out and hugged her, trying to soothe her. "If you gave him a chance, he'd be serious about you *and* Sophie."

With sniffle, Jeri mumbled, "He was really good with her when he babysat the past few days. Maybe I can think about it."

Sara tightened her embrace to comfort her and said, "Maybe is a good start."

CHAPTER 26

ROBERTA WAS AT HER DESK, working on the *quinceañera* article and giving it the "feel good" spin that would inspire others. It wouldn't be the first time that she'd done that kind of story, having covered multiple charity events and galas over the years. In truth, they were her favorite kinds of lifestyle stories and she preferred them over Marco's preferred lineup of articles filled with drama and conflict.

Having had this story with lots of juicy trouble turn into one with sweet human interest made her feel less guilty about what had happened earlier with the chefs. She hoped that she could somehow make it up to them with a wonderful piece about the event.

She tucked her keyboard drawer back under her desk just as her editor walked in, coffee cup in hand. Breadcrumbs, a remnant of his daily toasted Cuban bread, dusted the front of his shirt which stretched tightly against a growing belly. Probably because of all the carbs he ate.

She faked a smile and said, "Good morning, Marco. What can I do for you today?"

"I know you're working on the *quinceañera* story and I have some news to share with you."

His voice held a tone she didn't like, but she didn't let on that she was worried. She leaned back in her chair, adopting a casual pose. "I'm all ears, Marco."

He nodded, took a sip of his coffee, and then grasped the mug tightly with both hands, as if to steady himself. "Your recent write-ups caught the attention of one of the editors at a national channel. They want to do a short segment about the *quinceañera*."

She held a hand to her chest. "But *I* have an exclusive on the story."

"The *magazine* has an exclusive, Roberta." One eyebrow shot up as if to dare her to disagree.

"What does that mean, Marco? Am I not writing the story? And if I am, what's the sense of doing it after the national segment airs?" She'd been looking forward to how her article would highlight the girls' *quinceañera* as well as the two chefs, but she had also been looking forward to the attention it would bring to her.

"The magazine will be out after the national and hopefully we'll see more hits to the website and sales. Do you have an issue with that?" His second eyebrow joined the first, daring her to defy him.

She wanted to. Oh, how she wanted to blow him off and tell him to write the article himself, but she bit her tongue and dipped her head to acknowledge his request. Once he was out the door, she drew out her keyboard drawer, opened a document, and did the only thing she could after his instructions.

She wrote the kind of story that would set things right and give people hope. That would highlight friendship, family, and maybe a bit of romance as well. When she was done with that, she did the only other thing she could do.

She updated her resumé.

Tony was in the kitchen, his cooking journals laid out across the surface of the table. He'd set them aside in the last week while dealing with the last-minute rush for tomorrow's *quinceañera* celebration, but he'd been itching to get back to selecting recipes for a possible cookbook. With a short break before the madness that would start later that night, going through his journals would serve a dual purpose. It would help him relax and it would also keep his mind off Sara. He was happy with how they were once again talking and laughing. Happy that she'd said she loved him.

But he couldn't avoid the ticking time bomb staring him in the face, namely that once the *quinceañera* party was over, he was going back to New York. The Big Apple. The place where if you could make it there, you could make it anywhere. He'd made it there. Big. And yet now, it didn't bring him the kind of joy that working beside Sara did. Staying in Miami, however, was complicated.

Too complicated? he asked himself. Could he leave what he'd built in the hands of his staff in order to start over in Miami? It was a difficult question and one he had no answer to yet. But whether he came home or not, one thing he intended to do was work on the cookbook that had been on his mind for way too long.

Flipping open one of his earliest journals, he skimmed the pages and flagged some more recipes that would be good for the book with a little updating.

Tension left his body with each page that he turned and recipe he identified. He was about half-way done with the current journal when a commotion in the living room shattered his peace. Especially when he heard the creak of his father's recliner, warning that his old man had moved from his throne. That didn't happen all that often.

"*Mijo*," he heard his mother shout out followed by an almost bellowed, "*Mami. Papi.*"

Javi, he thought and rushed out of the kitchen. Sylvia and he had not given up hope that their brother was coming home for the party even though they hadn't gotten a firm commitment of any travel schedule from him despite various phone calls and texts with him in the last few days.

Sure enough, his older brother was trapped between his mother and father in an awkward embrace. As Javi saw him, he lifted his shoulders and smiled. "Tony, *por favor. Ayudame*," he teased in a mock plea for help.

There was no denying the joy on his parents' faces and the happiness on Javi's, although his brother looked tired. Dark circles like smudges of charcoal sat heavily beneath his eyes. Deep lines bracketed the edges of his mouth and fanned out from beside his grey eyes. The hair at his temples had silvered, making him appear way older than his thirty-five years.

Tony walked over; hands tucked into his pants pockets. "Sorry, *hermano*, but you deserve being trapped for keeping us guessing about when you planned on getting here."

Javi peered heavenward, as if seeking divine intervention, but their mother finally released her death grip on him and shooed her husband back to his recliner. "Javier, *Mijo*, why didn't you let us know you were coming?"

their mother admonished, and their father grunted his agreement and dissatisfaction with their middle child.

"Yes, *mano*. Sylvia and I only called you about what? A dozen times in the last week?" Tony kidded.

Javi shook his head in frustration and wrapped a muscular arm around his mother's broad waist. "It was more like a hundred phone calls and it couldn't have come at a worse time."

"*¿Porque?*" Tony asked, wondering what could have been so important that his brother couldn't take two minutes to tell them about his plans—especially when he *had* been able to take a minute to be there for Tony when he had been at his lowest about the situation with Sara.

Javi raised his hands as if pleading and said, "I think you should all sit down for this." He guided his mother to the ottoman in front of their father's recliner and urged her onto it. He faced Tony and said, "You too, *hermanito*."

"Out with it. No need for all the drama," Tony said. His brother, besides being absent-minded, always made a saga out of a novella.

With a flip of his hands, he said, "*Bueno*. I sold my company. You are now looking at our family's first billionaire."

As Tony's knees went weak, he thought that maybe he should have sat down.

Javier couldn't have chosen a worse day to come home and make his announcement. There was no time to catch up with his brother or to celebrate the big news because of all that Tony had to get done at the hotel. While his parents, Javi, and his sister were busy planning a get-together at Sylvia's later that night, Tony had headed to the venue to meet Sara, Jeri, and their staff, as well as the crew at the hotel. He hoped that he would be able to get away and join his family before it got too late.

When he arrived, the women were already hard at work on making the trio of flans while the hotel staff bustled to prepare marinade for the pork shoulders.

He found Sara in the midst of all the activity, enthusiastically making dough for the *empanadas* they'd added to the hors d'oeuvres. He held back for a second, just watching her work. Watching how she smiled at one of the other chefs laboring nearby. Her smile stole his breath and the passion in her grey-green eyes was magnetic.

He finally took a breath, told himself to get a grip, and apologized for being a little late. "I'm sorry, but you'll never guess what happened."

"Javi came home a billionaire," she said, surprising him. With a wrinkle of her nose at his questioning look, she said, "News travels fast in Little Havana."

He shook his head and laughed. "Apparently, it does. What are they saying about us?"

She chuckled, paused in her work, and said, "That we should stop messing around and admit what we're feeling."

With a dip of his head, he stepped closer and said, "What do *you* think we should do?"

She grabbed a towel to clean off her hands, then reached up and cradled his jaw. Ran her finger across his lips that way that she always did. A gesture that made his gut tighten and his heart skip a beat. "I think we already stopped messing around, don't you?"

"*Sí*, we did. I'm glad I told you how I feel."

"But that doesn't make things easier, does it? Once we're done here tomorrow –"

"I am going back to New York in a few days, but that doesn't mean I'll stay there," he finally admitted, though he was quick to add, "But it may take time." He didn't want to give her unrealistic expectations.

Her gaze shimmered with tears he hated putting there. "I told you I wasn't patient, but for you I can wait."

Tony nodded and smiled, joy spreading through him. He leaned close and brushed a kiss across her cheek. "*Gracias*. I promise I'll try. Hard. You're important to me."

Always the chef, Sara stepped away and said, "Things seem to be going well."

He tracked her gaze and couldn't disagree. Grateful for that, he said, "I was hoping to get away early since Javi is home. Do you think that's possible?"

She nodded. "Jeri and I can keep an eye on the preparations. The most time-consuming thing to get done tonight is the *ropa vieja* for the tamales."

With a quick nod, he grabbed an apron, and slipped it on. "I'll get them working on the *sofrito* for the sauce."

She smiled at him. "Thanks. I asked Matt to trim the brisket to help us out, but I'll get it boiling so that Jeri and my crew can shred it once it's tender and cooled."

"Perfect. Have they done the jelly for the flans yet?"

With a shake of her head, she said, "If you could get my pastry chef working on that it would be great."

He walked over to the hotel crew to get the line chefs working on the sofrito and other items they'd need for the *ropa vieja* sauce.

Once they were cooking and preparing the items, he tracked down Sara's pastry chef and helped her with the strawberries for the jelly. She was eager to learn, her process efficient, surprising him with her abilities since he knew she was one of Sara's trainees. Her skills mimicked someone who'd attended culinary school. Sara had clearly taught her well. When the pastry chef was well on her way with the task, he strolled around the kitchen to see what was happening. Satisfied that everyone was working efficiently, he tracked down Sara.

She was taste-testing one of the batches of citrus juices for the marinade. She smiled and nodded at the chef. "That's the right mix of sweet and sour. You've got the proportions for the rest of the spices, right?"

"Yes, chef," the young man said.

"Great. Once it's all mixed, it's time to add the pork shoulders and get them in the walk-in fridge until tomorrow morning," she said and wiped her hands clean with a towel.

When the chef walked away with the storage pail filled with the juices, she shot a quick look around the kitchen to see how things were going. With a smile, she said, "Looks like everything is going smoothly."

He placed his hands on his hips. "It is. Hopefully tomorrow will be the same."

"Hopefully, but somehow I doubt it," she said with a chuckle.

"If you don't mind, I'm going to sneak away now to go to Sylvia's. I can come back later to help finish the *ropa vieja*."

Sara brushed back a bang of reddish-brown hair that had fallen into her eyes. She scanned the kitchen again and said, "There's no need for you to come back. I think we've got this under control."

As she'd turned, he had noticed a smudge of flour on her cheek. He reached out, skimmed his fingers across the flour. A zing of awareness that only Sara seemed to create flowed through him. And her, he realized. Her eyes widened and darkened. Her breath hitched and while common sense told him to pull back, he double downed and cupped her cheek.

"I *want* to come back. I want to see more of you," he said.

She licked her lips and bit the bottom one, worrying it with her teeth, but then she nodded. "That would be nice. I want to see more of you, too."

"Good. I'll see you later then."

CHAPTER 27

A NGELICA DIDN'T KNOW WHAT TO make of her *Tio* Javi and apparently neither did Samantha, who had come over to help Angelica put the finishing touches on the favors for tomorrow's *quinceañera*. Earlier in the week Angelica had assisted Samantha with her bundles of chocolate cigars.

"He's a billionaire?" Samantha whispered dubiously and tucked a packet of orange-flavored candies into a cellophane bag. The candies would be nestled against the fresh fruits and flowers that were Angelica's centerpieces.

"He just sold his start-up to one of the Big Tech companies," Angelica whispered back. When Samantha handed her the bag, she checked to make sure it had all the contents. Orange candies, a mojito mix packet, and chocolates had replaced her earlier idea for the favors. Still Miami flavors, but much more guest friendly.

Samantha had been peering at *Tio* Javi as she worked, puzzling Angelica.

"Sam," she said, drawing her friend's attention. "What's up?"

"He's kind of nerdy, but he seems nice. I think Aunt

Bridget likes him," her friend said.

She did a double take between Samantha, her uncle, and Sam's aunt Bridget, who had come over to help with some of the final chores. As she took the time to really observe the interaction between them, she could kind of see what Sam was talking about. Her uncle had that cool-nerd look with his slightly crooked horn-rimmed glasses, thick finger-tousled hair, and lean muscular body. His shirt and khakis were wrinkled, as if he'd just gotten off the plane even though he'd been home for hours. It made you want to go over and get him straightened up which Bridget did at one point, smoothing the fabric of his shirt across his shoulders—earning an intense look and smile from her uncle.

"Maybe," she said with a shrug, not really sure about how well Javi and Bridget knew each other and if she was misreading the situation.

A second later *Tio* Tony rushed into the room and hugged her *abuelos*, mom, and Bridget. He clapped his brother on the back before giving him a bro-hug. She waited, hoping he'd brought Sara with him, but he was alone.

"Fail," she said to Samantha.

"Epic. I hoped he'd bring Aunt Sara."

"Me too," Angelica whispered back. "What can we do?"

She'd heard her mother say more than once that you could lead a horse to water, but you couldn't make him drink. She'd never really understood where a saying like that came from but recently, she was starting to understand it better. It seemed like no matter what they did to get Sara and Tony together, it just didn't seem to be working.

But she wasn't going to give up.

"Guilt trip," she said.

"What?" Samantha said, puzzled.

"You know the routine. We've gotten it often enough from our *mamis*. We make *Tio* Tony feel guilty that he's here instead of helping your aunt Sara."

Samantha looked from Angelica to the group of adults gathered across the room at the kitchen table. "I don't know, Angelica. Maybe it's just not meant to happen."

"I guess I'm a romantic."

"A drama queen," Samantha said with a laugh, but then shook her head. "I think Aunt Sara really likes Tony."

"Like, *like* or more?" Angelica asked as she filled one of the favor bags.

"More," Samantha confirmed with a nod.

Angelica finished tying a ribbon around the cellophane to seal it and held her hand up for a fist bump. "Then let's do this," she said.

Samantha hesitated, but then fist bumped her. "Let's do this."

Sara stretched to ease the ache in her back. It seemed as if she'd been working for days instead of only hours to prep everything they needed for tomorrow's big event. The pace and quantities had been far different from how they labored at the restaurant and far more tiring. Especially once Jeri and her staff had left to go back to *Munch* to work the dinner service. Tomorrow they would close the restaurant for the night so that everyone could work the *quinceañera* party. It would be a hit to her bottom line for the month, but it would be totally worth it to not only help out her brother's family and her sister Bridget, but also reap the benefit of the *South Beach Style* piece—and also the national segment they'd just learned would air about the event. She hoped that "the competition" that the magazine had stirred up was long dead now that she and Tony were working together. She also hoped that the focus would be on the girls, the *quinceañera*, and the wonderful thing the families were doing by donating some of the money they'd saved to Bridget's non-profit group.

Determined that everything would be perfect, she walked over to take a last taste of the *ropa vieja* before it would be chilled so they could work it into the *tamales* tomorrow. The beef was succulent and had absorbed the rich flavors from the tomato sauce spiced with the *sofrito* and the finishing touches of roasted peppers and peas.

In the walk-in fridge she examined the assorted flans nestled in their ramekins. For the dessert service tomorrow, they'd flip them over so that the caramel would bathe the flans with that sweetness. Satisfied that everything was in order, she exited into the kitchen, intending to head back to *Munch* to help with the last few hours of the dinner service.

But as she exited the fridge, she realized Tony had returned to the hotel kitchen.

She walked over, removing her apron as she did so. She ran a hand through her short locks to hopefully put them in some semblance of order, suddenly self-conscious.

"It's late. I didn't think you were coming back," she asked, puzzled, but happy to see him.

"I wasn't given much of a choice. Your niece and mine are experts at laying on a guilt trip. They didn't realize that they didn't need to work so hard—I wanted to come back and be with you," Tony said with a shrug. "But I see that you're all done."

"We are. I was just heading back to *Munch*," she said and gestured to the exit.

"May I walk you there?" he asked

"That would be nice."

Nice. What a lame word for how she felt whenever she was with him. He brought so many other emotions with his presence and she would miss them all once he'd gone. But she wanted to experience them as much as she could before then.

He smiled and placed his hand at the small of her back, the touch possessive. She knew he'd find a way for them to be together.

They walked out of the kitchen into a service corridor and finally out to the hotel lobby where an assortment of guests filled the space. Tony kept his hand at her back as they walked, and the touch was a reminder of his promise.

The hotel, a combination of a renovated Art Deco hotel from 1939 and a new tower that had been constructed in the mid-90s, was only a couple of blocks away from Lincoln Road and her restaurant on Collins. It made for a short walk, mostly conducted in silence, until they reached the door to *Munch*.

Tony stood by her at the edge of the crowded al fresco dining area, smoothing his hands down the fabric of his pants. He rocked back and forth on his heels and said, "I'm sorry I wasn't more of a help tonight."

She shrugged. "You had good news to celebrate and we were able to handle it."

He pursed his lips and dipped his head. "Thanks. Javi's really excited about his news. He's also excited because he's decided to come back to Miami."

Sara opened her eyes wide, surprised. Javi had left Miami years before Tony and had spent even less time there during the last decade. That Javi was coming back brought renewed hope about Tony's promise. "That's a shock. We all thought he was gone for good."

Tony expelled a rough breath. "You and me both. Maybe he got tired of the L.A. traffic and pressure and decided to exchange it for a more laid-back life in Miami."

"Maybe," she said, thinking that the Sanchez brothers had a history of leaving brokenhearted Kelly women behind. Her sister Bridget had confessed to her years earlier that she and Javi had had a thing, but then he'd left her to go work on the West Coast.

"Why do I think there's something you're not saying?" Tony asked, his brow furrowed as he examined her.

"Maybe because there is," she said, but Javi and Bridget's story was their own and not for her to share. She pushed up on tiptoes and brushed a kiss across his cheek as she said, "I'm just glad you came home and that you're planning to come back when you can."

He smiled, laid a hand on her waist, and kept her from leaving. "I'm glad too. See you tomorrow?"

She nodded and grinned. "For sure. I can't wait to work together." It would mean the world to her to be at his side in the kitchen tomorrow.

"Me too," he said and dropped his hand away to let her go.

She hurried into the restaurant, but as she risked a look back at him, she caught him smiling and couldn't tamp down the hope that continued to build in her heart.

Tony lay in bed, staring up at cracks in the ceiling of his old bedroom. Across the room the metal of the window air conditioner rattled and clanged like an offbeat conga band. The unit emitted a barely cold wisp of air into the room and across his body which was why he was lying in shorts on top of his sheets, praying for some relief.

A familiar knock came on the wall by his bed. *Javi*. It had always been their signal as kids so they could sneak into each other's rooms to talk or play video games. Smiling, he tapped back on the wall and within seconds Javi scurried into the room.

Tony popped himself up in bed, leaving room for Javi to join him as he had so often when they were younger. Like him, Javi was only in shorts to combat the Miami heat and humidity. His brother leaned against the wall and stretched his legs out in front of him.

With a sigh Javi said, "First thing I'll do with the money is buy *mami* and *papi* one of those new AC systems."

Tony laughed because he had been thinking about the same thing. "I'd chip in, but I don't think you need the money."

Javi shook his head in disbelief. "I never imagined anything like this. I mean, I'd hoped to be successful, but this...."

"You should be really proud, Javi. You worked hard for it," Tony said. "You're actually coming home?"

Javi tilted his head and focused on Tony's face in the dim light in the room. The only illumination came from the streetlight glow that eked in through a far window.

"I am. Esteban is going to look for a place and Sylvia will do the closing for me."

"Something nice and over-the-top on Star Island?" Tony teased. His brother could now afford the multi-million-dollar mansions they'd imagined owning when they were kids.

His brother shook his head. "No way. Nice and family friendly is what I want."

"Whoa, family friendly? Are you holding back, *mano*?" That was the last thing he'd expected to hear from his commitment-phobic brother.

Javi held his hands up to forestall more questions. "There's one special right now, but who knows? I plan on taking a few months off to relax. Get reacquainted with old friends and family."

"And after that?" He imagined that someone like his brother might be bored after only a few days with nothing to do.

With a shrug, Javi said, "I have an idea for something new and I was thinking of maybe starting a non-profit."

Which brought to mind a very special woman. "Like what Bridget is doing?"

Another shrug. "Bridget seems to be doing a lot of good with her organization, but don't go there, *hermanito*. Like I said before, water under the bridge."

Tony detected an emotion beneath his brother's words that hinted otherwise, but he left it alone. "Whatever you say, Javi. I'm just glad you're home," Tony said, leaning forward and tapping his brother on the arm.

Javi laughed and jabbed him right back. "What about you, *hermanito*? Sylvia says you're thinking about a second restaurant right here in Miami?"

"Maybe. It depends on a lot of things," he said, unwilling to say more. There was so much for him to do before he could come home. So much at stake given his feelings for Sara. He'd never felt like that about any woman and doubted he'd ever find anyone else who made him feel like Sara made him feel.

"If you need an angel investor, I'm your guy," Javi said and hopped off the bed.

"I appreciate the support, *hermano*. I'll let you know." Once Javi had gone he sank back onto the bed, pillowed his head in his hands, and stared back up at the ceiling. *Get some rest, tomorrow will be a long day*, he told himself, but it was tough to fall asleep as so many thoughts raced through his brain.

Tomorrow's menu. Sara. The reporters who'd be there. Sara. Javi's generous offer. *Sara. Sara. Sara*, he thought with a smile, conjuring images of her to warm his soul and lighten his spirit. It was so much better working with her than working against her in some trumped-up competition. It was too easy to picture collaborating more in the future, maybe even in their own restaurant. Armed with those thoughts, he finally drifted off to dreams filled with optimism.

CHAPTER 28

S ARA SURVEYED THE KITCHEN AS the combined staffs
of her people and the hotel chefs worked side-by-side
to plate the various hors d'oeuvres. She caught sight of
Tony working with one of the line chefs on the avocados
and lemons for the salad service. He had a smile on his
face and clapped the man on the back as they finished
the task, his stance easy-going. Quite a difference from
what he'd told her about how he'd been in his own
kitchen just a short month ago. It warmed her heart
that his time in Miami – with her – had worked such
a change on him.

He seemed happy, truly happy. She liked to think
she was the reason for that change. She liked to think
he would want to keep that change going and explore
a life with her. But first they had to get past tonight.

She checked what was happening with her *toston*
and *picadillo* first course. With a quick taste, she said,
"Delicious. We'll start plating at my station once the
quinceañera traditions are finished."

Sara hated the thought of not seeing Angelica and
Samantha go through the rituals marking their passage

into womanhood, but she had to be in the kitchen to make sure the first course came out on time. When she returned to her station, two of her women were already laying out the plates for the first course and prepping them with the first batch of *tostones* out of the fryer.

"That looks good, Diana. Sheila," she said to her chefs. Pride filled her at how her staff was handling things.

Jeri came rushing over from the pastry chef's station where they were decorating the plates that would later hold the trio of flans they'd prepared the day before.

"Everything okay?" she asked her partner.

"No, it's not. The girls are about to walk in, and you and Tony should be out there to see it. Get him and go," Jeri said with a shooing motion.

"But –"

"No, buts. We've got this," she said and once again urged Sara to go with a wave of her hands.

"Everything okay?" Tony asked as he walked over, a furrow of concern across his forehead.

"OMG, you two are like peas in a pod. Everything is okay and you should be outside watching your nieces," Jeri repeated, exasperation dripping from her voice.

With a quick look around the kitchen, Tony seemed satisfied that they could spare the time. "Let's go," he said and grabbed Sara's hand to playfully drag her into the ballroom where they stood by the kitchen door, watching the festivities. Still holding hands. *Together*, she thought, buoyed by their connection.

The MC for the band announced, "Would everyone please take their seats to welcome Angelica and Samantha and their *quinceañera* courts."

The guests hurried to find their places and barely a minute later, the band launched into the cover of a pop song both girls loved. The doors to the ballroom opened and the court consisting of the girls' friends and their dates danced their way into the room. After a brief pause for the MC to announce them, Angelica and Samantha walked in on the arms of their escorts, bright smiles on their faces. Each girl held a plush doll which they stopped to hand off to a youngster seated at a table before they walked up to where Matt and Esteban waited for them.

Their escorts helped them sit in the chairs positioned before the two fathers on the dance floor and then walked off. As the fathers came around, each holding a pair of high heels, the two girls lifted their dress hems to reveal they were wearing their soccer cleats, prompting laughter from their guests as well as Sara and Tony.

Since the tradition was meant to signify giving up childhood, Sara joked, "I sure hope this doesn't mean they're done with soccer."

"Me either, since Sylvia tells me their team might make it to the championships this year," Tony said.

The cleats came off and the high heels went on so that the girls could dance with their dads and it was as awkward as the girls had said it would be. The dads did an off-rhythm back and forth, barely moving. In a change-up to tradition, in the middle of the song the dads stepped away and let the moms dance with their girls.

"That's so nice," Sara said, her gaze wavering as tears of joy welled up in her eyes.

"It is. Maybe one day you'll do that as well," Tony said and when her gaze met his, she let herself hope that it might be their child she danced with. A child with her light eyes and his dark hair.

As the music ended, the next part of the ritual continued with each girl receiving the different items of jewelry that a woman would wear. A tiara from their mothers and a bracelet from a godmother. Her sister Bridget stepped in to slip the bracelet on Samantha's hand while one of Sylvia's best friends did the honor for Angelica. After, Bridget came over to her with a box holding the necklace Sara had for Samantha. She left Tony's side to take part in the ritual, easing the gold necklace with Sam's initial over her niece's neck before returning to Tony.

While the girls were receiving their gifts, the photographer from *South Beach Style* was busy taking pictures, a videographer tagging along with him. Sara craned her neck and finally took note of Roberta Lane standing on the edges of the dance floor, a pleased look on her face. She still was uncertain about the reporter's supposed about-face, but she guessed she would see once her article about the event came out. Whether good or bad, no matter who she featured, she refused to let it upset her.

With the ritual completed, the MC announced that the first course would soon be coming out which was their cue to head back into the kitchen. As they entered, Tony said, "Let's make this a meal they won't forget."

"Let's do this," she said, happy to be working with him. She was certain that the quality of the food would speak for itself and help them both with their businesses. In a moment of spontaneity, she dropped a kiss on his cheek before hurrying away to her station. When she arrived, she was pleased to see that the line chefs were already dishing out the *picadillo* over the Cuban toast and grating a little *cotija* cheese, a last-minute addition for visual appeal, over the dish. Another set of servers were loading all the completed plates onto serving trays and heading out to serve the first course.

With the first course well in-hand, she hurried over to another station where Tony assisted a different group of chefs with the salad preparation. She helped scoop, slice, and present the avocados while Tony handled the dressing and final decorations.

Finished with that, they were both about to oversee the main course when one of Sara's pastry chefs scurried over, a look of dread on her face. "Chefs, we have a problem," she said, hands fisted at her side.

"What is it, Brenda?" Sara asked patiently, not wanting to add to the chef's apparent upset.

"The strawberry jelly didn't set. I used the right amount of gelatin, I just don't know what went wrong," Brenda said, almost in tears. Wringing her hands with worry.

Sara laid a hand on hers to still the nervous motion and gave a reassuring squeeze. "These things happen. Let's figure out what to do." She walked over to the station with the chef where, sure enough, the assorted trays they'd laid out to set in the fridge were still not firm enough to cut into the circles they wanted for the banana flan.

With Tony beside her, she considered what to do. Shooting a quick look at Tony, she said, "We can whip up some cream, add the unset jelly, and make a mousse to pipe on top. What do you think?"

Tony nodded. "I think it'll work. I'll help you in a second," he said and in no time, they had put things to right for the dessert.

Just in time, Sara thought as the busboys had started bringing in the dirty dinner plates while the waiters and waitresses took out coffee and tea for the guests.

She and Tony stood by and watched the dessert plates fly out the door. When there wasn't a plate left to serve, they turned and faced the many chefs who had worked with them to execute the meal.

"Thank you, all. You did an amazing job," she said

and clapped her hands to congratulate them.

Tony smiled, and wrapped an arm around her waist. He drew her near and said, "It's been a pleasure working with all of you. Each of you is a true professional. Now let's get ourselves something to eat!"

With that the kitchen went into action to set up meals for the staff on some nearby worktables, but Sara was too wired to eat. She laid a hand over her stomach and said, "I can't believe we pulled it off."

"I can," Tony said and cupped her cheek. "You're an amazing chef, Sara. It's truly been wonderful to work with you."

Joy filled her, warming her heart with intense pleasure and pride at his recognition of her talents. With his support and his love. "You too, Tony. I'm glad the girls found a way to deal with everything so we could do this together," she said.

He ran his thumb across her cheek, his touch gentle. Soothing. "I'm glad too."

She crinkled her nose and he tapped it playfully, smoothed his finger across it as she said, "I hope that means that you and I can cook together again?"

Tony grinned, a broad welcoming grin that caused her heart to skitter, but then he lowered his hand to wrap around the nape of her neck and draw her closer. "You know Javi has said he might be interested in making some investments here in Miami. Like maybe in a new restaurant for his little brother. But I don't really want to go it alone. I'd rather have a partner to help me do it."

"A partner? As in—"

"You and me, Sara. I want to be partners in every way you can think of because I love you," he said and applied gentle pressure to draw her even closer.

"Not just *think* you love me? You *love* love me?" she

teased even though her heart was racing so hard, it was knocking against her ribs.

"I *love* you. I think this is the part where you say–"

"I *love* love you too, Tony. I want to be your partner in all things," she said, but then guilt jumped in.

"But what about Jeri?" she said, worried about her partner. Jeri and she had always worked together and she hadn't really envisioned that changing. But she was sure her partner would never hold her back, not matter how hard it might be for Jeri.

"I think Jeri can manage *Munch* on her own. Or with Rick helping her. So, what do you think?" he said, and his warm breath spilled across her lips.

Rick would only be too willing to help Jeri and maybe that would help her partner also move on with her life. Certain that they could make things right for all of them, she moved the last little inch until her lips brushed against his as she said, "I think you've got yourself a new partner."

He shifted his mouth over hers, deepening the kiss, and she let herself melt into the moment she'd only imagined as a young girl and then a teen.

It was far far better than any of those kisses she'd only dreamed about because he was there, in the flesh, and he was hers. Nothing could be better.

Two weeks later, Tony sat beside Sara at the News Café as they read the article in *South Beach Style*. He'd been dreading it and yet the article was incredibly upbeat on various levels. The focus on the girls and their *quinceañera*

was nicely balanced with the competition that had never really happened once the girls had combined their parties. Much like in the national television segment, there was nothing but praise for how the *quince* had helped Bridget's non-profit group as well as for Tony and Sara's skills. And to his surprise and pleasure, both of them had been equally featured in the piece as well as the national segment.

Within days of the segment airing, both he and Sara had been inundated with requests for more interviews about the *quinceañera* and also about their future plans. Since they had both discussed it with their partners and chefs, it had been the perfect time to talk up their personal and business partnership and what they hoped to do with a new, shared venue. That had generated a great deal of interest from various sectors and in no time, they had lined up the financing for a new restaurant.

"I'm surprised," he said and lay the magazine down on the table.

Sara swept her hand across the glossy pages with the pictures of the girls and the two of them at the *quinceañera*. The emerald and diamond engagement ring on her finger caught the Miami sunlight as she did so, bringing warmth to his heart just as it did every time he looked at it. She was his and in just a few months, she'd be his wife.

"I am too. I guess she was serious with her apology," Sara said and glanced at him, her grey-green eyes alive with joy. She smiled in a way that made his heart skip a beat and he knew it would always be that way between them. Exciting. Happy. Comforting.

"She was. And this article, like the national segment, is going to be a big help," Tony said.

"I can't believe how fast this is all happening. I mean

just a month ago –"

"We barely knew each other?" he said, took hold of her hand, and gave it a reassuring squeeze.

Sara laughed and wagged her head. "Kind of. And now, we've got our whole lives to get to know each other better."

"We do, but first we need to go check out all those locations Esteban has lined up for the new place. There's even one just a few doors down from *Munch*," he said, closed the magazine and pulled out the printouts with the details his brother-in-law had sent over.

Sara pulled out the listing for the location near *Munch* and perused it with a twitch of her nose. "It would be nice to be close, just in case."

Tony laughed and smoothed a finger across her nose and then down, across the tight set of her lips. "Now who is being controlling? Jeri can handle it. Deep down you know that. Plus we both know Rick will be there and Bridget too. Maybe even Javi, *sabes*."

"Yes, I know," she said and shot him a side glance. "Did you know Bridget and Javi were involved ages ago?"

Tony nodded. "Javi said it was 'water under the bridge.'"

"But you don't believe him," she said and then quickly added, "I don't either. You should have seen Bridget's face when she heard he was back and staying."

Tony paused, considering what Sara had said. With a chuckle and a shake of his head, he said, "So much romance. Jeri and Rick. Javi and Bridget."

Sara cupped his cheek and ran her thumb across his lips. "You and me. Forever, Tony. Side-by-side at the restaurant. In life. I can't wait to be your wife. I love you so much."

Tony leaned his forehead against hers and rubbed his

nose across hers. "I love you too, and I can't wait to start our lives together." He dropped a quick kiss on her lips, shifted away, and grabbed the real estate listing from Esteban so they could look at not only locations for a new restaurant, but for a home to share.

"Let's take this next step together," he said, rose from the table, and held out his hand to her.

She slipped her hand into his. "Together."

EPILOGUE

"*C*HICA, STOP MOVING AROUND," DOLORES groused around as she undid the bustle at the back of the wedding gown.

"I just can't help it," Sara said and peered over her shoulder at Bridget who was standing by the entrance. "Are they ready yet?"

"Patience," Sylvia said as she came to stand by Dolores. "You really outdid yourself with this dress, *amiga*," Sylvia said and hugged her friend.

"It had to be perfect for Sara and Tony," Dolores said and did a "come here" motion to Angelica and Samantha who had been standing off to the side in the anteroom of the church. "*Niñas*, one last look, *por favor*."

"*Mami*, chill," Samantha said and rolled her eyes as her mother did another inspection of the bridesmaids' gowns she had made for them.

"You chill. You want to look right for that celebrity magazine, don't you?" Dolores shot back.

"They are all going to look fabulous, and you won't be able to keep people away from the shop," Sylvia said. Bridget seconded the comment.

"You really are a genius, and I'm so appreciative of all that you're both doing with my ladies from the shelter," she said and hugged Dolores and Sylvia, who had been offering legal help to the group.

The music that had been softly playing inside the church stopped and a second later the wedding planner stuck her head into the anteroom. "The rest of the bridal party is on their way back here. Get ready for the walk down the aisle."

Sara sucked in a breath and couldn't resist sneaking a peek up the aisle to where Tony stood in his tuxedo, looking more handsome than possible. Her heart did a little skitter while her stomach fluttered in anticipation of her walk to meet him.

So much had happened in the last year. Dolores had been able to open her own shop, and it was doing well thanks in large part to a new article from Roberta about how Dolores was helping to train women from Bridget's nonprofit. The shop had also gotten some grants from Javi to smooth the way. The two teenagers, once rivals, were now the best of friends. As promised, Javi had settled down in Miami and provided part of the financing so that Tony and she could open a new restaurant that was a melding of both of their styles. Located at the furthest end of Lincoln Road, just blocks from *Munch*, *Fusion* offered high-end twists on family favorites and had been a great success. They had already won several local awards and been featured in a couple of cooking magazines. Those accolades had helped bring business to *Fusion* and to their other restaurants also.

But best of all, she was now getting married to the man she'd had a crush on since she was ten years old. A man who was kind, talented, funny and so many other things she hadn't even known but had come to learn and love over the last six months.

What could be better? she thought as the wedding planner signaled for everyone to get in line to begin the walk down the aisle.

Tony had his hands clasped in front of him and rocked back and forth on his heels as he waited for his bride to meet him at the altar.

The church was filled with friends and family, but Tony only cared about seeing Sara walking down that aisle to his side.

The months since he'd made his decision to stay had been a blur, but a happy one. After all the work to open their *Fusion* restaurant, he was back in the kitchen doing what he loved best. Even better, he was doing it with his absolutely brilliant and amazing Sara by his side.

As the opening strains of the Pachelbel Canon in D signaled that the bridal party would soon be entering the church, he drew in a deep breath and rose slightly on tiptoes to search for Sara. Beyond the flower girls, bridesmaids, and maids of honor, he caught a glimpse of Sara sandwiched between her mother and father, waiting to enter and join him at the altar to begin the rest of their lives.

His throat choked up with anticipation, his gaze locked on the back of the church until she finally walked in with a smile so bright it lit up his soul. Her gaze met his and didn't leave him during what seemed like an interminable procession up the aisle until she stood before him.

He held out his hand and she slipped her hand into his, locked their fingers together.

"Ready?" he mouthed, finding it difficult to breathe given how she'd stolen his breath away.

"Always," she said and together they turned to face the priest and take the vows to forever bind them in love.

THE END

TRES LECHES CAKE WITH BANANA AND COCONUT

A Hallmark Original Recipe

When two chefs, Tony and Sara, each cater a *quinceañera* on the same weekend, a local reporter positions them as culinary rivals. But the truth is, Tony and Sara are well on their way to a sweet romance. Here's the recipe for Tony's *tres leches* cake, delicious enough for a fancy occasion...but no occasion is required.

Prep Time: 20 minutes
Cook Time: 40 minutes
Serves: 12

INGREDIENTS
- 1 box white cake mix
- 1 1/4 cup water
- 2 tablespoons vegetable oil
- 3 eggs
- 1 cup mashed bananas (2 medium)
- 1 – 14 ounce can sweetened condensed milk
- 1 cup coconut milk
- 3 cups heavy cream, divided
- 1 teaspoon vanilla extract
- 1/2 cup powdered sugar
- Toasted coconut for garnish

PREPARATION
1. Preheat oven to 350°F. Grease bottom of a 13x9-inch pan.
2. In the bowl of an electric mixer, blend cake mix, water, vegetable oil, eggs, and bananas on low speed for 30 seconds. Scrape down sides of bowl and raise speed to medium for 2 minutes. Pour into pan.
3. Bake 40 minutes or until toothpick inserted in center comes out clean. Let cool 10 minutes.
4. With a long-tined fork, pierce the top of cake every ½ inch. In a medium bowl, combine sweetened condensed milk, coconut milk, and 1 cup heavy cream. Pour over cake evenly.
5. Refrigerate at least 1 hour and up to overnight, covered.
6. Whip remaining cream, vanilla, and powdered sugar on high until think. Cut cake into 12 pieces, top with a dollop of whipped cream and toasted coconut. Serve.

Thanks so much for reading *South Beach Love*. We hope you enjoyed it!

You might like these other books from Hallmark Publishing:

Wedding in the Pines
The Secret Ingredient
A Dash of Love
Beach Wedding Weekend
Sailing at Sunset

For information about our new releases and exclusive offers, sign up for our free newsletter at hallmarkchannel.com/hallmark-publishing-newsletter

You can also connect with us here:

Facebook.com/HallmarkPublishing

Twitter.com/HallmarkPublish

ABOUT THE AUTHOR

Caridad Piñeiro is a transplanted Long Island girl who has fallen in love with the Jersey Shore. When Caridad isn't taking long strolls along the boardwalk, she's also a *New York Times* and *USA Today* bestselling author with over a million romance novels sold worldwide. Caridad is passionate about writing and helping others explore and develop their skills as writers. She is a founding member of the Liberty States Fiction Writers and has presented workshops at the *RT* Book Club Convention, Romance Writers of America National Conference as well as various writing organizations throughout the country. You can connect with Caridad at www.caridad.com.

you might also enjoy

the Secret Ingredient

NANCY NAIGLE
USA TODAY BESTSELLING AUTHOR

CHAPTER ONE

KELLY MCINTYRE DIDN'T CARE IF the town of Bailey's Fork, North Carolina was too small in some folks' eyes. It was big enough to have kept the Main Street Cafe open through four generations of McIntyres. It also had bragging rights for the winningest high school football team in the region for ten years running and held the honor of the largest loblolly pine in both Carolinas, and that suited her fine.

The fact that she and Andrew York had professed their love by carving their initials in the bark of that tree had made Kelly McIntyre almost famous…for a little while.

Kelly straightened her short black-and-white apron and retied its red sash over her blue jeans. She lifted the tall glass dome from the cake people came from miles around to get and sliced a wedge, letting it fall over right into the center of the shiny red plate. Today's flavor—Southern Seven-layer Caramel. Her specialty. For that, she could still feel a little famous.

"Here you go." Kelly placed the plate in front of Fuzzy Johnston. "Mrs. Johnston out of town again?"

His eyes twinkled. "She'd never let me have this." He sank his fork into the frosting, then lifted it to his mouth. "Only live once, don't you know?"

"Your secret is safe with me," she teased. "You *are* going to eat some real food too though, aren't you?"

He nodded while swallowing the rich cake, then chased it with a sip of coffee. "I'll have the chicken-fried steak, please."

She jotted the order on her pad. "Do I need to even ask if you want mashed potatoes and gravy?"

"Nope." He grinned, looking quite pleased with himself. Fuzzy owned the biggest chicken farm around, and rumor had it his wife cooked chicken six ways to Sunday, which was why when she was out of town, Fuzzy always ended up here in the cafe for something a little different. "And fried okra."

"I'll put this right in." She tucked her pad into her apron pocket and headed to the kitchen. "Fuzzy's usual." Kelly pushed the ticket onto the clip and spun it.

Andrew snapped the order up and then stage whispered from the pass-through, "For someone who complains that his wife won't fix him anything but chicken, you'd think he might switch it up when he got the chance."

She loved that twinkle in Andrew's green eyes. His light brown hair was damp, which made that one piece of hair fall forward, giving him a tough-guy look. But she knew the ooey-gooey sweet side of him. "He did switch it up. He had cake as an appetizer." She spun away with only a quick glance back, knowing Andrew would pick up on the playful jab.

Andrew leaned forward at the pass-through. "He *loves* my chicken-fried steak and gravy."

"He ate a big slice of *my* cake, first," she challenged.

"Saving the best for last," he said with a playful smirk.

She turned and propped a hand on her hip. "I seem

to remember helping you get that chicken-fried steak recipe just right." Kelly had helped him with as many recipes as he'd helped her. It seemed like there was nothing they couldn't perfect together.

Andrew straightened, his white apron splattered with grease and barbecue sauce. "Did I tell you that you look real pretty today?"

She swept a loose tendril of hair behind her ear. "Now you have." She never tired of hearing him say that. With a smile on her face, she turned, and then looked over her shoulder. "Thank you." He still made her heart race. She swept her thumb against the band of the diamond engagement ring on her left hand.

"Hey," he called after her. "Mom texted me. She and Dad are coming in for dinner tonight."

Kelly walked back over to him. "Great." They'd hardly ever come in since Andrew had started work at the cafe. "What's up?"

"They want to celebrate. Mom said it's a surprise. Something about my great aunt."

"That's the one who lives in France, right?"

"We haven't seen her in a couple of years. Not since the last time Dawn and I went for the summer. Maybe she's coming for a visit," he said. "Mom would love that. Will you save some cake for them? They love your chocolate cake."

"Of course. I'll put two slices aside right now. I can't let my future in-laws down. How would that look?"

"Very bad."

"My thoughts exactly." She placed two slices in the cooler to hold for the Yorks.

"Thanks, beautiful." He blew her a kiss, then got to work on the order.

I'm the luckiest girl in the world. She and Andrew had

known each other since grade school, but it wasn't until high school when he'd landed a job bussing tables here at the cafe that the two of them had started dating. He loved to cook, and she loved to bake, so they spent nearly all of their extra time in the kitchen of the Main Street Cafe making up recipes and testing out ideas. They never tired of it, or each other.

The dinner crowd started to roll in, and the noise level grew exponentially. She pulled another order from the call window. With three plates balanced up each arm, she made it across the diner and dropped them off at table fourteen. "Can I get you anything else?" Everyone was already digging in, so she whisked back into the kitchen to pick up the next order.

Andrew tapped the bell at the window and shoved two more plates of the daily special under the heat lamp, giving her a wink before turning back to the cooktop. Kelly's dad barked an order, and Andrew hopped to it without a single grumble. Andrew loved being in the kitchen as much as he loved her, and she loved watching him cook.

Kelly spotted the Yorks as they walked in. There was no mistaking Andrew's father. Except for slight graying at the temples, father and son looked just alike. Tall, athletic, with wide lean-on-me shoulders, light brown hair and green eyes. His mom wore her signature cowboy boots, jeans and pearls with that ever-present smile and an air of kindness you could sense a mile away.

Read the rest! *The Secret Ingredient*
is available now.